Death in the Cotswolds

Death in the Cotswolds

REBECCA TOPE

Allison & Busby Limited
13 Charlotte Mews
London W1T 4EJ
www.allisonandbusby.com

Hardcover published in Great Britain in 2006.
This paperback edition published in 2008.

A CIP catalogue record for this book is available from
the British Library.

10 9 8 7 6 5 4

ISBN 978-0-7490-8064-8

Typeset in 10.5/14 pt in Sabon by
Terry Shannon

Printed and bound in the UK by
CPI Bookmarque, Croydon, CR0 4TD

REBECCA TOPE is the author of ten previous crime novels. She lives on a smallholding in Herefordshire, with a full complement of livestock, but manages to travel the world and enjoy civilisation from time to time as well. Most of her varied experiences and activities find their way into her books, sooner or later. For example, beekeeping, milk recording, spinning, arguing, undertaking and gardening. She is also currently the Membership Secretary of the Crime Writers' Association.

For everyone in the letter group:

Anita, Carol, Jo, Madelon, Margaret, Martha, Quenda and Sheila.

CHAPTER ONE

That October was much as usual – blowy, damp, mild, the leaves still green on the boughs, the sheep fat-bottomed and clean with their new fleece, complacent from the attentions of the tup. Odd, I suppose, that most people imagine the mating season to be the spring when in fact that's the time of birth, which is quite another matter. Conception can be any time from high summer to dark November for most mammals left to their own devices.

October, for me, was the dyeing season. Dahlia heads, sloes, the seeds of the golden rod and lichens pulled from the boles of old trees – they all have to be gathered and stored in the days of the first frosts or just before, and then steeped in pans with the raw fleece, mixing colours and trying in vain to get anything near a decent blue without resorting to indigo yet again.

* * *

I had known Phil Hollis since he was in his teens and I a clamouring infant of four and five, following him through the village, encouraged by his kindness. And here he was, finally due back that Friday afternoon to tackle his dead aunt's possessions at last.

The car arrived quietly, but I'd been listening for it and was waiting at my door before the engine stopped. He didn't see me as he got out of the driving seat and I was able to watch him go round to the passenger door and stand beside the woman he'd brought with him.

'*We should be there by six on Friday. I'll have Thea with me,*' he'd written in the letter he sent to tell me his plans. '*And three dogs. We'd appreciate it if you could air the bed and get some dry firewood in. Also, some basic provisions – bread, eggs, milk.*'

He knew that I wouldn't have any idea who Thea was, but the reference to only one bed made it clear enough. I imagined he wrote instead of telephoning in order to dodge any questions I might throw at him.

It was dark and my cottage was shielded by shrubs. I could have stood there much longer, quietly observing them, and they'd never have known. As it was, I only gave it a minute before going down to my gate and calling out, across the street. A minute, though, was enough to see that Phil had found his new lady, and she was just that bit less certain about the whole thing than he was.

Phil raised his head from the little woman – who must have been nearly a foot shorter than me – and met my eyes. He didn't smile. 'Hello, Mary,' he said. 'I like your hair.'

I swayed with the gust of rage that flooded through me. 'Ariadne,' I said loudly. 'My name's Ariadne. You know it is.'

'Sorry, sorry,' he put up his hands. 'I should remember by now.' He tilted his head towards his friend. 'This is Thea Osborne. Thea – this is Ariadne. She and I have known each other for ever. She was wonderfully kind to Auntie Helen before she died.'

The woman and I looked at each other like two cats. I'd known it would happen, of course. Phil had been single for over three years by that time, his misunderstood Caroline already remarried. He was fit, friendly, good-looking. A definite catch. And this person was just his type. Small, vigorous and lovely. And keen on dogs from the look of it. In the back of the car there was a whirl of bouncing, yapping canines. I shuddered. Dogs repelled me, with their great slobbering jaws and stupid fawning habits. One of these seemed to be a spaniel – a breed I loathed more than most. As it jumped from seat to seat I could see it was a cocker, with an undocked tail. I could almost hear my farmer father sneering at such a monstrosity.

'There's no power in the house, you know,' I said.
'You had it cut off, remember?'

'Of course. We've got a lamp and a camping
stove and a few candles. And there's always the pub
if things get desperate.'

'I've cleaned,' I went on. 'Not because you were
coming – I'd have done it anyway. The window
frame in the back bedroom's rotting.'

'You're a star,' he said. 'Thanks.'

They were hardly listening to me, wrapped up in
each other and their foolish adventure. Greenhaven
hadn't been lived in for a year, and even with my
regular visits for dusting and airing it was bound to
be clammy and uninviting. But Phil was behaving
like a schoolboy, already digging about in the boot
of the car.

'Can I let the dogs out?' said the Thea woman.

That was my cue to leave them alone. I retreated
without them even noticing, except that she gave
me one last look. Then she turned her pretty face up
at Phil and I could see her mouth shaping the word
hair, with a nasty smile. So what if I'd done yellow
and black stripes in it? What did it have to do with
them?

In another week, the clocks were going back, and
it'd be dark by four-thirty. As it was, the light had
all gone by the time Phil and Thea had arrived. I
had wasted much of the day thinking about Phil

and how it would be to have him across the street for a week, pottering about tidying my house when I should have been working in the garden, digging potatoes, picking up windfall apples for my pig. She was a very beautiful Tamworth, incidentally, called Arabella, living in a patch of old coppice I rented for peanuts half a mile away. Arabella was turning it over, uprooting a lot of brambles and nettles, which the owner thought a fair return for the loss of small saplings in the process. I'd worried that she'd be lonely, but it seemed she was too busy for that.

It was by then much too dark for working outside and a chill breeze had sprung up. I threw another few shovels of coal into the Rayburn and wondered about my supper. I'd got ham from my own pigs, and ridiculous quantities of home-grown vegetables. Living the way I did, it was never likely that I would run out of food. Nor wine, because I made my own. I should have had six kids, by rights, to help me dispose of it all. As it was I'd left a large basketful at Greenhaven – carrots, onions, spuds and beans. It all needed cooking, of course – something they'd have trouble with on a camping stove.

I went to Phil and Caroline's wedding, all those years ago. They had it in the church at Painswick, where she came from. Some of their friends showed up from Sussex and Surrey and raved about how gorgeous the Cotswolds were and how nobody had ever *heard* of Painswick, which they thought was amazing, because it had to be the most gorgeous place in England. They all ignored me, of course – a gawky fourteen-year-old with lank hair and huge feet. I spent the time despising them for their false laughter and expensive clothes. But Caroline was lovely to me; already we'd become friends in a gentle careful sort of way. It took me a while to appreciate how special she was to accept me as she did.

I actually babysat their two kids in the early years. Everything seemed to be sweetness and light in the Hollis household in those days. Phil was just an ordinary PC then, not much overtime, none of that stuff you see on the box where the wife goes apeshit because he's never there. That was twenty years ago – more, even. He's forty-six now. I know that for a fact. Ten years older than me.

His Auntie Helen had been great. She'd wanted me to move in with her when she got so arthritic and clumsy, but I compromised by buying the cottage across the road, which providentially became available just at the right moment. I was into my thirties by then and ready to own my own place. Nobody would give me a mortgage, of course, with no proper job and no man to bale me out. Although eventually one did – my father came to the rescue, selling the farm for close to a million, and offloading a chunk of the proceeds onto me. 'That's it, mind,' he said. 'There'll be nothing in my will for you, after this.' My brothers had grumbled about it for a while, but eventually persuaded themselves they'd probably get the best of it in the long run. Nobody owed them any favours, after all. They'd all been offered the choice of carrying on at the farm, but Robin opted for teaching, John went into the Civil Service and Graham set himself up as a motor mechanic. They all worked reasonably hard and made a decent living. Two of them were married with kids, the third, John, had never pretended to be interested in women. He had a close friend called Mark and nobody doubted that this was the only significant relationship in John's life. I suspect they all three felt guilty for abandoning the farm. Dad's grandfather bought it in 1921, so it had seen a lot of Fletcher history.

The thing I had not entirely bargained for was the distance that developed between me and the rest of the family once the farm had gone. Given financial independence, I somehow drifted away and made my own life, hardly ever seeing them. My mother kept in touch, phoning every couple of weeks, and I went along for the usual Christmas stuff, but something visceral had been severed. I think it wasn't just me, it was because the old life was over and my parents were having to remake themselves without all those sheep and bullocks. Now when it snowed or blew a gale, they didn't have to worry. Not worrying diminished them, even in their own eyes. My mother fell into the habit of hospital visiting, followed by regular work at the hospice. It was the closest she could get to her lifelong pattern of jumping out of bed to check the lambs, or help with the dipping, or any one of a hundred farming jobs.

My father found it even more difficult to adapt. He spent most of his time watching sport on the telly and most of his money on backing horses. He became a boring, irritable person.

All evening I kept glancing out of the front window, expecting to see something more of Phil. In the near-darkness I could see smoke starting to curl out of the chimney, and I could see the vague shape of the largest of the dogs as it ran round from the back, sniffing all the plants in the little front garden and cocking its leg against most of them. Male dogs have to be the most disgusting of all creatures. Their instincts are all centred on excrement and piddle and copulation. Cats aren't like that, nor sheep, nor pigs, nor *any* animal I can think of. Phil's perverse preference for dogs was one of the things about him that had put me off, even when I was mooning over photos of him and dreaming that he would wait for me to grow up and then we'd be

married. He already has his own pooch by the time
he was twenty: a fat yellow Labrador called Mavis,
of all things. Mavis and I disliked each other
relentlessly throughout her entire life.

I tried to imagine Phil and Thea in the house that
had been a second home to me for three years and
more. Before Helen died I'd spent a lot of my time
there, getting her meals, checking she'd taken her
pills, reading to her. Ever since my teens I'd taken
pleasure in watching out for old ladies. I even
worked in nursing homes, in advance of my mother,
on and off through my twenties, although the
routines and the careless cruelties drove me away
eventually. Since then I'd just had one or two special
favourites to focus on. Nothing formal, no stupid
Social Services vetting procedures or paperwork –
and not much payment either. Helen couldn't afford
to pay me, except with her company, although I
charged Phil Hollis for my attentions to the house
that now belonged to him.

Helen and I had agreed that she should stay at
home right to the end, keeping the medical people
at bay, fooling them into thinking she was much less
sick than the reality. It almost worked.

There were still some of my things there: rugs,
cushions and my tapestry weaving frame. I'd made
four big wallhangings in those last months, just
sitting and chatting to Helen, as she dozed and

dreamed. We'd played tapes of her favourite music – jazz, ragtime, anything American pre-1950. Neither of us had ever mentioned the future.

She left me most of her modest savings, which ensured I could carry on as I was for a while longer, before having to think about earning a sensible income. Now she was gone I had enough time and money to establish my new venture. Except it wasn't really new. I'd been knitting, spinning, weaving since I was six in a disorderly kind of way. Now I had some capital for better equipment and proper labelling and advertising. As a trial run I took a stall at the Stow Horse Fair in May. I sold everything I'd made in those years I'd spent with Helen: rugged jumpers in natural Cotswold colours, woven rugs, hats, scarves and two highly experimental wallhangings. I'd under-priced them, I realised. The Horse Fair was run by and for gypsies – who had no truck with my quirky handmade stuff. But there were plenty of tourists, in their cashmere and tweed and green boots. They turned up their noses at the gypsy wares – the gaudy cushions and glassware, the outrageous frills and flounces intended for small girls to wear – and fell on my stuff with relief. They assumed, of course, that I was Roma myself, with my black hair and the bright red headscarf I'd been wearing.

I'd only been allowed to have a stall at all

because my brother Graham, the car mechanic, had connections with one of the many Mr Smiths who organised the Show. I was put at the top of the slope, near a chap selling lurcher pups.

I'd tried to clear all my stuff out of Helen's house when I heard that Phil was coming, but somehow the things hadn't wanted to leave. Her furniture was still there and without the throws and hangings and cushions it would have looked impossibly stark and cold. I hadn't the heart to take them away, which was ridiculous, considering that Phil's sole purpose in coming was to dispose of the entire contents and get the house put up for sale. Rather him than me – that was how I settled it to myself. I never liked getting rid of things.

It was unfriendly weather that day, more like late November than October. Really, it was the first chilly day of the autumn, which was bad luck for Phil and his lady friend. I revved up my Rayburn a bit, pulled the windows shut, and wondered what it would be like in Greenhaven with no proper heating. Helen had never wanted an Aga or Rayburn, relying on an open log fire for extra cheer, but essentially dependent on central heating fuelled by oil. And now, with no electricity, it wasn't going to work.

Cold Aston was often windy, exposed from most sides, on the upper levels of the wold. They

used to call it Aston Blank, probably due to the
chalkiness of the soil – or the festoons of old
man's beard along all the hedges, the white seed
heads like snow for part of the year. Blank – *blanc*
– get it? But blankness wasn't so different from
whiteness, and I often got into a mood where the
place did indeed seem empty of that energy or
whatever you want to call it that other places
have. Cold Aston was beautiful, of course, like
everywhere in the Cotswolds. It got prizes for Best
Kept Village, and any new building was
rigorously controlled, to ensure it matched what
was already there. The remaining farms were all
huge ranches with endless acres of corn and
grassland. You could stand on the high ground at
Notgrove and scan the views in all directions and
barely see a living creature, man or beast.
Another reason for calling it Blank, now I think
about it.

But they changed it to Cold Aston, not so long
ago – or so they think. The signs all keep Aston
Blank as an alternative, and I don't believe either
name will ever really disappear.

It was as good a place as any to live, and all the
better for not being on the tourist trail. There was
at least the normality of a school, and a pub and a
fair number of small houses for not-so-rich people
to live in. The farms were mostly approached by
plain rutted tracks, left open and unannounced to

the road. There were avenues of trees on all sides, remnants of driveways to country mansions, in many cases. If there was frost overnight, I thought, the leaves would have lost their green within a couple of days.

Just as it was getting properly dark and Thomas, my big tabby, had come in from the cold, seeking out the fire I'd already lit for us both in the back room, there was a knock on the door. Phil was there, eyebrows raised in a sort of mock drama, holding a broken oil lamp chimney.

'We've made a bad start,' he grinned. 'Baxter knocked this over with his tail.' I didn't need to ask who Baxter was. 'It's useless now. I don't suppose you've got one anywhere, have you?'

'An oil lamp,' I said slowly. 'You're asking me if you can borrow an oil lamp.'

'I know – it sounds a bit like a fairytale, doesn't it. It's just that they cast such a lovely romantic light.' He cocked his head sideways, coaxingly, infuriatingly. 'Besides, there are only four candles. We forgot to buy a new boxful.'

'Well, sorry, but I haven't. There might be one in your attic, though. Helen kept all sorts of junk up there. You should keep those dogs under better control.'

'You don't have to tell me that – but I've never found a way to stop them wagging their tails. Even

Hepzie – that's Thea's spaniel – can do some damage with hers.'

'Cut them off,' I said. 'Now...' He was letting the cold in, and I was cross with him for being so soppy. The Phil Hollis I remembered had never been soppy. He was a senior policeman, for heaven's sake!

He blew out his cheeks, still playing the same game, helpless little boy, appealing to an earlier version of me, fishing for some old shared childhood that had never really existed. 'It'll be awfully dark in the attic,' he whined.

'So use the candles for the rest of tonight and have a look up there tomorrow. It's got a skylight – you'll be able to see quite well by day.'

'Oh, well, thanks, um, Ariadne.' He worked his lips and repeated quietly, 'Ariadne. I must remember to say Ariadne.'

'Oh, go away,' I said, and pushed the door shut in his face.

It wasn't as bad as it sounds. If we were playing a 'reversion to childhood' game, then this was entirely in keeping with the rules. He would tease me, I stuck my tongue out or punched him, he retreated and forgot all about me. It had been a regular pattern for decades and I'd have been lost if anything had changed. The presence of a love interest on his side made no difference. Whatever it was between Phil Hollis and me, it definitely wasn't love. For love, you had to have equality, respect, attention, seriousness, understanding – and about fifty other qualities which were utterly absent from our relationship, such as it was. Instead, on his side there was a decency, a good heart – and a kind of unimaginativeness which prevented him from working out that I might be bad news. For me there was a curiosity about his life, along with our shared history and an uncomfortable knowledge of secrets. Secrets that Detective Superintendent Hollis certainly would rather I hadn't known.

CHAPTER TWO

Before ten the next morning he was back, wearing a quilted bodywarmer over an inadequate nylon jumper, and looking pinched with cold. His lady friend hadn't managed to create much heat, then, I thought, while wondering whether she'd had the sense to pack more substantial clothes than he had.

Without giving him time to speak, I ushered him into my house and sat him down beside the Rayburn. 'Stay there,' I ordered, and went through to the back room. It didn't take me long to find what I was looking for.

'Here,' I told him, proffering a thick jumper in handspun Cotswold wool. 'That'll keep the cold out. I've got a pot of tea made, too, if you'd like some.'

He didn't demur, just grinned and shivered. 'I didn't think it could be this cold in October,' he said. 'How do you cope in January?'

I didn't bother to reply. He might never have

lived in Cold Aston, but he knew the area well enough, so acting like a soft townie didn't cut much ice with me.

'Does your friend want a jumper as well?' I asked, once I'd put boiling water in the teapot.

'We'll buy them off you, of course,' he said, standing up to put the jumper on. It fitted perfectly. 'Must be worth quite a bit.'

'You don't have to. I wear them myself before I sell them. Just don't spill red wine down it, or blood, and you can give it back when you go if you like.'

'But I want to keep it,' he insisted. 'I love it already.'

I shrugged. Everybody loved my jumpers – which was why I'd been forced to employ a team of spinners and knitters to keep up with the demand. It took a lot of the satisfaction out of the business, but also most of the pressure. There'd been a time when I'd knitted for twelve hours a day, turning out three full-sized jumpers a week, and that'd been no fun at all.

'D'you want to ask her over for some tea, as well?' I invited. 'Or is she frying sausages on the camping stove?'

'I'll go and get her,' he said. That was always a thing I'd liked about Phil – he didn't waste time on polite nonsenses, like *well, if you're sure it's no trouble*. He took people at their word. Sometimes I wondered whether this was a good trait for a policeman. Might he not be missing some of the undercurrents, if he believed whatever his witnesses and criminals told him? When I said this to Caroline once, she laughed at me and said I'd got him completely wrong. 'He never stops trying to spot the hidden agenda,' she told me. 'That wide-eyed look works a treat, putting people off guard.' She seemed to be saying it had worked rather too successfully with her at times.

Before they came back, I fetched another jumper for the woman. This was a smaller version of Phil's in the golden brown you get from dyeing fleece with dead dahlia heads. It wasn't one of my favourites.

She came in looking as if she'd only just got out of bed. Her hair was messy and her cheeks very pink. Phil followed her into the kitchen, standing behind her and putting his hands on her shoulders. She pressed back against him, angling her head up and sideways to see his face. I thrust the jumper at her without saying anything.

She accepted it with a big smile and immediately put it on. I poured tea for them, without offering coffee. I dislike coffee myself and seldom keep it in the house. All I had was some very stale ground beans that had to go into a proper coffee machine and there was no way I could be bothered with all that.

The woman was curious, looking round the

house with no shame. 'It's more recent than Auntie Helen's house, isn't it?' she said.

'By a century or so,' I confirmed. 'This one barely dates further back than the 1880s. It was built for a farm worker and his family, I think.'

She nodded seriously. 'Very likely,' she said. 'Have you always lived here?'

I shook my head. 'I grew up on a farm, near Charlbury, not really in the Cotswolds at all.'

She nodded again, as if this information fitted her expectations of me. *Just a country bumpkin,* she was thinking. *Probably left school at fifteen.*

'So what do you do now?' she asked. 'Besides making gorgeous jumpers?'

I shrugged. 'All sorts of things. Gardening, watching out for old ladies, lending a hand at lambing time. Keeping pigs. Making wine.'

She blinked, trying to make something of me, to fit me into a pigeonhole. Phil rescued her. 'Oh, M— Ariadne's a woman out of her time,' he laughed. 'Always has been. Babysitter, shepherd, home help, and now expert craftswoman.'

I hadn't missed the near-blunder over my name, but gave him credit for correcting himself in time. I didn't mind that he was patronising me. What he said was accurate enough.

'He's left out the most important bit,' I said lightly.

They both looked at me expectantly, and I felt

strangely foolish. 'I'm a pagan,' I mumbled. 'We've got a group here. I more or less started it.'

'I didn't know there was a group,' said Phil. 'Is it flourishing?'

'Depends on what you mean. It's healthy enough.'

'I've always liked the sound of paganism,' said Thea, not very convincingly. 'Although I don't know much about it.'

'There's no mystery,' I said, with a look at Phil.

Thea was still being gushingly polite. 'It must have been wonderful to grow up on a farm,' she said next.

I smiled. 'It was, actually. We mainly had sheep, and I didn't get very involved except at lambing time, when I was in big demand. From when I was twelve or thirteen I was the best at it. More of mine survived than anyone else's. It just seemed to come naturally to me. Plus I've always had strong hands.' I was boasting shamelessly, trying to get a reaction from her, wanting her attention for some reason.

She smiled at me, a fresh sincere smile. It was as if she kept a neatly laundered stock of them somewhere, ready to produce a new one every minute or so. 'That must have been quite something. And you still do it now, do you?'

'Yup,' I agreed. 'Still the best, ask anybody.'

'Actually,' said Phil, with typical male clumsiness, 'I came over to ask you a favour.'

'Oh yes?'

'You know the attic in Helen's house? Where you said there might be a lamp? Well, we can't find how to get into it.' He laughed. 'Is there a secret door somewhere?'

I'd forgotten that he had hardly even been to his aunt's final home, even though she lived there for eighteen years. When he did visit, it was just for an afternoon, Helen treating him to tea and scones and gratitude for his trouble. His life had been on its own track, with wife, kids, parents, job.

'Fine detective you are,' I teased.

'It's really quite a big house,' the woman defended. 'I was surprised. I mean, just for one old lady. She must have rattled about in there.'

'She loved it,' I said, feeling a pain behind my left breast. 'I've never known anybody love a house like that before. She was always polishing and dusting, and just – well, *loving* it.' I sighed.

'But Phil says she was quite old when she came here to live.'

'She was sixty-eight. Her husband had just died. She wanted to make a new start in a new place.'

Phil's friend looked out of my kitchen window, where there was a view of open fields, stretching down the slope to the south. 'It's much more open than most Cotswold villages,' she murmured. 'The others I know all seem to be situated in hollows or valleys. There's a lot more sky here.'

I didn't say anything. Phil drained his mug, and wriggled his shoulders inside the jumper. She read his mind instantly, and downed her own drink in one gulp.

'Work,' she said. 'We've got work to do. Ariadne—' she said it easily, with no sign of any effort or reluctance, which earned her a small hike in my estimation '—the attic. We really *can't* find the way into it.' She went to my front door and stared across at the house. It obviously had three storeys, although lacking the dormer windows that were such a common feature of Cotswold houses. A Velux skylight had been set into the steep roof, though, betraying the presence of a useable roof space. Thea shook her head.

'It's crazy – putting in a window like that and then hiding the access.'

'It isn't really hidden,' I said and led them back to their side of the street.

I showed them where it was with a ridiculous feeling of pride. There was in fact a narrow stairway to the upper floor, not some newfangled loft ladder, or removable rectangle of plywood covering a hole in one of the ceilings. To get to Helen's attic, you pushed aside a tallboy beside the chimney breast in the third bedroom, and climbed a flight of steep brick steps which followed the tapering line of the chimney itself. Then you turned tightly, to step onto the boarded floor of a large space which ran the entire length and breadth of the house.

Phil and his Thea pressed right behind me, making daft jokes about the secret stairway and wondering what they'd find under the roof.

But they had to wait. As I turned, ready to climb the last few inches into the attic itself, I stopped. The light was quite good, streaming in through the roof window. It showed a transformation that made no sense at all to me.

'Why've you stopped?' demanded Phil. 'What's the matter?'

'Somebody's been here,' I said, my heart pounding at the strangeness of what I was seeing.

'What?' He couldn't hear me, stuck halfway up the narrow stairway.

I tried to bend towards him, but it was difficult. I couldn't bring myself to take the final step. 'It's all different,' I said, a bit louder.

'Well, move then,' he snapped at me. 'Let me see.'

I crawled clumsily onto the boards and sat close to the top of the stairs. I felt cold and scared.

Phil's head appeared, and he swivelled, trying to find me. 'Look!' I told him. 'Look at it.'

He came up higher, turned and hopped up to my side. Only then did he inspect the attic, spread before us like – well, like a film set, perhaps. Or the scene of a very peculiar crime.

It wasn't so much a crime scene, I corrected

myself, as a clinically organised hideout. As Phil and I slowly shuffled over, to make space for Thea, the three of us obviously had very diverse reactions to what we were seeing. For myself, I was quite simply stunned. What lay before me was impossible. It was a joke, a cleverly constructed display designed to confuse. For Phil the policeman, it was deeply suspicious. He moved first, walking with head bowed to avoid the low beams of the roof, hands clasped behind his back, giving everything a forensic inspection, careful not to touch. Thea inhaled loudly, excitedly. 'It's so *clean*,' she said. 'Surely…? I mean…?'

She was right. Everything sparkled in the morning light. None of the dust and cobwebs that even Helen had permitted up there, and which would inevitably have accumulated in the year since her death without a human hand to remove them. The clutter that I had expected to see had all disappeared. 'Where are her *things*?' I demanded. 'They've all been stolen.' I thought about the stamp collection, the photo albums and boxes of letters.

Phil was halfway towards the far wall. 'No, I don't think so,' he said. 'There's a whole lot of stuff behind this curtain.' He tweaked at a huge dark blue swathe of chenille. Then he started to enumerate the objects that were carefully arranged on the clean floor in full view. 'Cushions, lots of them. Silver candlesticks. Tins of food. Paper and pens. Books. China plates. Folding table. My God, look here!' His hands had become unclasped, and he was using a ballpoint pen, with its cap still on, to flip things open or nudge something aside for a better view. I stared into a neat cardboard box containing objects that I immediately realised had a particular significance. Phil, too, had understood what they were and our eyes met in a startle of memory and apprehension.

I rubbed my toe on the two-by-eight boards on the floor, which I remembered as having been covered with fine dust the last time I saw them. Now they were insanely clean. I peered down for a closer look. 'They've been *sealed*,' I realised. 'Or varnished. Why would anybody do that?'

'And when?' Phil added. We both stared at the floor, until I spotted faint lines in the varnish. When I looked at Phil, it was plain that he'd seen them already.

'What are they?' I asked.

'Something's been marked out,' was all he would say.

Thea was standing under the Velux, scanning the whole space. She moved to a Tesco carrier bag, lying on its own in the angle made by the roof. Bending down she retrieved it and looked inside. 'What's this?' she said, pulling something out.

Phil beckoned her to where he was standing, not wanting to have to crouch in the lower part.

'Masking tape,' he said. 'All scrumpled up.' He tilted his head at me. 'This is what made those lines,' he explained.

'Why would they unpick it? Why not just leave it?'

He shrugged. 'They probably change. Maybe it's just some sort of rehearsal.'

Thea looked from him to me and back again. 'What are you talking about?' she demanded. 'Is this making more sense to you two than it is to me?'

She bent over the cardboard box, reaching out a hand. 'Don't touch anything!' Phil warned her.

She blinked at him in surprise and then turned her attention back to the objects. 'Jewellery,' she said. 'Is it the stash of a burglar or something? This must be his booty. Phil – there are probably fingerprints on it all. You'll have to call the police.' Then she giggled, hearing herself. 'Except, you *are* the police, aren't you?'

'Not really,' he muttered, inattentively. 'I haven't got a fingerprint kit with me, for a start.' He and I must have been acting strangely because Thea quickly picked up our reaction. 'What?' she demanded. 'What's the matter with both of you?' She gave the box a sharp kick, shifting the contents. 'A gold ring with a sort of sunburst pattern on it. And a watch with a bird design in the middle. Something made of blue silk with stars on it.' She shook her head. 'Nice things.'

'It's a blazing star, not a sunburst,' I said. 'It stands for the Great Being.'

Phil gave an intake of breath. Even after all those years it upset him for the secrets of the Lodge to be spoken out loud. He glanced around as if expecting the All-Seeing Eye to materialise between the roof beams.

'Great Being?' Thea repeated. 'I'm sorry, but you'll have to explain. If you don't, I might have to scream.'

Phil spoke to her. 'It isn't a burglar, Thea. This stuff must belong to the...intruder.'

She frowned at him. 'How do you know?'

He sighed. 'They're Masonic things. My guess is that there's a man living locally who doesn't want his wife to know he's on the square. So he keeps all his regalia up here, where she won't find it. He comes here to learn the ritual as well, making marks on the floor, to be sure he gets it right. These are Masonic books with the things that have to be learned. It takes time, so he'd stay overnight, eating out of tins. These cushions would make a tolerable bed.'

'How ridiculous!' she exclaimed. 'Pathetic.'

Phil sighed again. 'You could say that,' he mumbled. 'Most people think that way these days.'

'Don't you?' She widened her eyes at him. 'All that secret handshaking and pretending to bury each other alive. It's childish nonsense.'

I drew back, wincing on Phil's behalf. Even now, with much of their mystery exposed and the one-time pervasive nervousness around them dissipated, it felt dangerous to criticise them too openly. At the same time I was wondering whether Phil was going to be honest with her. He knew that I knew what he ought to reveal, the air crackling with our shared memories.

'They take it very seriously,' was all he said.

Thea tossed her head and made a tutting sound and I gave Phil a look which he met full on. 'Have you any idea at all who did this?' he asked me with a frown.

I'd already been asking myself the same question. One or two names had forced themselves into my mind, but I had no intention of uttering them to a Detective Superintendent until I'd had more time to think.

So I acted dumb. 'It doesn't make sense,' I said. 'How did they get in? And *why*? What's the point?'

'It's lovely, though, isn't it?' said Thea. 'Everything just right.' She smiled at us like a child. 'He can't have known we were coming, can he? We must have interrupted him.'

We went down again after that, Phil leading the way. Their three dogs were all waiting at the foot of the stairs, the spaniel bouncing about with a loopy grin on its face. The corgi, I noticed, also had its tail undocked. What *was* it with people, thinking they knew better than age-old custom? Bad enough leaving the tail on a cocker spaniel. On a corgi it looked even more ridiculous. It made me realise how long it had been since I'd lost touch with Phil. I no longer knew his dogs, or his girlfriends, or what he thought about anything.

Somehow we all managed to get downstairs and into the kitchen, which was cold and musty-smelling and rather dark. It was at the back of the house, with a small window, across which a broom had grown. Helen had been fond of that particular shrub, despite its ill-considered position. In the year since her death it had grown in all directions, reducing the light considerably.

'Do we have to report it or something?' Thea asked. She was subdued but fighting it, fully aware that something strange had happened that I understood better than she did. She persisted in asserting her stronger claim on Phil. 'Presumably a crime's been committed – someone breaking in without permission.'

Phil closed his eyes for a few seconds, leaning back against one of the worktops. 'It isn't a very serious crime,' he said eventually. 'And he isn't going to come back while we're here.'

I snorted. 'You mean somebody has to get themselves murdered before you take it seriously.'

They both seemed to go very still when I said that, catching each other's eye. I remembered the news headlines, in the summer. Something about a boy murdered down near Chalford, somebody telling me Phil had been involved.

'Am I missing something?' I asked them.

'Not really,' said Phil. 'Just that Thea and I both hoped not to hear that word for the whole week.'

'Well, excuse *me*,' I flounced.

'What are we going to do, then?' Thea repeated doggedly. She had become upset, agitated. And disappointed, as if something she'd looked forward to had been snatched away.

'I'd like to know how he got in, at least. If we can make the place more secure I'll feel happier,' said Phil.

'I suppose we should,' said Thea.

'Let's check the windows,' Phil said, pushing himself away from his perch. He moved heavily, and his eyes looked small and sunken. I knew why, but his girlfriend had no idea.

It didn't take very long to find evidence of illicit access to the house. There was a ladder lying alongside the garden fence, not hidden at all. Phil scanned the back wall of the house, and pointed to some scratch marks on the stone just below the bathroom window. He propped the ladder up, climbed to the window, and gave it a yank. It came open easily, both halves of the casement flipping outwards as if he'd cried *Open, sesame!* to them. There was just space for an adult to climb through and into the house.

I felt a flicker of alarm. I, after all, had been entrusted with the security of the house. Phil had even paid me a few quid to keep an eye on it. I couldn't remember ever having inspected the bathroom window's fastening, although I had noticed that the wood on some of the window frames was going rotten. This had not been one of them.

We went back indoors, without talking. The other two seemed very glum, sighing and looking into each other's eyes. I thought about it from their point of view. Obviously, this had been intended as a romantic little holiday for them, at the start of their relationship. They didn't want policemen clumping about, checking window catches and bagging up the stuff in the attic. They hardly even wanted *me* there.

It was plain they weren't going to say anything about what they intended, so I waded in and said it for them. 'Don't worry about me,' I started. 'I mean, I can pretend this never happened, if that's what you want.'

I'd stepped onto dangerous ground all right. But then Phil ought to remember that I was always doing exactly that. He tucked his chin into his neck and looked at me like a schoolmaster.

'Oh, bugger it.' He smacked his hand on the table, and stared at the floor. It didn't sound like a straight answer to my question.

'It's me,' said Thea. 'I'm a jinx. I knew I was, after the last time.'

'Don't be stupid.'

I watched her response to this. Was she going to stand for such rudeness? He hadn't said it gently or fondly, but as if he meant it just as it sounded. The skin tightened around her mouth and eyes, but after a deep breath she nodded. 'You're right. Sorry.'

'Well, I can see I'm not needed,' I said, not wanting to witness much more of their mutual adjustments. It didn't matter to me whether or not they got it together and settled down for the rest of their lives, but I was no marriage counsellor and I found the details embarrassing.

'Thanks for showing us the attic, anyway,' said Thea, as if something had been decided. 'We can let you get on now.'

'You'll have to see if you can buy a new lamp,' I said. 'There wasn't one upstairs, after all.'

'We'll just get lots more candles, I expect,' said Thea. 'Or we might even try and get the power reconnected on Monday. It seems a bit silly struggling to manage without it, now we're here.'

I had my hand on the door latch when Phil seemed to wake up. 'Wait! Mary, wait a minute.'

I can only say that I *growled* at him.

'She's called Ariadne,' Thea said swiftly.

'Oh, to hell with that nonsense.' He looked at me like a grown-up tired of playing the make believe

game the children had roped him in to. 'Don't you
know *anything* about what's been happening in the
attic? Can't you even guess? Wouldn't you have
seen movement, or lights, or something, through
the skylight? Or heard them?'

I straightened my spine and returned his look. 'I
have changed my name to Ariadne,' I said loudly. 'It
is now my name. I'm not asking you to like it or
approve of it. Just have the basic respect to *use* it.
And no, I have never seen or heard anybody in this
house since Helen died thirteen months ago. Is that
clear enough for you?' If I'd felt a sneaking guilt
about the things I wasn't telling him, it had quickly
evaporated in the heat of my anger.

He did not drop his gaze. I remembered that he
spent much of his working life asking questions and
weathering a wide range of hostile and intemperate
replies. But I felt amply justified in the stand I'd
taken. And I was more interested in Phil's new
girlfriend's response than I was in his or my own.
Most women would have been embarrassed, tried
to smooth things out, even taken sides. Instead,
once she'd corrected him about my name, she just
backed away, turning to her wretched spaniel and
ignoring me and Phil completely. She started
picking at the dog's ears, and muttering quietly to it.
The big black and tan thing sidled up to her, its nails
clicking on the tiled floor, and she gave it a quick
rub between the ears. I didn't think she was

embarrassed at all – just happy to leave us to settle things between us, without making any sort of judgement.

'I'll have to go now, anyway,' I said. 'I've got somebody coming for lunch.'

I sounded ungracious in my own ears, almost resentful, and disliked it in myself. I wasn't usually like that. It was all about Phil and his knowledge of me as a sullen teenager. Somehow that earlier me – who he had known as Mary – was still lurking somewhere, and I couldn't keep her out of sight. And I hadn't just been sullen; I'd been nursing a powerful passion for him, which I hoped then, and continued to hope, had been invisible to him and everybody else. In my adolescent dreams, he had kissed me and vowed undying love, and left me tingling and confused in the morning. The reality, which I sometimes had difficulty in holding on to, was that he had been friendly, amused, relaxed, even interested – but not emotionally connected. I had hung on every word he spoke to me, and repeated them again and again afterwards. I knew Phil Hollis well – or thought I did.

CHAPTER THREE

It was true that I was expecting a visitor. One of my knitters, Gaynor, was coming for lunch. I'd made soup from my own vegetables, and a pork stew from a small part of one of Arabella's sons, slaughtered earlier in the year. Providing food for visitors was not something I got aereated about. There was always plenty in my pantry. Everybody constantly told me that I lived like someone from the 1940s, with my meat safe and hams and egg rack and huge collection of jamjars – not to mention the racks of homemade wine, which even I couldn't drink as fast as I could make it. I mostly shrugged them off with a laugh, pointing out how much money I saved from never going near a supermarket.

Gaynor and I had one major thing in common: we lived alone and had few calls on our weekends. Her parents were dead and mine were otherwise engaged. We did not have boyfriends or partners or children to occupy us. We were in that awkward no-man's-land of the mid-thirties, no longer young enough to be silly, nor old enough to panic about the rest of our lives. If we'd lived in London or Liverpool, we'd undoubtedly have been totally different people. As it was, we'd squared our shoulders, settled down, and made some progress on learning what it was we did best.

She arrived at half past twelve, smiling faintly, carrying chocolates. 'What a lovely smell!' she said, sniffing the air.

'Parsnip and dill,' I told her. 'Do you want some sloe gin?'

Gaynor only drank when she was with me. It frightened her, as did many things. It came with all kinds of associations to do with social gatherings and protocols and unpredictable emotions. But it was all right with me. She trusted me not to take any kind of advantage. She perhaps knew that I drank more than was good for me, but not the exact extent. It wasn't that I made any attempt to hide it, with the demijohns burping away in the back of the kitchen and crowds of empty bottles all over the place. Perhaps the tubs of fermenting blackberries and sloes and apples were a kind of camouflage. They diverted attention more into the production and less into the consumption. She nodded her acceptance of the gin.

'Did you finish the coat?' I asked.

'Obviously not or I'd have brought it with me. Those buttons won't be any good. I'll have to get some different ones.' The straight talking surprised me, although I chose to take it as a mark of our friendship. Nobody could be as completely submissive and mousy as most people thought Gaynor was. I had seen evidence of strength buried inside her on many occasions, although it took a close acquaintance to recognise it.

I spoke carefully. 'Really? I thought they were fine.'

She twitched, her head jerking sideways in a characteristic mannerism. 'They're too big, Ari. The thing's heavy enough as it is – chunky buttons aren't right.'

Knitted coats were, of course, risky. They could all too easily look like baggy dressing gowns. But when they worked, they were divine, as luxurious as fur, and almost as hard-wearing. We'd adapted some Kaffe Fassett ideas, reducing the width that made several of his things unwearable and playing with collars and pockets. It took Gaynor a month to knit one, and I paid her two hundred pounds. The wool was my own handspun. So far I'd sold three for three hundred each to a fabulously upmarket emporium in Broadway, which added a disgraceful mark-up of its own. I was in a hurry for the next one. October was the best month for selling warm woollen garments. People believed there might actually be some wintry weather for a change. By January, they'd realise their mistake.

Although we'd known each other for so many years, I still had to watch my step with Gaynor. I had to rein myself in, pretend to be less competent than I actually was. Even my size could intimidate her, if I stood too close. She believed herself to be a failure in the important areas of life, viewing expert knitting as hardly worthy of notice. She was doggedly insistent on her own uselessness. My impression, gained from my earliest knowledge of her, was that she'd be fine when she got to about fifty. She could settle down then into being what she truly was – a good-natured misfit, born out of her time, living a simple solitary life with her knitting.

In an effort not to overwhelm her, I had to avoid talking about books I'd read, because she didn't read. I couldn't talk about the evening classes I ran in Cirencester, teaching women the secrets of dyeing and spinning and felting. 'I don't know how you can cope with all those people asking questions, and wanting you to tell them what to do,' she'd shuddered, when she'd come to hear about it. My stripy hair had strained things between us, drawing people's attention as it did and making me an object of remark. She'd gulped painfully at her first sight of it, finally asking who'd done it and how long it would take to wear off.

But one thing besides knitting that I could talk

about to Gaynor was the pagan group. She would never have had the courage to join it herself, but she was extremely interested in our activities and was acquainted with all the members, having met them at my house a number of times. My role in the group was as the specialist in country matters, unravelling the ancient meanings behind superficial modern rituals. I had made it my business to keep the focus on the connections between the natural world and human beings. It came, I suppose, from my farming childhood and a deep impatience with present day religion. The group did not make any attempt to conceal its existence and most local residents seemed benign towards us. Some thought us daft, others obviously liked the local colour that we contributed. They never showed the slightest concern, in any case, recognising that we were a harmless outfit, not interested in attacking or even challenging anybody's genuinely held views. There were the usual jokes about full moons and nakedness, but not much beyond that.

'I've been busy with the Samhain stuff,' I told Gaynor. 'There's going to be a divination session. Do you want me to ask anything for you?'

She went rather still, looking at her gin as if into a crystal ball. 'Well, I sort of do, as it happens,' she said quietly. 'Except you'll think it's silly.'

'Try me.'

'You know Oliver Grover?'

I nodded patiently at this rhetorical question. She knew I knew Oliver, although it was more accurate to say I knew Oliver's grandmother, old Sally Grover. I knew her very well, having taken her on at much the same time as Phil's Auntie Helen. She lived in Naunton, only a mile or two away, and in summer I would walk up there via Arabella's coppice. I liked Sally almost as much as I'd liked Helen. She was nearly ninety, perfectly active and alert, but prone to giddy spells. Oliver had sought me out to take some of the burden off his shoulders, his mother having gone to live in Spain with a new husband. He lived in Bourton-on-the-Water, quite close by, but Sally had refused to allow him to take on tasks that she regarded as strictly woman's work. I was glad to be asked. It felt good to have somebody else to think about, to wonder how the old girl had slept and whether she'd tried the soup I'd made for her.

'Well,' Gaynor told me blushingly, 'I think he might be trying to...you know. It's shy he is, like me, but he *looks* at me...you know.' She sighed. 'I wouldn't mind, you see. He's got lovely eyes. And he talks to me as if he likes me.' She looked as if she wanted to say something else, but I doubt if my expression was very encouraging.

Gaynor had been a very late child. Her mother was forty-eight when she was born, and her father fifty-five. They were Welsh, but had come across the border when her father lost his job in the coalmines. The migration must have taken all the courage they'd possessed, and they never managed to find a comfortable place for themselves in the Cotswolds. They were like a family of Hobbits living in the wrong universe. Small, nervous people who kept themselves shut away. I met Gaynor in the sixth form, where she was taking Latin and Ancient History A-levels. She still had her Welsh intonation, and would often say 'is it?' at the end of her sentences. Her parents had died before she was twenty, having taught her almost nothing about how to get along in the world. It was a wicked waste of a perfectly good person, although nobody else seemed to see it that way.

'You want me to find out whether there's any future for you and him?'

'Something like that. Can you? I mean, is that something...?'

The simple old-worldliness of her plea gave me a pang. So did her allusion to Oliver Grover, a self-employed accountant in his late thirties. Without anyone making much overt reference to it, it was common knowledge that Oliver was gay. He was a classic example, only son of a single mother, quietly amusing when you got him talking, and carrying that complicated air of having a secret that made him rather prickly. Gaynor's suspicions that he was casting amorous glances her way could only be deluded. I wondered how she could have failed to realise.

'Where have you seen him?' I wondered. She had made it sound as if she saw him regularly and I couldn't think how that could happen.

'At the bridge club, of course,' she said with a little twitch of impatience.

I consistently forgot that Gaynor played bridge. She seldom spoke about it and it seemed so contrary to what I knew of her that it perpetually slipped out of my mind. I had similarly forgotten that Oliver belonged to the club, as well. Card games did not feature in my life at all. The whole thing struck me as a complete waste of time, something people did to while away empty hours when they could have been far more constructively engaged. My pagan soul disapproved of cards, if I stopped to think about it. The associations with gambling and deceit only deepened my disfavour.

'He's quite often my partner,' she went on. 'That's when Leslie can't come. Usually they're together, of course. And I'm with Brian. But Brian's leg's been very bad for months now, so we've had to rearrange things.'

Brian was an elderly buffer who I scarcely knew. As a bridge partner for Gaynor he sounded ideal. And even less interesting than Oliver.

'Leslie,' I repeated. 'Is that Leslie Giddins? From the pagan group?'

She nodded. 'He joined at the same time as Oliver. They both turned up without partners, so we put them together. They make a great pair, actually.'

Later, this snippet of information acquired a great deal more significance than it did at the time of telling. Leslie Giddins was married to a sweet girl and was a reliable member of the pagan group. The fact that he partnered Oliver Grover at bridge seemed unremarkable, as did his sporadic attendance. Presumably there were often better things to do. All my attention was concentrated on how to deal with Gaynor's sudden pash for the unobtainable Oliver.

'I just need a bit of help,' she went on. 'I mean, what should I do next?'

'I'll think about it,' I said feebly. 'But don't get your hopes up. I suspect Oliver's a confirmed bachelor by now.' Yet again I retreated from the task of explaining something to my friend. It was as if she lacked some crucial mental function. Once or twice I had wondered if she might be mildly autistic, unable to grasp anything unusual or subtle, incapable of seeing things from another person's viewpoint.

Stella, another friend, had accused me of 'rescuing' Gaynor in order to boost my own status. She'd been drunk at the time, and I'd tried to laugh it off as the booze speaking. But I couldn't forget it, and nearly every time I saw Gaynor I asked myself whether it was true. Eventually, I admitted it probably did explain why I stuck with her, despite there being so many drawbacks. Besides, she was a brilliant knitter.

'There's a car outside Greenhaven,' she noted, looking out of my front window. I was in the kitchen, but I heard her clearly enough. I only had to tilt my head to see her as well.

'Yes, Phil's there. Didn't I tell you he was coming?'

She seemed tense all of a sudden. 'No,' she said. 'Is he by himself?'

'Actually, no. He's with some bit of fluff.' Even as I spoke, I felt a kick of shame in my gut.

'What?' She frowned. 'You mean he's got a girlfriend?'

'So it would seem.'

'Is the electric on again, then?'

'Nope.'

'They must be *freezing*. How long are they staying? What are they *doing*?'

'They've come for the week, to sort out Helen's things, before putting the house on the market. I expect their love's keeping them warm. Plus the logs and the jumpers I've given them, of course.'

'Jumpers? Which ones?'

'She's got that brown thing that Maddie did. I gave him the blue crew-neck.'

'No! Not the slubby one?'

'He might give it back when he goes. It'll be all right. Just a quick shake in the fresh air, and nobody'll know it's been worn.'

'Ari!' she giggled. But her amusement didn't last. A few seconds later she was sighing and drifting restlessly around my small room, glancing out of the window every few seconds.

'What's the matter?' I asked her. Usually she sat tidily in one of my saggy chairs, her ankles crossed like a debutante. 'Is it Oliver?'

'Oh no,' she said. 'I suppose that's just a bit of silliness. He wouldn't be interested in me.'

Nobody could have done differently. 'Rubbish,' I told her. And then I got stuck. I couldn't for shame tell her she was interesting or beautiful or even particularly clever. She had failed all but one of her A-levels, for a start, and never managed to qualify for anything since. The truth was that she didn't appeal to men, not only because of her mousy looks, but her self-effacing manner. She couldn't look a person in the eye for long. Something always seemed to fail inside her in the middle of a promising conversation. As if she remembered her place, her inadequacies, and gave up all effort.

'I have to pull myself together,' she murmured. 'I can't go through life like this.' I had to shake my head to convince myself I'd heard correctly. This was a sudden departure from the Gaynor I knew.

'Like what?' I said, coming out of the kitchen. 'What do you mean?' I confess that my first thought was that I might be about to lose my best knitter.

'I need a *focus*,' she said, using a word I never thought I'd hear coming from her lips. 'Something outside of myself, with other people.'

'But you've got the bridge club for that.'

'That's not much of a challenge any more,' she said. 'Although it's going to the bridge club that made me see the possibilities.'

I was lost. The beans were boiling fiercely and I retreated to the Rayburn to rescue them. Gaynor never talked about *challenges* or *focus*. Who, I wondered, had she been listening to? What on earth had come over her?

We had our lunch, and she raved about how fabulous it all was, and how she'd have only had some bread and cheese if it hadn't been for me.

Before she left, having run out of conversation, I remembered the discoveries in Greenhaven's attic. 'Guess what,' I said. 'Somebody's been making free with Helen's house.'

She blinked at me. 'Pardon?' Her voice came out thickly as if through a full mouth. But her mouth was empty – we'd finished lunch minutes ago.

I pointed across the street. 'We found a whole lot of stuff in the attic this morning. Somebody has really been making themselves at home up there – varnished the floor, kept all the cobwebs and dust cleared away – and stashed away a lot of Masonic stuff.'

'Masonic? How do you mean?' Her voice still sounded obstructed.

'A ring, some sort of banner, lots of books. I can't remember all of it. Everything's got the usual emblems on them. I remember from when Phil was a Mason. He showed me some of the stuff then.'

'He wasn't supposed to do that, was he?'

I shrugged. 'He was never very good at sticking to their idiotic rules. He'd never have joined if Caroline's father hadn't insisted. He only did it to please her.'

'Caroline?' I became aware that Gaynor had done little but echo my words since I started the story.

'You know. Phil's wife. Ex-wife, I mean. She and I were great friends for a while. I'm sure I must have told you. She's married again now, to that Xavier bloke who does garden design or whatever it is. Lives near Painswick.'

'Johnson,' she said. 'Xavier Johnson.'

'That's right. I didn't think you'd know him.'

She shook her head and avoided my eye. 'I've just seen his boards up, that's all. It's not a name you'd forget.'

'I wonder if he's on the square,' I murmured. 'Caroline would be pleased, if he is. She's always loved the Masons, silly cow.'

Gaynor coughed and went to the kitchen for

some water. When she came back, she started talking again about buttons for the knitted coat, and then went home at about half past three.

I tried not to think of the forlorn solitary evening that lay ahead of her. She lived in a flat in Stow, part of a large house that had been converted. When her parents died, I'd expected her to simply carry on in their house, but she'd explained that it was too big for her and she didn't like living on two floors. When I queried this, she said she could always hear noises – from upstairs during the day, and from downstairs during the night. 'I'm scared all the time,' she admitted. 'I just want a nice ground floor flat, with a little bit of garden. I think that would be perfect.'

She found it effortlessly, two minutes from the centre of Stow with open fields at the back. She banked the rest of the money she'd made selling her parents' house, vowing not to touch a penny of it unless she became desperate. 'I can make enough to keep myself, while I have my strength,' she said, sounding touchingly old-fashioned. The flat had one bedroom, a living room and a kitchen-diner. My little house was small enough, but I had twice the space that Gaynor did.

As for myself, I had plenty to do to prepare for the meeting that evening. Living on meagre amounts of money made me odd in the eyes of the modern world, especially being of the generation who had not the least idea of how to survive. It also kept me busy. My garden was small but densely packed with produce. It needed constant vigilance, the seasons galloping ahead of me if I allowed my attention to waver.

I put two bowls of flour and yeast to warm by the Rayburn, and went outside to spread mulch around the currant bushes. From the back, I had no view at all of Helen's house, and managed to forget, for several minutes at a time, that Phil was in there. When he did force himself into my head, it was mainly to wonder what he would do about the amazing state of the attic.

The mulch-spreading took all of twenty minutes, by which time my hands were cold. Nagging for my attention was the forthcoming Samhain season. Despite my emphatically prosaic approach to paganism (and most other things), this was a time of year I found exciting. I had learned such a lot during the Samhain ceremonies of previous years that I was now convinced that it really did have some very special features. The way it was usually expressed was to talk about the blurring of boundaries between two realms. The thinning of the walls, the porosity of the divide between *here* and *there*. Since Pullman's book *The Subtle Knife* had been published, this idea was easier to grasp. The 'curtain' became more flimsy and we could glimpse other realities.

It had happened to me when I hadn't been expecting it: when I had seen a ghost. An apparently three-dimensional person who ran through a dense hedge as if it wasn't there at all. I found it thrilling, conferring on me some kind of privilege that I felt no need to talk about. I nursed my warm secret, bringing it out every October to remind myself that there was something right and true about my pagan beliefs, regardless of the materialistic world around me.

Samhain is the time of death and sex, where ordinary individuals glimpse something of the relation between these two. Human babies tend to be conceived at Beltane or Lammas – the spring and summer festivals where inhibitions are quelled by music and drink and the weather impels them to excess. But this is not the way animals operate. They resist the farmer's knife, surviving the cull triumphant, copulating to express their survival. Die or procreate – the eternal option.

This is all perfectly ordinary stuff. So obvious it ought not to need stating. But people have a tendency to create dramas and conflicts out of ordinary matters, and some of the antics committed in the name of paganism glory in the nastier side of our natures.

It might be merely the power of suggestion, but when a person knows a curse has been put on him, he's liable to react strongly. It will haunt him, making him swagger defiantly, while using whatever strategies he can to forget. And the person imposing the curse doesn't escape, either. We fear those we hurt, and it becomes curiously difficult to look our victim in the face.

I should know. I've been there and done that.

CHAPTER FOUR

The weather was persistently grey, with a hint of drizzle in the air. Twilight came early, as it had the day before, and I could see the yellow glow of candlelight coming from the windows of Greenhaven, and no let-up in the smoke surging from the chimney. What were they doing in there, I wondered. No television or hi-fi. Possibly a battery radio, but I doubted it. They'd be cuddled together on Helen's leather sofa, talking sweet nonsense, hour after hour, until drifting entwined to bed. They'd eat bread and cold ham, drink wine and finish with fruit and chocolates.

I'd kneaded my dough, and left it to rise. Early in the morning, I would put it in to bake, ready for breakfast. Probably I'd take a loaf across the street. They'd be impressed.

Then, half an hour before people were due to arrive for the moot, Phil came knocking on my door again. This time I recognised who it was from the rhythm of the raps.

'Me again,' he said when I opened the door.

I kinked an eyebrow at him but said nothing.

'I've been back up to the attic. We can't just ignore it or leave those things there. I've got to decide what to do about it.'

'Why tell me?'

He took a step forward, barging into my living room without being invited. He was holding the cardboard box from the attic. 'Listen,' he said. 'This is a very odd assortment. Nothing to suggest a Master or even a Past Master, except for this.' He held up the blazing star medallion. 'But it's not quite right – see?'

I didn't even pretend to examine it. 'Phil, I'm not that familiar with the intricacies of Masonic symbolism,' I reminded him. 'I'm surprised you remember so much detail.'

He grimaced. 'So am I,' he said. 'But seeing all this stuff takes me right back.'

I could see he was hating the whole thing. He wouldn't meet my eye, worried perhaps that I'd remind him of the drama that his resignation from the Lodge gave rise to.

'Why not just throw it away?' I asked. 'What do you care about upsetting some deluded little hypocrite? Isn't that what you called them?' I gave him an innocent smile. 'Good phrase, that. Very memorable.'

He shuddered. 'I've still got them under my skin,

even now,' he admitted. 'Thea doesn't understand it, of course. How could she?'

'You've been trying to explain it to her?'

'All afternoon,' he said. 'Told her the whole story.'

'Heavens!'

He smiled ruefully. 'Heavens indeed. Sun, moon and seven stars, you might say.'

'I don't know who the Masters in the local Lodge have been in the past few years,' I told him, reverting to his initial request. 'I try to ignore them these days, though it isn't easy. Once you become aware of them, you can't escape. Even Oliver Grover's into it now, according to his Gran. She thinks it's a sign that he's got a great career ahead of him.'

'Who's Oliver Grover?'

'Local accountant.'

Phil snorted. 'No surprise there, then,' he said. 'But I must say they've cleaned their act up a lot since all that trouble in the late Eighties. To the point where they hardly seem to matter any more.'

'Damned by indifference,' I said. 'Poor things, they must really hate that.'

'I doubt if they've noticed,' said Phil.

I hadn't asked him to sit down or have a drink. He did not seem to notice that I had my chairs arranged in a circle, that there were candles and bowls of water and bundles of herbs on the table in the middle of the room. I only had a few more minutes before I needed to get rid of him.

'Why don't you just chuck it all in the bin?' I said, indicating the box.

'I can't,' he said. 'I know how much store they set by all these knick-knacks.'

'Bibelots,' I said, using a word I'd always loved.

'Gewgaws,' he contributed, playing along. For a policeman, his vocabulary wasn't bad at all.

But it couldn't last. 'Phil – I've got some people coming,' I said. 'Don't leave that stuff here, whatever you do. Somebody's sure to sniff it out. Let me have a think about it and I'll come over in the morning and we can talk about it then.'

He went willingly enough back to his girlfriend. On the way to the front door, I saw him pause at his car, open the tailgate and dump the box of Masonic trinkets inside. What did he plan to do with it, I wondered.

It was bound to be an irritant to them, the mystery of the attic, when all they wanted was to be left in peace. They wanted time together, away from the unpleasantnesses of his work, or the strangeness of human behaviour.

I didn't blame them. It didn't matter to me. I no longer yearned for Phil's attentions. On balance, I wanted him to be happy. The woman seemed harmless, apart from her deplorable dog. I couldn't stop them selling Greenhaven, much as I might like to. Not only would I lose a useful little retainer in my capacity as caretaker, but I might acquire undesirable neighbours who would be noisy and interfering and intrusive. But that was some time off yet, and I could always retreat to the garden behind my house if the people over the street offended me.

My tasks occupied me as usual. The cat curled on his stool by the Rayburn, and I pottered about the room, making everything tidy and ready for the coming moot.

Phil had gone and I forgot about him for a few hours.

Six people came to the moot. Four women and two men, plus me. The group included a couple – Kenneth and Pamela – who were planning a full-scale pagan wedding at Imbolc. We'd all argued for Beltane as far more fitting and traditional, but they insisted. They shared a birthday on February 3rd, and had a strong liking for the quiet optimism of Imbolc, rather than the uninhibited carryings-on of the May celebrations. In any case, it gave us all something unusual to look forward to, and their obvious affection warmed the atmosphere every time they entered a room.

We began by sharing thoughts and insights concerning Samhain. Pamela started us off, in her light chatty voice, looking round at us in turn, face all bright and enthusiastic. 'I don't know where this came from,' she said, 'but I suddenly noticed that in French, sex and death sound the same. *L'amour* and *la mort*. Isn't that amazing! It sparked off a brilliant meditation, where I wove the symbol of Cupid's arrow with an arrow of death, and then I pondered the changes that both bring to us. The transformations. But I couldn't bring them together—' she looked at us again. 'I can't find a way to unite sex and death meaningfully.'

I watched the others' reactions to this, wanting to jump in with some clever summary, but finding my tongue paralysed. Surely I'd known about *l'amour* and *la mort*? Didn't everybody? Try as I might, I couldn't recall ever having been aware of it until that moment.

'There's "the little death",' Kenneth put in hesitantly. 'You know – it's what they say about orgasm.'

A frisson ran round the circle. We were all wary of overt references to sexual matters, myself included. We would make jokes and indulge in innuendo sometimes, but despite the image of pagans as free spirits indulging in all sorts of hedonism, our particular group shied away from it most of the time. When it did intrude itself we were generally very solemn about it, searching for deeper meanings and links with nature. Pamela and Kenneth were careful not to flaunt the physical side of their relationship in public, which I thought was sweet of them. Besides, they were both in their late thirties and not at all inclined to giddiness. On top of that, Kenneth had some peculiar bone condition, which meant they broke easily. He habitually moved carefully, avoiding any risk of knocks or falls. I had never heard anyone make the obvious jokes about what it might be like to have sex with him, but I'm sure it was in all our minds.

'But that's only men, isn't it,' said Ursula, the granny of the group at forty-five, with a mild stare at Kenneth through her bifocals.

I interposed. 'We're following a wrong path here. For a start *l'amour* means love not sex. I think we ought to concentrate on the importance of Samhain as a time of cleansing and preparation for winter. We clean our houses, and our minds. We put away the pleasures and indiscretions of the hot seasons, and turn to serious matters of survival.' The language came naturally to me, the words dropping into my mind like those of an experienced priest's prayers. It delighted me to give these homilies at our moots, to keep everyone's attention where it ought to be. It made me feel that I'd tapped into the true meaning of life, constantly stressing the rootedness of all living creatures in the realities of the soil. A pity, then, that the great mass of human society so obstinately ignored or resisted my doctrine.

Even, sometimes, my own fellow pagans.

'Survival,' Pamela echoed in a tone that suggested a whiff of scorn.

I faced her squarely. 'I know what you're thinking. There's no need to struggle any more, to find enough food for the winter, to keep warm, to protect our livestock. That's true. And – ' I glared at her ' – and it's the reason we so often sound mad to most people. Most people think it doesn't matter any more what season it is, what the weather's doing, how we relate to other species. They think all that's old-fashioned and obsolete.' I sighed. 'And they become diminished, their spirits withering, as a result.'

Pamela wriggled rebelliously. 'I wasn't thinking that at all, actually. I was thinking about what we need to survive these days. Like money.'

An inhalation of breath from Kenneth drew everyone's attention. 'Pam,' he said, sounding weary and apprehensive.

'Well it's right, though, isn't it? Without money we can't do anything. It didn't used to be like that. People could live and eat and travel around without needing any actual cash.'

'Yes,' I agreed. 'But where's this taking us?'

Kenneth clutched his hands together, though not too tightly. 'Nowhere,' he said. 'I'm more interested in your ideas about what happens to people who abandon all contact with the seasons and the soil.'

'They become Freemasons,' said Daphne bitterly.

She had the air of someone who had been waiting to speak for some time. 'All allegory and symbols and totally ignorant about anything solid and real.'

Everybody groaned. Then I smiled and said, 'Hey, Daph, that's almost a record. Fifteen minutes before you mentioned the Craft. You must be getting over it.'

It was a risk. Daphne saw nothing to joke about in the subject of the Brotherhood. Her husband had joined several years previously in the face of her strident objections. She had made it as difficult for him as she possibly could, given that the active co-operation of the wife was one of the central requirements for membership. But Eddie had been determined. He was the ideal type for a society of the self-important. He loved the dramatics of it, the bonding and the ritual. As Daphne became more hysterical, he became more committed, until the inevitable happened. He left her with two teenage children, and moved to Gloucester where he quickly gained initiation to the third level at one of the big Lodges there. Daphne followed his progress obsessively on their website, broadcasting his activities everywhere she went, with caustic mockery. He was a recurrent presence both actually and figuratively, visiting his children, and driving between the Cotswold towns and villages in a bright yellow convertible that everybody knew.

His profession was Town Planner, and he had a

senior position on the Council that involved writing influential reports for planning appeals, inspecting doubtful extensions and offering expert guidance on the quality of differing types of Cotswold stone. Eddie Yeo was a man everybody claimed as a friend, but nobody ever took for granted.

When Phil and Thea and I had found the Masonic artefacts in Helen's attic, my first thoughts had turned to Eddie. He might well have been afraid to store his regalia and equipment when he was still living with Daphne at home, knowing that his wife was quite capable of destroying it when his back was turned. Perhaps he had sneaked into Greenhaven to use it as a secret storage place. But the timing didn't work. Helen's attic had been used only days ago, and Eddie had been a free agent for over a year, with no need to hide anything from anybody. When Phil had made his guess about a clandestine Mason, it had rung all too true to me. There had to be other couples like Eddie and Daphne. My problem was discovering just who they might be.

Daphne was a compulsive proselytiser. She gave talks about paganism to any group she could persuade to have her. She wrote articles for mainstream magazines, correcting misapprehensions and claiming nothing less than the future of humankind and the entire planet rested in the beliefs and values of pagans. She was a good writer, able to convey serious points with an accessibly light touch, and I had great admiration for her. My only reservation was that much of what she did and said came as a direct reaction to Eddie and his behaviour. Eddie liked secrecy so Daphne threw everything open to the public gaze. Eddie liked abstractions, so Daphne got physical. Daphne, by nature rather academic and bookish, killed hens and rabbits with her bare hands and prepared them for the pot in true medieval fashion, guts and severed heads all over her kitchen. Daphne went out along the hedgerows gathering sloes and blackberries, getting scratched and chilled, long after I had given up and retreated to the fireplace. She collected slugs and snails in messy traps and tried to feed them to my pig, nicely spiced with the beer she'd used to drown them. The fact that Arabella steadfastly rejected them seemed a mere detail. Daphne had recently established a tannery in a large shed in her garden, in which she cured sheepskins. The smell of animal fat and saltpetre never quite left her. She let her black curly hair grow long and seldom tied it back from her face. Her children saw her as deeply embarrassing and her friends trod warily. On a personal level I found her scratchy and unpredictable, but this didn't stop me from teasing her.

I was fortunate this time. She merely tapped a finger on the table in front of her and sat back in her chair. The message was one of suppressed impatience.

We went on to plan the ceremony for Samhain, which required careful preparation. It was to take place in the very convenient Long Barrow at Notgrove, which was an ancient Megalithic burial ground dating back to 3,000 BC or thereabouts. As old as Stonehenge, anyway, or so Kenneth claimed from something he read. For a ritual centred on death and the passage between the different realms, it was perfect. The bodies once buried there had long ago disappeared, but the atmosphere remained – or so we assured ourselves. English Heritage, nominally in control of the site, paid us no heed, so long as we left no obvious damage. The local people were mostly unconcerned about our activities, despite Daphne's attempts to awaken their interest. They had their own bowdlerised version of the great festival, all the dafter for being over and done with long before midnight – the moment when its entire meaning was made manifest.

Hallowe'en – as Samhain has become known in the general population – is a festival of contradictions: silence and feasting, sacrifice and survival, fire and blood. It overflows with material for effective and focused rituals. Children dressing as caricature witches and knocking on doors with empty threats is a bewildering corruption. Their confused parents and teachers, timidly dodging anything 'incorrect' make no attempt to explain what lies behind. Even references to ghosts carry nervous over-the-shoulder glances, for fear the authorities will accuse them of needlessly frightening the little ones. The idea that in times of acute hardship and bitter winters superfluous infants themselves might have been despatched to the spirit world hadn't for a moment occurred to the merrymakers. Even in our own wiccan circles, I never heard it mentioned.

We agreed timings and the wording of the incantations and prayers, and then I produced the food. Shy Leslie, the youngest of the group, who had barely said a word during the business part of the evening, followed me into the kitchen, and without having to be told, began to arrange the cold meat, coleslaw and cheese on plates. It took me a moment to remember where his name had recently cropped up, in some quite different context. Then the snippet from Gaynor about his partnering Oliver at bridge came back to me. I almost said something, but it seemed intrusive, irrelevant to the moment.

He was a pleasant boy in his mid-twenties, much cleverer than at first appeared. His pagan convictions ran as deep as could be, brought up as he'd been by a wiccan mother who had never attempted to conceal her beliefs or way of life. He was married to a pretty girl a year or two older than himself, who came to our moots from time to time, but plainly held none of the required convictions. 'No Joanne today?' I said, just to make conversation.

He shook his head, without meeting my eye. 'Nope,' was all the reply I got.

Just as everybody started eating, I remembered Gaynor's request. 'Hang on,' I said, waving for hush. 'I forgot to say we've had an application for a divination.' And then, to my shame, I told them who and why and what. Strictly speaking, this was not necessary. More than that, it was breaking a confidence to reveal Gaynor's feelings towards Oliver Grover. The response was predictable.

'The little fool,' said Verona. 'Doesn't she *know* he's gay?'

Ursula quickly disagreed with her. 'People can change,' she said. 'It's a complete fallacy to think sexual orientation is immutable. Just a modern fad, that's all that is. Good luck to the girl, I say.'

Verona, almost as retiring and silent as Leslie, but immeasurably less shy, gave a little laugh. Everyone turned to look at her. When Verona laughed, it made you stop whatever you were doing. The sound pierced to your marrow, raising ripples on your skin, shivers in your guts. Verona laughed as if to tell you that she had just glimpsed your destiny, and it was as amusing as it was unpleasant.

Kenneth, in possession of thicker psychological skin than most, raised his eyebrows at her. 'What's funny?' he asked.

Verona shrugged with a fleeting glance at me, full of her usual sly superiority. 'Nothing much,' she said. 'Only that I hear they've been seen around together a few times. We oughtn't to be so quick to laugh. I vote we do the divination, just as she asks.'

'And I say good luck to her,' Ursula endorsed.

I had glanced at Leslie in the middle of these jumbled reactions, and been shocked by his expression. It seemed to me to comprise an unsavoury mixture of disgust and anger. I realised that he knew Gaynor and Oliver rather well, and had had the unique privilege, amongst those in the room, of seeing the two together.

'What do you think?' I asked him. 'Does Gaynor stand any chance of winning him over?'

He said nothing for a long beat. Then, 'We'll have to wait and see, won't we?' he managed.

Pamela, sitting next to him, gave him a little nudge with her elbow. 'Go on,' she teased him. 'Commit yourself, why don't you? Make a guess.'

He didn't look at her, but twisted away, staring down at the floor. His mouth moved, but he didn't say anything.

Kenneth came to his rescue. 'What would he know about it?' he said.

Leslie lifted his head as if this was a direct

challenge, or a final intolerable straw. 'I know them both,' he said, rather loudly. 'That's not it.'

He was like a tortured adolescent, embroiled in unmanageable emotions. With one accord, the whole group released him from the painful spotlight of their attention. Ursula got up to take some empty cups out to the kitchen. Verona began talking to Pamela about childhood memories of bobbing for apples at Hallowe'en. Kenneth jingled coins in his pocket and seemed to have some urgent private thinking to do. Leslie's tension receded, and he was soon himself again, asking for precise timings and duties during the ceremony.

They left before eleven, going out into the dark night quite quietly. I watched the last car drive away, satisfied that we'd had a good moot, reinforcing our ideas, marking the season, preparing for the climax to come.

CHAPTER FIVE

Sunday morning was even damper than the previous days had been. A mist hung over everything, and I could scarcely see Greenhaven, only thirty feet away. But regardless of the weather, I heard Phil and Thea load their dogs into the car and drive off before nine. That seemed rather odd. If they wanted to give the beasts a run, they only had to turn right outside their gate and have an ideal cross-country walk to Notgrove. An arrow-straight avenue of young beeches comprised most of the way – perfect for dogs as well as horses. The almost total disappearance of livestock from farming in this part of Gloucestershire made things much more relaxed for dog walkers than they would have done in the era of wholesale sheep husbandry.

Besides, I remembered I had told Phil I would call in and talk to him about the Masonic things from the attic. Wasn't it rather rude of him to swan off like that without waiting for my visit?

Giving myself a shake, I turned to my morning tasks. Another batch of bread had emerged as crusty and redolent as anyone could have wished. I'd been planning to take some over the street, before realising they were going out. Helen actually had a workable brick oven attached to the rear of her house, but I could hardly expect Thea or Phil to stoke it and get baking when only staying a week. They probably hadn't even seen it, or if they had they might not understand what it was.

I wanted to phone Gaynor and get her assurance that the coat would be finished by the middle of the week. Knowing her hesitancy over shops, her stubbornness over the buttons had come as unwelcome news. I worried that she might take ages to work up to choosing and buying replacements. Meanwhile, I had decided to show the finished garment to one of my best-paying customers in Nailsworth, who hadn't yet seen the coats we made, in the hope that some well-heeled shopping party would be tempted to make some early Christmas purchases. Parts of the Cotswolds were virtually colonised by upper class associates of the Royal Family. Several of them had a gratifying partiality to my products.

But Gaynor did not answer the phone when I tried her. With a *tut* of frustration, I turned to other chores.

All finished by ten-thirty, and noting that the mist had lifted, my attention switched to the undertakings I had given the pagan group. I had a lot of notes about Samhain, the underlying meanings and the more constructive and serious ceremonies that were attached to it. Despite a persistent sense that I was completely out of kilter with the times, I retained a deep commitment to preserving the ancient connections between humanity and the soil. Without that connection, we became aliens on our own planet. Every time I went into a city, I realised that this moment had very nearly arrived. The vast majority of people living in the 'developed' world had lost any sense of the rhythms and tides of nature. Sometimes this made me smug about my own awareness, at others it drove me to despair.

But the pagan group could have a similar effect on me at times. There were always some who believed they could make impossible things happen – usually to do with acquiring great wealth or power. They looked for danger and transgression. They wanted there to be fairies and werewolves and flying broomsticks. They read Harry Potter as if it was literal truth. And the serious ones could be even worse. Some of the men seemed to think they'd signed up for the Freemasons, and made great play of secrecy and hidden signs of other realms. And I could not help but be aware of matching tendencies in both organisations. A lot of pagans dubbed themselves high priests of this or that Egyptian deity, and wandered off to do bizarre researches into wall paintings from some temple or other in the Valley of the Kings. Freemasons also adopted great chunks of esoteric Egyptian flummery, which to the uninitiated would look and sound much the same. The would-be pagans I'm referring to wanted special clothes and symbols and incantations. Most of them moved on quite rapidly when they realised there was no naked dancing on the wold, and no surefire ways of getting promoted beyond their abilities. A few probably ended up in the Masons after all.

My notes prompted me to think about that year's setting for our central ritual, where we confronted death in all its forms. That is the core meaning of Samhain, which stretches back to the days when mankind first kept livestock, and understood the implications of the coming winter. With the turn of the season, many creatures had to die, including human creatures. The weak and dispirited reached their lowest point, finding themselves unable to face the cold hungry months ahead. There was no need to invoke the supernatural to make something large and important of this. Death was in no way unnatural, after all. Despite the universal fear felt by every living thing throughout their lives, death itself was unexceptional. A fly will evade it with all its strength, a rabbit will flee from the fox, pigs scream in terror as the truth becomes clear to them. Everything loves life and resists death. People are only different in the strategies they employ.

So it seemed to me that the persistent aura of death that manifested in the last days of October and early November arose from thousands of years of custom across the northern latitudes. And whatever the explanation for ghosts and previsions in that season, I had no doubt that they were a part of it. Traces of powerful feelings, perhaps. A slackening of the fortifications we kept in place against the certainty of death, so we permitted ourselves glimpses of truth, in the shape of phantoms and spectres created by our vastly over-active imaginations.

I mused over these thoughts, trying to turn them into a kind of sermon. That was my role in the group. I distilled meaning for them, aiming for clarity and honesty. I wove in stories, linking ideas together, explaining and illuminating. Nobody had ever labelled me as a priest, and I had remained careful not to be seen as any sort of a leader – but at the major ceremonies, I was usually the one who spoke. I was good at it. I could make them laugh and cry and above all *think*.

After nearly an hour of that, I was ready for some air. Outside the trees were blowing about, the first autumn leaves coming off in clouds, banking up along the sides of the street and collecting in gateways. The villagers didn't like that. They brushed and gathered and burnt great sackfuls, adding to the misty smoky atmosphere on windless days.

I set out towards the north, past the village church, up the lane to the little gate that opened into the beech avenue.

It was noisy under the trees, but fairly sheltered, considering the wide exposed sweeps of land on either side. Farming had grown to an industrial scale in our area, with fifty-acre fields a commonplace. Hedges and copses had been ripped up, gateways widened or removed entirely, for the massive machinery required to harvest the corn and other crops.

Ahead of me lay Notgrove, a smaller village than Cold Aston, with a very different history. Notgrove had a special claim to my attention during Samhain, because of the Barrow. The burial chambers had been excavated a long time ago, exposing the stones that were part of the construction. But then the powers that be had deemed it prudent to protect the site from vandals, and had covered everything up again. They called it *backfilling*, which seemed an oddly technical word for what they'd done. Many of us considered it little better than another form of vandalism. I had never seen the stones, except in photographs. Ursula, and one or two others, disagreed with my point of view on the subject. 'It's much more authentic as it is now,' she said. And she did have a point, I suppose. All you could see was a small hillock, with grass and wild flowers growing on it. To the south side was an indentation, and all around were big trees. The northern edge was bordered by the A436 – a horrible road, with traffic zooming along and no proper footpath.

People came to see the Barrow in all seasons, courtesy of English Heritage, who put no restrictions or charges on visitors. The mere fact that it dated back 4000 years was enough to attract Americans and other tourists, although I daresay they found it disappointing when they got there.

I went in through the small gate, with my head full of death and the clever inventions that people have used to make it bearable. I thought about this burial place, the care lavished on the bodies, the impossibility of ever truly understanding the ideas and hopes of those who constructed the place.

I walked to the top of the hummock, where the summer grass now lay limp and mushy. Hogweed seedheads rose eerily all over the site, the brittle stalks bare of leaves by that time, looking like the skeletons of triffids. In summer, you could see flattened circles where people had picnicked or had sex – or both. In October, such activities had ceased and the place had an abandoned air, despite the unseasonal mildness and the surprising greenness of the trees. The Samhain ceremony would be conducted at the highest point, in full view of traffic from the road, if they chose to look. Almost nobody ever did, being far too intent on overtaking each other on the sudden thrilling section of straight.

Then I did what I usually did, which was walk down the side of the hillock, towards the bowl-shaped hollow that had formed to the south, probably unintentionally, giving shelter from observation.

My mind was still on death, so it seemed at first no more than a slightly more concrete manifestation of my thoughts when I observed a form, lying tidily in the hollow, frosted slightly with the morning's drizzle. A hedge sparrow perched on its shoulder, as if on a tree stump. I blinked and looked again, and my heart thumped huge and loud in my chest.

Facing away from me, on her side, was the inert body of a woman. When my brain finally informed me of this fact, I had to sit down on the wet sloping edge of the depression, fighting a giddiness I'd never known before, summoning the courage to move closer. I had to see the face, to know exactly what I was looking at. Until then it could be a dummy, or a living person sleeping off drink or drugs. But a living person wouldn't lie like that on the wet grass, so utterly unmoving, offering a perch to a wild bird. With a sick horror I gave thanks that it hadn't been a crow or a magpie, seeking the unexpected bounty of a juicy eyeball. In February it would not have taken them so long to snatch such a prize.

Moving at a bent, crabbed angle, as if suffering from acute stomach ache, I skirted the perimeter, keeping a few feet between me and the thing in the grass, until I was staring down at its profile. Half hidden by hair and a few dry stalks of dock, it was still quite easy to identify.

My friend Gaynor was lying dead in Notgrove Long Barrow, with a long slender piece of metal protruding from her body. Her hands were folded together against her throat, her feet precisely parallel to each other and at right angles to her lower legs. The knees were tightly bent. It was the attitude of a sacrificial victim.

CHAPTER SIX

I didn't have the mobile with me. There was a phonebox in the middle of Notgrove, only five minutes away, if I ran. But how could I leave poor Gaynor there in the long grass, where crows might peck at her? Fighting to calm down and think rationally, I squatted beside her and put a hand on her shoulder, where the sparrow had been.

She was wearing a sleeveless body warmer over a shirt. The ghastly weapon sticking out from her front coalesced as I stared at it, horrifying me all over again when I finally understood what it was. Grey, with a neatly shaped head at its end, I finally identified it as a knitting needle. A slender 2.5 mm knitting needle, which must have been pushed with great force through Gaynor's ribcage. Pointed they might be, but certainly not sharp enough to kill a person easily.

There was a small patch of blood at the site of entry, but no more. Didn't that mean she'd died instantly, before there was time for any bleeding? From what I could see of her face, she didn't seem to have suffered any terrible agony. Or did the dead features simply relax into blandness, whatever the final few moments had been like?

The flesh was cold and hard under my hand. There was a smell of damp, an oddly *dirty* smell. Her eyes were open, filmed over appallingly like an animal you might see in the butchers. She was so completely other – not in any way the friend who'd eaten lunch with me only the day before. Whatever I might have thought I understood about death before this moment became ludicrously inadequate. I had not had the least idea of the absolute transformation from life to death. I had seen it in animals, but never in a person. It was beyond words, almost beyond acknowledgement. I found myself quivering with shock and fear and horror.

Somebody had killed her. This detail had slipped away into a less important place as I tried to commune with the remains of my friend. Unless – I examined the weapon again, the way Gaynor was lying – unless she could have done it to herself. But no – if that had been so, she'd still have her hands on the length of steel – or whatever they make knitting needles of these days – and would be lying awkwardly, legs sprawling. Instead, she had been neatly arranged, or so it seemed to me, by other hands. Placed squarely in a space created thousands of years ago for another dead human being, whose bones had been carried off to a museum, or excavated by rodents before the archaeologists reached them.

Recoiling at the implications, I stared dumbly at the scene. Somebody had put Gaynor there deliberately, as some kind of Samhain message. That appeared as obvious to me as if a large announcement had been pinned to the body. Somebody who knew what was planned for the Barrow in a few days' time and had wanted to sully it. Somebody who had a powerful animosity towards paganism perhaps. But why *Gaynor*?

I knelt there trying to understand, before I could summon assistance. I needed to have some sort of explanation for myself before I could speak of it to anybody else. Because I knew already that the police would never understand unless somebody like me talked them through it. They would hear the word *pagan* and get no further than that. They would think this was the work of one of my group.

In a sort of fugue state I paraded the individual members before my mind's eye. Pamela, with her bright smile and cheerful enthusiasm; Ursula, argumentative and frustrated; Verona, mystical and inscrutable – and Daphne, the wife abandoned for the Freemasons. The two men, Kenneth and Leslie, hovered more faintly behind these four women. Kenneth was kindly, colourless and very gentle. I had never heard him speak angrily or seen him make a violent gesture. I liked Kenneth in an unthinking casual sort of way. I believed everybody did. Leslie was similar in his lack of overt masculinity. Quietly intense, was Leslie. I realised I hardly knew him, or what he was capable of.

At last I got myself out of the little gate and onto the verge at the side of the road, where I started trying to flag down a passing car. It felt over-dramatic, almost ridiculous, but I kept at it, and the traffic kept storming past me. Five minutes later somebody finally stopped. It was a local man who I knew by sight. He left his car in a layby some yards further ahead and came running back to me. When I dragged him to the concavity and showed him my discovery, he took over with admirable efficiency. He called the police on his mobile, and in no time there were uniformed men and women running about, asking questions, including whether I knew the dead woman, taking photographs and notes, speaking into phones, tying yellow tape across the Barrow. The trauma of all this activity was greater than that of finding Gaynor – or if not greater, then different and barely tolerable. They trampled the Barrow, not knowing what it was. They shouted and moved jerkily in their excitement at having a full-scale murder on their hands. I hated them so much I could hardly hear or see or speak. Somebody put me into the back of a car and drove me home.

I was shaking as they walked me to my house, unable to properly understand what was being said to me. There was a constant muttering going on, with glances at me that seemed to contain suspicion, concern, kindness, wariness, impatience in a dreadful kaleidoscope. I wondered whether they thought I might have killed Gaynor, and would shout at me until I confessed. And then I remembered Phil Hollis.

I had a friend in a high place. This thought was briefly reassuring, something to hold on to in a world that had gone insane. I kept feeling Gaynor's shoulder under my fingers, stiff and cold. I kept rerunning the previous day when she had been alive, walking, talking, knitting, breathing. She might have been annoying at times, demanding an uncomfortable level of sensitivity from me, but I couldn't grasp that she was *dead*.

Somebody joined me and the police officer on my doorstep, as I groped for my key. I looked at her blankly, unable to remember who she was. Then it came to me. It was Thea, Phil's new girlfriend, the woman with the dog.

'I'll sit with you, if you'll let me,' she said. Her voice was pitched low, but sounded full and sweet, a voice you could rely on.

'Thanks,' I mumbled. 'I'll be all right soon.'

There was more muttering and then the two of us were in my living room, sitting at the table. I glanced at the sofa, wondering why we hadn't gone to it first. I'd crammed a lot into this main room to leave space in the small back room for all the wool stuff. This was where sitting and eating and talking all happened.

'I know I shouldn't say this,' Thea ventured, when the police people had all finally gone. 'But I do know what it's like. It's happened to me twice this year.'

I wasn't interested. Her experience meant nothing to me. I was struggling to escape from all the sights and sensations and *smells* of Gaynor dead. It all reran, over and over, making anything else seem distant and insignificant.

She went into the kitchen, the tiny area where there was a sink and a couple of cupboards and a place for chopping things. I heard mugs clinking and then the electric kettle starting to boil.

'I never use the electric,' I said confusedly. 'There's hot water on the Rayburn already.' It annoyed me that she hadn't the sense to see this for herself.

'Does it matter?' She side-stepped into the doorway so she could look at me.

'Not really.' I held my hands out in front of me, wondering at the shaking. 'Look at me! Isn't it weird.' I laughed raggedly. 'I'm supposed to be the one who's all right with death. I give *talks* on it.'

'I don't think anybody's all right with death,' she

said quietly. 'I'm going to put sugar in this tea, if I can find some.'

'That's all right. I take sugar anyway.' And for some reason this seemed immensely funny and I began to laugh. Then I found I couldn't stop and there were tears everywhere and Thea was cradling me against her front.

We talked after that for an hour or more. I told Thea all about Gaynor, her shyness, her fabulous knitting skills, her inoffensiveness. 'Just a timid little Welsh girl, out of her natural environment,' I summed up. 'How could anybody possibly want to kill her?'

Thea asked very few questions and supplied no answer to this one of mine. She just shook her head and glanced at her watch.

But my own words were echoing in my head. *Who?* I stared at the blank screen of my television across the room. There was nobody. 'It must have been a total stranger,' I decided. 'Somebody up to no good at the Barrow and Gaynor saw them.'

'Did she often go to the Barrow?'

How was I to explain? I looked at her helplessly. 'It's Samhain,' I said.

'I'm sorry. I don't know what that means.' She did look genuinely sorry, as if she'd put me to a dreadful lot of bother.

'The old pagan festival to mark the end of

summer. Bonfires, slaughtering the livestock, all that. It's around November the first, but it really gets going from the middle of October.'

'Hallowe'en,' she said.

'Sort of,' I sighed.

'So – Gaynor was a pagan?' she prompted.

'No. But she liked Samhain. Ghosts and divinations. She thought it was exciting, I think. Took her out of herself.' Speaking about Gaynor had acquired a horrible significance. For the first time I had to really think hard about every word I said. I couldn't simply wheel out all the usual unexamined phrases as if they were pure truth. 'I'm not sure,' I admitted, hanging my head. 'I think I might have known her less well than I thought I did. It's a scary feeling.'

Most people would have come out with some truism about nobody really knowing anybody else. Instead, this woman took my hand, holding it lightly in hers. 'I know how that goes,' she said. 'I'm afraid it gets worse. You forget exactly what they looked like.'

I tested this, finding to my relief that I could conjure Gaynor's face with very little effort. The clear blue eyes, wide-spaced; the thin lips and pointed chin. 'I can still visualise her,' I reported.

'I'm still not sure about the Barrow,' Thea said. 'It's a pagan site, is it?'

'It's a burial place, pre-Christian. It's quite

atmospheric in the early mornings, before the traffic gets going. The traffic spoils it.'

'Traffic spoils everything,' Thea muttered. It felt like a lapse into something personal. Then she remembered herself. 'So that's why Gaynor went there? For the special atmosphere?'

I stared at the sheepskin on the floor in front of the Rayburn, noticing a grubby mark on it. 'I don't know,' I said, forcing myself to think. 'Even if she hadn't been – you know – I'd have been surprised to see her there. I've never known her to go there before.'

'Perhaps somebody took her there by force.'

'Maybe. But that would be difficult, wouldn't it? She could have screamed or run away.'

Thea nudged my tepid tea towards me. 'Drink up,' she urged.

I took a half-hearted sip. 'I think she must have gone because of the thing with Oliver,' I decided. 'And interrupted something going on and got killed for it. By a total stranger.'

Thea didn't pick up the reference to Oliver. Instead, one eyebrow kinked upwards in a gentle scepticism. 'I think it hardly ever is a total stranger,' she said. 'The myth of the bogeyman and all that.'

'Right,' I nodded. This was more familiar ground. 'It's easier to think that, isn't it?' I tried to embrace the notion that somebody I knew had murdered Gaynor. It was impossible.

'Phil's likely to be back soon,' she said, rather wistfully. 'They'll want to ask you lots of questions, I expect.'

It took me a while to catch up with the meaning behind this. Eventually I got it. 'He's doing the investigation?'

She nodded, with a sigh. 'It's technically in his area.'

I struggled to think. 'So why wasn't I taken to the police station? Why this wait?' I was still very cloudy-minded. 'What's going to happen next?'

'They have to do all their forensic work and take Gaynor for a post-mortem and inform her family. The questioning is the next stage.'

'You know a lot about it.'

'I'm afraid I do,' she said, with no further explanation.

'She hasn't got any family. I'm probably her closest friend.' I remembered a few of the questions at the Barrow. Did I know the deceased? Did I have her full name and address? I had supplied the facts automatically, without the need for thought. I supposed that henceforward it would be much less simple.

'How did she earn her living?'

'Her father left her a bit and she sold the house and got a little flat. She manages quite well; I pay her as one of my knitters and she does other handiwork. She can make lace and braid. This is a good area for that kind of thing. There are still a few people who want everything done by hand.' I heard myself using the present tense, knowing it was wrong, but unable to correct it. It was difficult enough to explain Gaynor, without getting my grammar right.

Thea breathed in deeply, seeming to brace herself for something. It took me a few seconds to notice. 'What?' I asked her. 'What's the matter?'

'This is going to seem like a wanton change of subject, so tell me if it's too much for you. But I suppose we've got to talk about something while we wait.'

'Go on,' I invited, guessing what was coming from the flush on her cheek.

Thea looked away from me. 'You and Phil knew each other quite well, didn't you? When he was married?'

'Before that. He lived near us and was best friend to my oldest brother for a bit. They moved down here from Stoke when he was twelve – he never entirely lost the accent, did he? He was always nice to me. Our paths seem to have crossed on and off ever since.'

'What's Caroline like?' She gave a furtive glance towards the door, as if afraid Phil would come in and catch her asking. I felt a surge of warmth towards her, forgetting for a moment the grim events of the morning.

I hesitated, wondering how best to reply to that. How was it possible, anyway, to sum up a whole person in a few selective remarks? And how could I leave out my own feelings towards the woman? Whenever I thought of Caroline, I felt a cold wriggle of guilt, one of the worms escaping from its can. 'She was lovely in the early days,' I said. 'She and I were chums when she first had the children. I used to go and play with them when they were very small, and Caroline would sit there with some book or other, half reading, half talking to me.' I trailed off, seeing again the typical scene on those afternoons. Twenty years ago, and more – it was hard to recapture any detail. But Caroline had always been relaxed around me, telling me what she was thinking and planning. I'd always felt oddly flattered by her friendship, wondering what was in it for her.

'And?' Thea prompted. 'Aren't you chums any more?'

I shook my head, forcing myself to speak steadily. 'I hardly ever see her now. She changed a lot. We drifted apart, as people do,' I added, trying to rationalise it into being true. 'She always wanted too much, somehow. From everybody. Phil, me, the kids. Nothing was ever enough for her.'

'Hard for Phil,' Thea murmured.

'Right. He could never really cope with it. She couldn't accept that his job needed him to work at strange times, even though she was thrilled every time he got a promotion. She still wanted him at home where she could see him and where he could take his share with the kids. Mind you, I took her side a lot of the time. His mind never seemed to be properly on her and what she was saying. It was obvious that she found it desperately annoying.'

'Typical husband,' Thea smiled.

'Really? That's your experience, is it?' I had assumed from the start that she was divorced and would therefore have plenty to moan about where husbands were concerned, just as Caroline did.

'Actually, no. Or only occasionally. I'll tell you about that another time. Let's stick to Phil and Caroline.'

'Well, there was other stuff. A lot of other stuff.'

She nodded knowingly. 'He told me about when he resigned from the Freemasons.' She made it sound as if he'd walked out of a job. Then she added, 'But he must have loved her.'

It sounded so naïve, put like that. I shook my head helplessly. 'To begin with, he did, absolutely. Anyone could see it. And she loved him. She was utterly happy to begin with. It was ever so sad when it changed. Most people thought it must be his fault that she got so sour-tempered. He thought so himself and stuck with it when anyone else might have given up. She was so inconsistent, that was a lot of the trouble. She wanted him to climb the ladder and earn a lot of money, but she resented the time he was out of the house.'

'And did he understand that it was because she loved him?'

'Depended on him, more like,' I corrected her. 'She's never had much life of her own, I suppose. Never really had what she wanted. I don't think she makes friends easily, now or then. And then she and I fell out over the whole idiotic business of the Masons, and we were both the poorer for it.' I stopped, worrying that I was saying too much.

'You stuck up for Phil when he left the Lodge?'

'That's right,' I agreed, not feeling up to an account of those days. It sounded stupid, anyway, so long after the event. The way people got so bothered about it was hard to credit, all these years later.

'Didn't she go out to work?' Thea continued her cross-examination. She obviously wanted me to cram as much information as possible into the time available.

'Not properly. A few little jobs in offices, which never seemed to last.' I looked her full in the face, and took the plunge. 'But then it all got much worse, when – you know what happened, of course. After that, I think he switched himself off entirely.'

'Mmm,' she murmured, with a sideways flicker of her eyes that made me wonder just how much of Phil Hollis's story she did actually know.

'Some men never reveal themselves to anybody, of course,' I added, hoping she wouldn't notice my fishing.

'My husband did,' she said. 'But then, he didn't lose a daughter.'

Ah! So she did know at least the basics.

'It was what finally split them up – him and Caroline,' I elaborated. 'He would never talk about it. Not to her, anyway. And then somehow I got pulled over to his side, and that was the final straw. Caroline saw me as a double traitor, I think. She gave me some very dark looks whenever I bumped into her after the separation.'

'But that was *ages* after the Freemasonry thing.' She was obviously keeping up well, I noted.

'I suppose so,' I mumbled, trying to reckon the years. 'But time's a funny thing, isn't it? We're all still here, remembering everything that's happened. It feels as if it's all part of one continuous picture, if that makes any sense.'

'I'm not sure it does,' said Thea. 'I tend to date everything before or after Carl died, as if there are two very different pictures.'

'Right,' I said. 'So he died, did he?' Thea was a widow. 'Well, maybe I've got it wrong then. But my point, I suppose, is that I've never really managed to be close to Caroline and Phil at the same time. I've always had to choose one or the other.'

'Or neither,' she said, a bit sharply.

'Don't worry,' I assured her. 'I'm happy enough now for it to be neither of them. My friend now, for the record, is a woman called Stella.'

'Sorry.' She turned on the charm. 'Just me being insecure.'

'There's no need,' I insisted. 'I've never been a threat to anyone, believe me.'

She nodded, and left a tactful pause, before returning to the death of Phil's daughter. 'It's not four years ago yet,' Thea said. 'It must be pretty raw for them, still.'

'Probably,' I said, vaguely, remembering Gaynor again like a sudden nausea. My mind did its best to dodge the facts, to smooth over the horror, but could find no escape. Helplessly, I confessed to Thea. 'I was thinking about death,' I said, looking at the floor. 'When I found her. Thinking I understood it, somehow.' I snorted at my own folly. 'We can *never* understand it, can we?'

She said nothing until I met her eye. Then, 'I think probably that's where we go wrong,' she said softly. 'Trying to understand it, I mean. Isn't it actually blindingly simple? Literally blindingly. Life stops. Permanently, totally. That's it.' She stretched her arms out from her sides in an odd gesture, and let them drop heavily. 'No more to be said.'

I tried to give this some thought, catching scraps of insight and losing them again, as she watched me.

'Take us,' she said. 'You, me and Phil. He's lost a daughter, I've lost a husband – and now your friend's dead. It seems unusual, doesn't it? As if we're somehow coincidentally suffering from some rare disease. But it isn't at all rare. It's universal. It's what always happens.'

I frowned at her, absorbing the revelation about her husband, while wanting to keep to the central point. 'No it isn't,' I objected. 'Those people all died far too young. That's what's unusual. They should have had decades of life to go.'

'Maybe,' she almost shrugged. 'I wonder sometimes whether that makes any difference.'

'It does,' I shouted at her. 'Of *course* it does.'

And then Phil Hollis came in through my front door without knocking.

CHAPTER SEVEN

He was different: taller, more serious, slightly alarming. 'All right?' he asked Thea.

'Yes, thanks,' she said, with a note in her voice that seemed to be warning him that he was striking the wrong tone.

He looked at me, square on. 'You'll have to be interviewed formally at the station, I'm afraid,' he said. 'There's a car outside.'

My heart began to thump uncomfortably. I'd walked into some weird realm where anything might happen and nothing could be trusted. Even Phil had turned into some heartless professional who showed no sign of caring how I might be feeling.

'Can't you do it here?' I whined.

'It won't be me.' He was so curt, almost angry, making me feel accused. That was when I began to shake. Perhaps I would be accused. Perhaps they thought *I* had killed Gaynor. I stared at Phil's face trying to find reassurance.

'Why?' I said, finding it hard to speak, choked with fear and bewilderment. 'Why are you so *cross*?'

Thea put a warm arm around my shoulders. 'He's not cross with you,' she said. 'It's just – well, we were meant to be on holiday.' Her suppressed sigh tightened the arm. 'It makes us feel jinxed. Now, come on. It'll soon be over and done with.'

That part wasn't true at all, of course. I knew that even as she spoke.

Phil put me in the back of a police car, while two uniformed officers occupied the front seats. Before we drove off, he asked me if I was warm enough and whether I'd had anything to eat. It occurred to me that I should be asking him questions – where was Gaynor? What was going to happen? – but it didn't seem important to know such details. Very little seemed important at that stage.

I was interviewed by a man who said he was Detective Inspector Baldwin, with a young woman beside him, who was Detective Sergeant Latimer. I gave them my attention and memorised their names – Baldwin was going bald, which helped, and Latimer had a sort of Latin look about her. I'd taught myself the technique years ago as a sort of game and it had quickly become a habit.

There was a lot of stuff about confidentiality and voluntary assistance that I carelessly agreed to, before they got down to the real business. 'How long have you known Miss Lewis?' 'What was your relationship to her?' 'When did you last see her?' 'What sort of mental and emotional state would you say she was in?'

It gradually became harder to answer simply. I remembered Gaynor's remarks about Oliver, and had to make a rapid decision as to whether to tell them about that. Nothing could have prepared me for the great wave of self-disgust that washed over me as I described our conversation over Saturday lunch. I was betraying Oliver by giving his name to the police, just as I had betrayed Gaynor when I told the pagan group about her attraction to the accountant. I rushed to minimise the damage.

'But he won't have had anything to do with this. He's a really nice person,' I babbled, hoping desperately that Oliver had a solid alibi that would quickly render him beyond suspicion. 'I mean – it was all fantasy on Gaynor's part. He wasn't in any sort of relationship with her. You asked about her mood, and she was a bit agitated, that's all.' I forced myself to remember Gaynor pacing the room, staring across the street at Greenhaven, talking about challenges. 'Actually, she was really quite agitated,' I said. 'More than I've ever seen her.'

'And you think that was about this Mr Grover?'

I thought hard. 'No,' I said. 'It seemed to be about the house across the street, if anything.

Where your Superintendent's aunt used to live, as it happens. Gaynor was surprised to see somebody staying there. But I don't think it was just that, either. She was saying odd things about her own life.' I wished I had paid more attention. I might have found out much more if I'd asked Gaynor what she meant. I looked at DI Baldwin helplessly. 'I don't know,' I whimpered. 'I can't believe she's gone and I can't just *ask* her.'

They seemed to find the subject of Gaynor's mental state the first interesting thing in the interview, and I understood something of the frustration and helplessness felt by uncomprehending police detectives trying to understand the subtleties of human interactions in the context of a murder.

'Right then,' said Baldwin. 'Miss Lewis was behaving strangely yesterday lunchtime. Restless, worried, confessing to a secret attraction to a local man. Is that right?'

'Yes,' I said with a strong feeling of reluctance. They made a delicate half-observed atmosphere into some clumping bit of police suspicion. 'Sort of,' I added uselessly.

'Could you give us Mr Grover's address please?' said Latimer, pencil poised.

I obliged readily enough. They could have found him without my help. But I continued to regret having mentioned him. 'It can't have been him,' I pleaded. 'There wouldn't have been *time* for anything like that.'

Baldwin frowned. 'Anything like what?'

'Well, for Gaynor to speak to Oliver, or for him to get angry – or anything.'

They cocked their heads in unison. 'No?' said Baldwin. 'You said she left you around three-thirty yesterday afternoon and we know she was killed very early this morning. That leaves a lot of time unaccounted for.'

I wrestled with the clash between mundane temporal matters and the all-consuming starkness of death. Gothic images of Oliver Grover stalking Gaynor with a knitting needle were foolish fancies that occupied police minds, but they scarcely mattered to me – or to Gaynor now.

But I had implicated Oliver and there was no taking it back. I was a blabbermouth and deserved to suffer for it. But why, I asked myself, why in the world *had* I mentioned him? Something to do with being a good citizen, a good witness. Having something to produce for these eager interviewers would earn me their approval. I wanted them to regard me as completely cooperative. Surely they could understand that?

'Who else did Gaynor know?'

I widened my eyes at this. 'Well,' I attempted, '*lots* of people, I suppose. But she didn't have many real friends. She was basically rather lonely.'

Latimer asked the crucial question, then. 'Who else knew how she felt about Mr Grover?'

It was almost telepathic and I stared at her. 'Um – well, actually, I had a group of friends at my house last night. I mentioned it to them.' I congratulated myself on remembering to withhold the word 'pagan'. They would discover it soon enough, of course. Meanwhile it would only distract and alarm them. The general population of rural Gloucestershire might be comfortable and relaxed with our practices – the British police were liable to be quite another matter.

They wrote down the names and addresses of everyone who had heard me reveal Gaynor's romantic aspirations, details that I gave with a sense of naming fellow travellers at a McCarthy investigation. All these people would be visited by police officers and they would all blame me for it.

'They all knew her, then, did they?' Baldwin checked.

I nodded minimally. 'Not very well, in most cases. But they'd seen her at my place a few times. They knew who she was and what she did.'

'Knitting,' said Latimer. The way she said it brought the murderous 2.5mm needle vividly to mind.

'But you can't think of any reason why anybody – in particular any of these six people – should want to kill her?'

I shook my head, feeling the nausea return. 'No, of course not,' I muttered. 'None at all.'

Suddenly he smacked the table, not so much in anger as impatience. 'Come on, Miss Fletcher – Ariadne – we need *help* here. We've never met your friend. We don't know her habits or interests or the company she kept. We have to start from a clean sheet, building up a picture, tracing her movements. We can't do any of that without the help of people like you.'

'But...' I met his small blue eyes. 'How do you know it wasn't just some random senseless killing? Somebody with mental problems thinking she was somebody else.'

'You don't believe that,' he accused flatly.

I sagged back into my original posture. 'No,' I admitted, as I remembered the careful, almost ceremonial, way Gaynor had been positioned at the Barrow. 'I suppose that hardly ever happens.'

'It happens,' he disagreed, 'but when it does, you don't get – well, let's just say it doesn't look particularly random to us.' He paused. 'Why do you think she was at the Barrow in the first place?'

It was the question I had hoped he wouldn't ask; the one I'd been dreading. I paused as long as I dared, his eyes on my face, Latimer likewise, her head cocked slightly, keen with interest.

'I – this sounds bizarre, I know – I think she was

just – sort of – searching for some special atmosphere,' I said.

Their expressions did not change. Two frozen faces stared at me blankly.

'Could you say a bit more about that?' Baldwin asked at last. So I spent several minutes trying my best not to explain about Samhain and the thinning fabric between the living and the dead, the winter preparations that involved slaughter and trickery and some latterday Christian muddle to do with saints. I fought to keep my language vague – *the early morning mists, planning for Hallowe'en, local folk tales*. I still ducked the word 'pagan' completely. When I'd finished, the expression on the faces of both detectives were sceptical and confused.

'But what did she expect to see?' asked Baldwin.

'Nothing in particular,' I told him. 'I don't even know if I'm right. She didn't tell me she was going there. I could have got it completely wrong. I think I've said too much. I've probably led you up the wrong path. Entirely the wrong path.' I was talking at random, babbling a lot of stupid suppositions that couldn't possibly help them in finding Gaynor's killer. 'Sorry,' I added.

'You said something about the early morning,' Baldwin backtracked. 'What time would that be, do you think?'

'I honestly have no idea. It isn't anything specific.

But *if* she wanted to have a bit of quiet time there, it would have to be before the traffic got going. And on a Sunday, that would be later than other days.' I could feel the ground crumbling beneath my feet. This was almost as bad as fingering poor Oliver Grover. Worse, in some ways. When they learned that Oliver was gay it would come as little surprise or cause for alarm. Paganism was something else – the average jobbing copper had only the most distorted grasp of what was involved – despite several of them being steeped in Masonic mumbo-jumbo and therefore at least *au fait* with the general business of symbolism. I could see they didn't entirely trust me. I'd answered all their questions in language I'd hoped they could understand. I'd bitten back a dozen sarcastic remarks, but a few had slipped through, in spite of my efforts. I had tried to make them see how upset I was at the slaughter of my harmless little friend. 'Gaynor couldn't possibly have been a threat to anybody,' I insisted. 'She was quiet and shy and never hurt a living thing.'

In the end I found myself wishing they'd leave me alone and turn their attentions to the others. My shame at having named them quickly transmuted into an eagerness for them to share my discomfort. It wasn't fair that I should have to put up with this on my own. In any case something about the questioning had sown some dawning suspicions in my mind. I wanted my fellow pagans to be roused by the police hammering on their doors as they enjoyed a lazy Sunday afternoon because as I went over it all again, forcing myself to confront the probabilities, it seemed that Gaynor's killer was very likely lurking behind one of those very doors.

A policeman drove me home again, asking me very politely not to leave the area without notifying them. 'What happens next?' I asked him.

'In what way?' He raised his eyebrows as if the question might be regarded as impertinent.

'Gaynor's house. Who's going to clear out the cupboards, turn off the electric, collect up the junk mail?'

'Nobody yet, for a while,' he said. 'It'll be searched first. In the course of the investigation,' he elaborated.

'I think it will have to be me, eventually,' I said. 'Will you tell me when you've finished with it?'

'Give DI Baldwin a call, at the end of the week,' he advised.

My phone was ringing as I went back into my house. Somehow it felt as if it had been ringing for much of the time I was out. The walls seemed to echo with it.

When I picked it up, it was Kenneth. 'Ariadne?' he breathed, as if he'd been holding his breath for a long time. 'Where have you *been*?'

'Helping the police,' I said. 'I suppose you've heard?'

'That girl – the mousy one with the Welsh name. Is that right? She's been murdered at the Long Barrow. Everybody's talking about it.'

'Her name's Gaynor, as you know perfectly well. We were only talking about her last night. What do you want me to say?'

He went quiet, breathing just audibly enough for me to know he was still there. 'Is it right that you found her?'

'Who told you?' I asked.

'Nobody – not exactly. I was passing through Notgrove this morning, and saw something was going on, so I stopped to ask. They've set up a police incident room in the village hall.'

Kenneth lived in Lower Slaughter. His reason for driving through Notgrove on a Sunday morning was not instantly apparent. But then, if it was suspicious, presumably he would not have mentioned it.

'Ken,' I said, feeling cold – and breaking his rule about never shortening his name, 'I had to give the police your name. And Pamela's, of course. They interviewed me a little while ago. They want to talk to everybody who knew Gaynor. I imagine they just feel they have to start somewhere and we're as good a place as any. The group, I mean.'

He spluttered at that. 'But *I* didn't know her. I can't even remember her name half the time.'

'I know. Sorry. Just tell them that, then, and it'll be fine. I didn't go into the whole business of us being pagans.'

'Why would you? What does that have to do with anything?'

'They found her at the Barrow, Kenneth,' I reminded him. 'She was curled up, very tidily and stabbed with a knitting needle.' *Oops*, I reproached myself, the moment the words were uttered. It would probably have been better not to have revealed that detail.

He made a sound, half disgust, half amusement. 'Good grief. They must think you did it, then.'

'It's not funny,' I said, feeling more offended than I ever had in my life. 'She was my *friend*.'

'Yes, I know. Ignore me. I always turn flippant in times of crisis. I'd better get my act together before the rozzers show up on the doorstep, hadn't I?' He paused. 'Maybe I'd better pretend I don't know the bit about the knitting needle while I'm at it. You didn't ought to have told me that.'

He was still being much too jokey for my liking. 'Suit yourself,' I said.

'Okay. Let's be practical for a minute. Are we going ahead with the Samhain ceremony? Will they seal off the Barrow somehow?'

'I have no idea,' I said tiredly. Then I revived

enough to ask him, 'Have you ever seen a dead body, Kenneth?'

'No,' he said, serious at last.

'Well, it's nothing like the films or the stories. It changes everything. The whole world becomes different. Do you know what it made me think?'

'No,' he said again.

'That everything we've been doing is childish nonsense. Games and silly rituals that we all know, these days, have no power and precious little meaning. It's time we all grew up and stopped fooling about.'

'You're wrong,' he said. 'Completely and utterly wrong.'

'Well, I don't think so.'

'It's bound to be a test of faith,' he said, sounding like a vicar. In some ways, Kenneth was rather like a vicar, anyway.

I made an impatient sound, but found that his words had had a mildly soothing effect.

Then he said, 'And Ari—'

'What?'

'Sorry I was so – inappropriate. It must be really grim for you. Pamela's going to be horribly upset when I tell her about it. Now listen, kid – be gentle with yourself, okay?'

I put the phone down in a blur of tears.

CHAPTER EIGHT

It was quite late in the afternoon when Thea came back across the street and suggested we go for a walk before it got dark. 'I've got to exercise these dogs,' she explained. 'They're getting hopelessly stir-crazy. We took them out early this morning, but it obviously wasn't enough.'

I remembered them driving off, a thousand years ago. 'Where did you go?' I asked, thinking confusedly that if they hadn't done that, everything might have been different.

'Phil wanted to show me Guiting Power in the morning light. We gave the dogs a run at the same time.'

'Guiting Power?' I blinked at her. 'Why?'

'He loves it,' she said simply. 'And Temple Guiting. We were still arguing about Freemasonry, and he wanted to demonstrate to me that there's a lot of real history woven into the nonsense.' She stopped herself. 'You don't want to hear it all now, but it was fascinating stuff.'

'Where's Phil now?' I wanted to know.

She rolled her eyes, trying to keep things light. 'Where do you think?'

'But he's on holiday, surely?' I was still confused as to Phil's role in the investigations.

She smiled patiently. 'Well, it seems that when somebody's as senior as he is, and on the spot like this, holidays don't really count. It might have been different if we'd gone to Easter Island or Vladivostock.'

'I'm not very good with dogs,' I said.

'What – you're scared of them, are you?' Her eyes had widened, as if I'd revealed some unsavoury perversion.

'Not at all. I just don't like them.'

'Oh.' She blinked. 'Well, you don't have to do anything. They'll run off on their own and we can forget about them. Assuming we can find somewhere without roads or pregnant sheep.'

'They chase sheep?'

'I'm not sure. They might, for fun.'

'I imagine Phil's got his better trained than that.'

'You don't have to come. I just thought...' she turned wistful and young, looking up at me with her pretty face.

'No, it's okay. Tell you what – we can go and see Arabella. She's due for some apples. You can help me carry them. We'll have to be quick, though. There's only an hour or so of daylight left.' Fortunately it was a bright day, and walking in the last light of the day was one of my greatest pleasures.

'Arabella?'

'My pig,' I explained, ignoring the amazement on her face.

I gathered the apples and some other leftovers, and grabbed my jacket from the back of the door. Thea was wearing the brown jumper I'd given her. It seemed weeks earlier that they'd arrived at Helen's cold dark cottage. The jumper reminded me of Gaynor.

I led the way past the primary school and off to the right, when the ground sloped downhill slightly and became rather less exposed. Arabella's woodland was far from densely provided with cover, but she had permission to dig it over as much as she liked, the mature trees easily withstanding her predations and the brambles and bracken were deftly removed by her powerful snout. She lived the life of pigs a millenium ago and more, except for one detail. She was all alone, a solitary creature starved of companionship. I tried to make it up to her by visiting three or four times a week.

I explained some of this to Thea as we walked, relieved to have a topic so far removed from Gaynor's death.

'Don't you have to give her extra food?' she asked. 'Pig swill or something?'

'I do in the winter months, but it's amazing how well she copes with what she can forage. Mind you, she'll have to move soon, or she'll start doing more harm than good. Geoffrey wants to put bluebells and snowdrops in, and I doubt if they'd last long with Arabella there.'

She kept Phil's two dogs on leads until we were clear of the village, letting her own long-tailed spaniel run free. It seemed to understand what to do when a car passed by. Once we were off the road, she liberated the others, and I half expected to see them disappear over the horizon. Half hoped, as well, if I'm honest.

'I hope they'll behave,' she said, with little sign of anxiety.

'I remember the first dog Phil had,' I said. 'Just before he got married. Mavis, he called it.' I was drawing breath to describe the horrors of Phil's Labrador when I remembered that Thea liked dogs. It seemed silly to deliberately irritate her.

'He told me,' she nodded. 'She sounds a dear old thing. Lived to sixteen, he says. I hope Hepzie lasts that long.'

'Hepzie?'

'It's really Hepzibah. My spaniel.'

I bit back the sarcasm. It seemed we'd finished the pig conversation, and I didn't want it to move on to dogs. The inevitable happened, of course. After a short silence Thea asked, 'How are you feeling now? Still a bit shaky, I expect?'

'Yeah. I haven't really got to grips with it yet. I keep seeing it, over and over. I s'pose I'll dream about it – if I ever manage to get to sleep.'

'How did it go at the police station? Being interviewed, I mean?'

'Weird. Not at all like I'd have imagined. They don't really know what to ask, do they? I mean – it seemed quite confusing, a muddle between the basic facts like times and places – and trying to get a handle on who Gaynor was. Sorry, I'm not explaining it properly.'

'I know what you mean. There's always such a lot going on in a village that isn't visible to an outsider. Stuff everybody takes for granted, and doesn't think can be relevant.'

'But Gaynor didn't live in Cold Aston. Or Notgrove, come to that. She's nothing to do with the village.' I found myself speaking loudly, trying to make her understand. 'The place isn't relevant at all.'

'Oh?' She was much more interested than she sounded. Her eyes were full of questions and quick thinking. 'What then?'

'I don't know. Gaynor always seemed so – simple. Shallow, even. She never got involved, never seemed to take much notice of anything or anybody. I mean – she hadn't even the sense to realise that Oliver Grover was gay!'

'Uh?'

'Oh, well, it's just an example. She'd taken a fancy to a local chap, trying to get me to do some work on it – when it was as plain as anything he was never going to be interested.'

'Some work? What does that mean?'

Too late, I wished I'd spoken more carefully. I would never have made a secret agent, the way my mouth blabbered of its own accord.

'Oh, you know. There are things you can do. Country lore, that's all. Most of it's very silly. But – well, there *are* things you can do.'

'Witchcraft?' Her voice rose, partly amused, partly alarmed.

'We call it Wicca, these days. It really isn't a big deal. It's only that most people have completely forgotten a whole dimension of existence. They're operating as if blindfolded.'

'Hmmm. Or is it just that reason and science have developed to a point where magic spells have been exposed for the wishful thinking and superstition they really are?'

'Whoa!' Her outspokenness came as a shock. Wasn't it supposed to be out of order to cast scorn on another person's belief system? 'That's a bit strong.'

'Is it? Look, Ariadne...' For the first time I heard my chosen name as fatuous, a mouthful as dopey as Hepizibah for a spaniel or Arabella for a pig.

Thea pronounced it deliberately, every syllable enunciated, not rushed as most people said it. 'Look,' she repeated, 'I didn't mean to be rude, but I think I'm well qualified to judge. My husband was killed eighteen months ago, and believe me, I went through all that stuff about his spirit lingering, trying to reassure me that all was well, the vital spark persisting in some other realm. And I found out, by first-hand experience, that it's all nonsense. He's gone, forever, and I won't ever see or hear or feel him again. It's finished. He's just bones in the ground.'

'I'm not talking about spirits,' I argued, wasting no time on sympathy, saving the questions for later. 'I don't believe in an afterlife, either – not in the sense of individual survival, at least. This is something much more ancient, centred on the soil, the energies that connect us all. The life force, if you like. It isn't possible to deny that it exists. It's all around us.' I stopped walking, and took hold of a convenient sprig of holly, with a few early berries on the stem. 'Look at this. Berries say it all, if you think about it. Actual and symbolic. They protect the new seeds, they've got colour and sweetness and nutrition—'

'Okay.' She held up her hand. 'I get the point. Everything connects. That still seems to me a long way from whatever "work" you're talking about doing for Gaynor. A very long way indeed.'

'Maybe it is. Gaynor never really understood what was possible, anyway. She thought the same way a lot of Christians do – just get your prayers properly formatted and God'll send you whatever it is you want. Like getting the right combination on a safe. I'd given up trying to explain to her that it wasn't like that at all.'

Thea just murmured something monosyllabic at this, and we walked on in silence for a bit. 'The police are going to interview everybody in the group,' I said, still worrying about it. 'They won't like it, some of them.'

'How many people?'

'Six. Two are a couple. Actually Kenneth phoned me earlier on. I warned him.'

'Why did he phone?'

'He'd heard what happened. They probably all have by now. He knew I found the body.'

'How?'

It was a deceptively simple question. I didn't know what news reports there might have been on local radio or TV. The car driver who stopped might have described me, or even remembered my name. 'Somebody told him, I suppose. It's not a secret, is it?'

'There hasn't been any news coverage yet.' Thea frowned. 'They'll be doing a press conference either this evening or tomorrow morning, once they're sure there's no family that needs to be notified.' She spoke as if all this was ordinary to her, familiar procedure hardly worth talking about.

'Incident room,' I said. 'Kenneth said they've set it up in the Notgrove village hall. There were people milling about outside.' I found myself quailing at the idea that they were all uttering my name in the same breath as Gaynor's. I would be forever linked with murder in their minds, which was not an image I would have chosen.

'Amazing how that happens,' said Thea. 'They come buzzing around like flies and the story gets passed along with all sorts of mistakes and wrong assumptions.'

'And theories about who did it,' I said glumly.

'That too,' she shrugged. 'You'll soon find you start suspecting everybody you meet.'

I stared doggedly ahead. 'I don't think I will,' I said.

'So who do *you* think killed her?'

The question was like an ice-cold knife right into my guts. It brought back the image of my friend's body, laid so neatly in the Barrow. And by some association with neatness perhaps, I remembered the bizarre appropriation of Helen's attic.

'I have no idea,' I said. Then I looked at her. 'But I have a sudden feeling it might be the same person who's been using the attic in Helen's house.'

'Ah!' she said. 'I thought you'd forgotten about that.'

The dogs handsomely lived up to the press Thea

had given them – they behaved perfectly and allowed us to pay them no attention for almost the entire walk. Claude, the Welsh corgi, turned out to have some character traits that even I found appealing. He followed in the rear, constantly checking that the party was complete, nodding to himself in satisfaction, and bumbling along on his short legs like a quick yellow caterpillar. The setter, on its rangy legs, ran ahead, long coat flying, head held high, only to stop every few minutes and wait for us all to catch up.

'Why don't you like dogs?' Thea had said at one point.

'They demand too much,' I replied briefly.

'That's true. Sometimes I can do without them myself.' I was learning that Phil's new lady had a knack of disarming criticism or disagreement, even though she could rubbish my pagan opinions so categorically. I had to admit, as well, that I liked her far more than I'd expected to at first sight. She wore her widowhood and consequent suffering lightly but conspicuously, conveying an impression of courage and self-sufficiency that made her very likeable. She was direct and brisk, in the way small women often are.

'But I'm afraid I'm hopelessly sentimental about Hepzie. She's such a good friend. I shudder to think what would have become of me without her over the past year and a half.'

'Well, we can't all be the same,' I said, rather stiffly. 'I've got a cat.'

I heard the next question coming. 'No boyfriend, then?' It was light, uttered in a breath, floating off even as she spoke it.

'No boyfriend,' I confirmed. 'Not for quite a while now.' To tell her about Lawrence, so many years after the event, would have been pointless. Even at the time he hadn't been particularly important. His significance had all been in the things he had taught me about human folly. But I was grateful to Thea for the question. It cleared a blockage out of the way, if nothing else.

'It's a rotten business, this murder, isn't it?' I said. 'For you and Phil, I mean. Is he going to have to go off every day and do his detective work? Will you want to stay at Greenhaven without him? I mean – there's still no power. It's sure to be chilly and bleak there.'

She sighed. 'I don't know, yet. I expect he'll try to keep the work to a minimum. But he can't dodge it altogether. He knows you, for a start.'

I hadn't seen it like that – the way I formed a link in a chain between Phil and Gaynor, and potentially, at least, provided him with an insight into the people involved.

'He thinks I might know the killer, does he?'

She chewed her lower lip worriedly. 'Well, you must understand,' she said haltingly. 'There's bound to be a question mark over your head, in their minds. I mean – you were on the spot. She was at your house yesterday. The Barrow's a special place for you.'

I had no idea what she was trying to say. 'And I found the body,' I said. 'So?'

'Well, you seem to be the only person who was in any sort of relationship with her. You might even have been the last person to see her alive. These are all pointers. That is—'

'I keep getting the feeling you're trying to warn me,' I said, 'against police suspicion that *I* killed her. Is that what you're trying to say?'

'Not quite. But I imagine you're quite near the top of their list, so to speak. At least until they learn more about her and the people in her life.'

I gazed around, at the spreading grasslands, the oppressive sky, the straggling smothering blankets of old man's beard on the hedges. Somewhere there must be comfort, reassurance. 'But...' I burbled. 'But I *didn't.*'

She put a small hand on my arm. 'You don't have to convince me. I'm not accusing you.'

That wasn't enough. That was like the defence lawyer who demands that his client withhold any incriminating truths. I wanted wholesale trust and unqualified friendship. But, I reminded myself, I had friends. I had Stella, and – at a push – Pamela and Daphne.

'And there's this Freemasonry stuff,' Thea added, as if prompted by a careless afterthought. 'What's that all about?'

'It's not *about* anything,' I snapped. 'But it has been a powerful factor in this area for centuries. We're all aware of it in the background, even if we don't actively think about it. I thought you said Phil had explained it all to you.'

'He tried. He told me the story of how he resigned from the Lodge and how furious everybody was with him. And you said something about it when I asked about Caroline. But I still can't get a proper idea of why it was all so important.' There was something touching in the way she spoke, a hesitant child wary of venturing into adult realms.

I nodded. 'It was all rather ghastly, actually. They don't like people to resign, you see. They did their best to punish him for it. And I told you Caroline was livid.'

'It must have been at the same time as all the scandal and publicity around Masons and the police,' she said. 'Exposing their corruption and back-scratching.'

'That certainly didn't help. Poor old Phil, he was trapped between a whole lot of hard places.' I recalled a long summer night, when I was twenty-one or thereabouts, and Phil had driven me home after an evening's babysitting. He'd had a few drinks –

nobody bothered much about drinking and driving in those days, at least in quiet areas like ours – and Caroline had seemed shirty about something when they'd come home. We'd sat in the warm dark car in the farmyard outside my parents' house and talked for half an hour or more. All I had to do was listen. He scarcely knew who it was there beside him, anyway. He'd discovered some sordid bit of business going on amongst the Masons, which had confirmed his decision to give it up. But their hooks were well and truly in him, and detaching wasn't easy. 'You leave a lot of skin behind where you tear yourself away,' he said. 'They're expert at tying you in – as bad as any cult. It's like walking over your own children's faces or cutting your father's throat to get away from them. Worse than that – it's like giving up your own soul. That's what happens when you make those oaths – just like Faust selling his soul. Everything's fine while you play the game. You can have the world. But if you break away, you're done for. You spend the rest of your life in outer darkness, lost forever.'

His language was full of images of torment and fear, which I assume he got from the rituals and ceremonies at the Lodge. Most of it frightened me, but I didn't understand a quarter of what he said.

At the end, when I opened the car door, he looked at me as if waking up from a nightmare. 'It's like choosing to live without a whole dimension,' he said. 'Can you imagine that?'

In my clear-sighted innocence, I met his eyes. 'If it's a dimension of evil, then you should be glad,' I said.

He laughed at that, bitterness mixed with a sliver of relief, I thought. 'Thank you, Mary,' he said, with the deliberate enunciation of the drunk. 'That's exactly what I needed to hear.'

I didn't even try to describe all this to Thea. Instead, I evaded any real discussion of the subject, aided by Arabella, who came thundering through the bushes at the sound of our voices.

A full-grown Tamworth sow is a large and very heavy object, and there was nothing between her and us except for Thea's spaniel. The dog was slow to realise what was bearing down on it, even when Thea tried to raise the alarm by calling its name. With only a yard or two to go, it noticed and started to dodge the oncoming leviathan. At the same time Arabella, perfectly well aware of the obstacle in her path and planning to politely circumvent it, also dodged in the same direction on an inevitable collision course. The dog howled, the pig squealed and Thea screeched as if she was ten times more hurt and shocked than the animals had been.

It was quickly over, Arabella snorting reproachfully at me for introducing such a brainless bundle of hair into her domain. The spaniel crept quiveringly on three legs to its mistress, who gathered it up and crooned idiotically as she examined the bones of one foreleg.

The other dogs gathered, eyeing the pig with surprised wariness. Arabella was orange, with a good coat of wiry hair, huge flapping ears and very small screwed-up eyes. In fact she seldom opened her eyes enough for anyone to see the pupils. She moved on delicate cloven trotters, which preferred soft mud to hard-baked summer ground. She spoke in a wide vocabulary of grunts, which turned into a purring croon when I scratched her cheeks.

I tipped the apples and carrots and cabbage leaves onto the ground, and Arabella forgot everything in her joy.

'Isn't she wonderful?' I said, competing fondly for Best Pet Award. 'She had eleven babies last year. That's a lot for a Tamworth. She's due again soon.'

'Oh?' Thea made little effort to show an interest. 'What happened to last year's?'

'Sold, bartered, eaten,' I summarised. 'There's half a one in my freezer still.'

'Right,' she muttered palely, still preoccupied by the limping spaniel.

'Pigs and dogs don't mix very well,' I tried to explain. 'They have very different world views, I've discovered. A pig doesn't care what its people think of it. They're marvellously self-sufficient. The babies are hilarious in the first month or two.'

I forced myself to stop eulogising on Arabella's gentleness, her curiosity and willingness to accord human beings the benefit of any doubt.

'She's very handsome,' said Thea at last. 'Pleased to meet you, Arabella,' she added. The pig squinted closely at her, wondering whether she might have another apple somewhere about her person.

The spaniel soon recovered and we turned for home in the fading light. Thea was very quiet, which I supposed was all about the dog, but when she finally spoke I realised my mistake.

'Why was Caroline so cross when Phil left the Masons?' The question burst onto my thoughts which had been entirely on Arabella and where I might move her when the woodland owner banished her. I had to switch rapidly back to the Hollises.

'Because of her father. He was the Grand Master, you see. It was all supposed to be kept in the family. Even poor old Steve was being groomed, from the age of about ten, regardless of their claims that they never actively recruit people. That's one of the big jokes about them – the difference between what they say and what they do.'

'Their son,' Thea remembered, ignoring my calumnies. 'And what happened? Did he join up?'

'Not as far as I know. He's only nineteen now, which is still a bit young. The whole business became taboo in the Hollis family, as far as I could tell. You'll have noticed that Phil still hates talking about the Craft.'

Thea thought about this, before saying something startling. 'Craft,' she repeated. 'Isn't that what pagans – or wiccans – call their activities as well?'

I choked. 'Well, yes. But it's completely different. With us, it really is a craft – something we *do*. In Freemasonry, nobody ever does anything. It's pure abstraction. It's different,' I insisted.

'Is it?' was all she said to that.

When we got back to the village Phil was standing by Helen's gate, talking to a woman I knew. It would have been surprising if I hadn't known her, actually, since I knew just about everybody in the neighbourhood. But this was Ursula Ferguson, who I knew rather well.

Greetings were exchanged, and questioning glances thrown in all directions. 'Ari!' Ursula exclaimed, hurrying to lay a hand on my upper arm, squeezing firmly, almost painfully. 'What an *appalling* thing to happen!'

I nodded and pulled away from her grip. She surged on, all the usual platitudes about it being unbelievable and terrifying and incomprehensible. Phil watched her closely, virtually ignoring Thea and the dogs.

Ursula lived in Turkdean, only a couple of miles

away, with a teenage daughter who cared for nothing but horses. The bulk of Ursula's income apparently went towards feed and equipment for a rangy hunter that the girl had insisted on acquiring. She was a familiar sight in all the villages, a solitary rider oblivious to everything but the equine muscles moving between her legs. Ursula was a schoolteacher, poor wretch, vainly trying to inspire her daughter's peers with the delights of geography at one of the big urban comprehensives. Sometimes she looked transparent with stress and exhaustion. But there was always some deeper reserve of energy, as was evident now, on a late Sunday afternoon in Cold Aston, with the light fading and a murder adding massively to the ghosts and shadows of Samhain.

'But *Gaynor*,' she wailed at the end of her threnody. 'That *poor* girl.'

I didn't think it was especially perverse of me to itch to correct her. Gaynor was not a girl, she was thirty-six. She was no more or less pitiable than anybody else unfortunate enough to be murdered. Her death, in fact, had appeared to be comparatively painless. I uttered none of these thoughts, but they made me wriggle and step further away from the group. I felt impatient and antisocial.

Phil rescued me. 'It's getting cold,' he said, overtly to Thea, but I felt myself included. 'We should get inside.' He looked at Ursula, and added, 'Thank you for talking to me, Mrs Ferguson. You've been very helpful.'

Belatedly I wondered what in the world she could have said to him. She knew Gaynor only as everybody else knew her – a peripheral figure, loosely attached to me, but not participant in any activity that concerned the pagans. Had the irksome matter of Oliver Grover been mentioned again?

Thea led Phil and the three dogs into Greenhaven and I crossed the street to my cottage. Ursula made a sound which I took to be valedictory. I looked at her. 'Are you walking?' I asked.

She nodded. 'It's not completely dark yet. There's a moon, anyway.'

The thought was inescapable. There was a murderer out there, and the way to Turkdean led down a bridlepath known as Bangup Lane. It was not a prospect she could possibly relish. On the other hand, she must have known what she was in for when she set out on foot, unless an expected lift had failed to materialise.

'I'd better drive you,' I said. Then I wondered about Phil, so casually letting a lone woman make her own way home after nightfall, without asking if she'd be all right.

Ursula protested half-heartedly. I ignored her and went to fetch my car keys.

There was no garage attached to my cottage so I

kept the car on the street outside. There was never any competition for parking space, with almost all the other properties boasting accommodation for vehicles as well as people. Ursula waited beside the car until I let her in.

I was tired. Weariness washed over me as I clumsily did a three-point turn in the street, running onto the pavement outside Greenhaven's gate. 'Careful,' said Ursula, as we jolted over the kerb.

I almost turned off the engine right there and let the ungrateful cow walk, after all.

But instead I drove too fast down the quiet twilight lane to Turkdean. Ursula clutched the door beside her, but wisely remained silent. It took barely five minutes to get to her village by car. A tiny place, much smaller and more compact than Cold Aston, it boasted nothing more than a church and a telephone box besides a handful of very beautiful houses. Ursula had a classic example, with front garden full of shrubs and perennials. It had taken me years to discover how she came by it. It turned out it was the usual pattern, albeit with one interesting variation. She had had an older brother, who made a handsome sum in the City. He bought the Turkdean house with his profits, in the mid-80s. Then he'd got himself run over by a speeding metropolitan police car, and Ursula had inherited the house, since the brother was unmarried and the parents comfortably settled in a hilltop hideaway near Montpellier.

Only as I drew up outside her gate did she speak again. 'They seem very interested in Oliver Grover,' she said. 'Mr Hollis asked ever so many questions about him.'

There was something about the way she said his name. 'Do you know him?' I asked. 'Phil, I mean.'

'Vaguely. I taught both his children in Year Nine. I remember him from the parents' evenings. And his wife, of course. And I was at Emily's funeral. Terrible business.'

'Ex-wife,' I said, automatically. 'But...' I was trying to keep a grip on the thread. 'That doesn't explain why you were at Cold Aston just now.'

'I walked over to see him,' she said, as if this was too obvious and simple to warrant explanation.

'How did you know he was there?'

'I saw him last night. When we left you, we stood around outside for a bit, the way we always do. He came to the door of the house opposite, and I recognised him.'

She spoke impatiently, as if answering a particularly obtuse pupil. I hadn't the energy to ask anything more, but I still didn't feel I had the whole story. Luckily, Ursula seemed to feel I needed her to continue.

'When I got there this afternoon, he invited me in and gave me a cup of tea,' she said.

My surprise was completely genuine. 'Brewed on the gaz?' I spluttered.

She laughed. 'That's right. Very atmospheric, it was, with the candles and everything.' She looked up at her own house, with little sign of impatience to get indoors. 'Of course, I already knew he'd become a Detective Superintendent, so I managed not to make any blunders.'

'How?' I mumbled, thinking she might have seen it in the local paper, but wondering at her noticing or remembering when he must be just one of thousands of parents she'd dealt with over the years.

'Funnily enough, it was Sally Grover who told me. You know – we both go to Bernadette in Naunton for our hair. She does us both on Saturday mornings, and we often get chatting. She's doing ever so well, isn't she, for her age? Wonderful woman.'

Shut up, I wanted to scream. The air felt full of watching eyes, following all my movements, spreading gossip, telling tales. And it was all my own fault. I'd gossiped to Sally about Phil quite a lot over the years, in connection with his Auntie Helen and Greenhaven. I'd even told her about the new lady friend and we'd speculated about what she might be like.

'Oh,' was all I said.

'Poor you,' she suddenly sympathised. 'It must have been *ghastly*. Finding her like that. They're all talking about it.'

I wilted even further. Whoever 'they' might be, they'd apparently got the story more or less right. 'Mmm,' I mumbled.

'Anyway, thanks for the lift. It was kind of you. Now I'd better go and see if Annie's home yet.'

There were no lights on in the house, which seemed a clear enough answer to that particular question. Eager to avoid any further involvement in Ursula's life, I put the car into reverse, for another turn in a village street. This time I executed it without any jolting, and was quickly back in my own front room. Thomas was waiting, tail flicking irritably, green eyes fixed on the cupboard containing his food.

CHAPTER NINE

If I had to identify my very best friend in the world, it would have to be Stella. By all normal definitions, she would qualify. I was most relaxed in her company, able to converse in a kind of shorthand where we finished each other's sentences, and understood all the references. We could be rude and careless with each other, accepting failings and small crimes. The only problem was that we seldom actually saw each other because she gave top priority to her job, followed by her husband and small son. I never doubted that I was her best friend, just as she was mine, because I was the only person she had any time at all for. And not everybody, it seemed, wanted to have an undertaker for a soulmate.

She lived and worked in Stow, in a handsome house with a huge mortgage on it. She worked full time plus as a partner in a local funeral director's business. That was how I met her – going with my mother to arrange my Gran's funeral, seven years previously. Although it had been a perfectly ordinary service, followed by burial, I had somehow got talking about pagan death rituals, which Stella had found interesting and informative, to the point of asking me to go back later and tell her some more.

Now, on a Sunday evening, I took the risk of phoning her. As expected, she answered with 'Brown Brothers. How can I help you?' in a creamy voice that was perfect for conveying unflappable professionalism and calm sympathy for the newly bereaved. I had long ago exhausted all the flippant responses that said I'm-your-friend-damn-it-I-don't-want-a-funeral. She was on call most of the time out of office hours, thereby saving having to pay anyone else to do it, but mercifully liberated from her own four walls by the handy invention of the mobile phone. Or so I kept insisting. The reality was that she very seldom left the house during the on-call hours. 'I'd need to take a whole mass of paperwork everywhere,' she said. 'People phone at midnight to ask when and where their cousin's funeral's going to be. Or there's a call from Nigeria needing a body repatriated, and I have to look up the procedure.'

'Stell? It's me,' I said. 'I don't suppose you've heard what's happened.'

'Er – that woman getting murdered? Your friend

Gaynor. I was going to call you about it.'

Stella of course made it her business to keep abreast of all the local deaths. Very often she was actively involved, sending Brown Brothers men to collect bodies from scenes of sudden death as well as from family homes and residential institutions.

'Don't tell me your people removed her,' I groaned. I had not stayed at the Long Barrow for long enough to witness the collection of the body. It hadn't occurred to me until then that Stella might have taken the call from the police.

'Actually, no,' she said. 'But we had a traffic accident around the same time, and Paul heard the story at the mortuary. He told me about it and I recognised the name.'

Another strand in the news network, I realised. The bush telegraph that ran from hairdresser to undertaker, school gate to public bars, and a dozen other points where people gathered together. It made me feel sticky, like a fly encased in spider's web. The invisible threads of gossip all seemed to connect to me, and I didn't like it.

'I found her,' I said, half expecting her to know this already.

'What? My God!' Her surprise was at least slightly gratifying. 'At the Barrow? But – why? I mean, what were you doing there?'

'Checking it out for the Samhain ceremony.' The police had asked the same question, of course, and

I had given them a much less definite answer. With Stella I could be frank. 'She was stabbed with a knitting needle,' I burst out, half crying. 'Can you believe that?'

'Hey, steady on,' she soothed me. 'You sound really upset.' She paused, and I could hear the thought processes in the silence. Could she spare an hour or two for me? Where was Johnnie – could he watch out for the kid? Was the mobile reception okay at Cold Aston? Stella always had to think hard before taking any action. 'Do you want to come over here for a bit?' she asked, finally. 'I'd come to you, but Johnnie's gone out, and I can't leave Zak.'

'No, it's okay,' I said. 'I'm too tired to go out again this evening. Where are you tomorrow? I might drop in and see if you're free, if you're at the new office.'

Brown Brothers had recently opened a smart new premises in Northleach and Stella sometimes spent a morning there, hoping for passing business.

'I'm not,' she said. 'It's going to be a busy Monday at Stow, from the look of it. There've been three nursing home removals over the weekend. Actually, love, I ought to get off the phone in a minute.' Any call lasting longer than five minutes made her twitchy, worrying that somebody might be trying to get through and would go to another undertaker if the phone remained engaged.

'Right, right,' I said, without rancour. 'I'll try and catch you sometime. It might be Tuesday.'

'Are you sure you're okay?'

'I will be,' I said. 'Probably. See you.'

I spent the next hour or two spinning beside the open log fire in the back room, a Leonard Cohen CD crooning softly at me for part of the time. There's nothing like spinning for opening up some of the dustier corners of the mind, releasing old memories or weaving fanciful plans. There's no place for strong emotion when you have to keep the wheel turning steadily, never gripping the fibres too tightly or letting them get pulled onto the spool too quickly. It's a regular rhythmic business, which promotes quiet thoughts in a stream that echoes the endless strand of wool, hair connecting to hair. Only a few animals have hair that is spinnable. It has to have tiny hooks along its shaft, which hold onto each other like Velcro. There are a few breeds of dog which produce the right sort of coat – bearded collie is the best of them all. Alpacas and Angora goats will do nicely too. But humans are useless. I liked to think of early women frustratedly experimenting with their spindles and the combings from their long-haired cattle or cats or daughters.

I couldn't prevent myself from thinking about Gaynor, but it was a more peaceful meditative approach than before. I reviewed her life and the mark she had left on the world. She had made dozens of beautiful garments, which people would wear for years to come. She had created a small garden in a neglected corner of the space she shared with neighbouring flat-dwellers. She had brightened the jangled lives of her ageing parents. She had, I believed, done no harm. I mused on the pagan doctrines of connectedness, working against the extreme individualism of contemporary thinking. People needed each other in ways they seldom acknowledged. They needed to be observed and heard in order to achieve any sort of identity. The image of an invisible underground root system, to which every person was connected, had always appealed to me. Spiritual nourishment flowed up, down and along this matrix, without our being aware of it. With Gaynor gone, we were all the poorer. I hoped she had understood that in her final seconds.

After a strange night where I plunged in and out of deep sleep and fuzzy reruns of seeing Gaynor's curled-up body, I was awake at seven the next morning. I bustled about, opening up the Rayburn and replenishing it with fuel, setting the kettle to boil and eyeing Greenhaven across the street. There was no sign of life, the house in total darkness.

I found myself considering Thea and what I had learned about her so far. It was obvious that Phil had found a treasure and I was impressed accordingly. There had to be something about him that had attracted her – something reliable and mature while at the same time interesting with auspicious hints for future satisfaction; all those qualities that a man must have if he's to hold the regard of a woman over forty. I found myself feeling a flicker of pride at my own appreciation of him, even from his callow days. He'd improved with age and might very well continue to do so if things went well with Thea.

I admired their courage, too. They'd both be well aware of the hazards ahead, the pain and misery that might befall them if things went badly, and yet they'd made some sort of commitment simply by coming here together, for all the world to see. Thea Osborne might be out of her immediate locality, and not especially celebrated even at home – but Phil Hollis was a senior police detective, with a reputation to protect. Even his private life was hedged about with restrictions.

It wasn't possible to be a practising Wiccan without believing in some sort of power to cast curses. Whenever some disaster occurred I automatically assessed it for its impact on me personally. Perhaps everybody does that? But in my case, I would also review my connection to the victim, checking to see whether they had ever annoyed or impeded me; whether I had ever even fleetingly wished them ill, and thereby perhaps brought about their trouble. Very often, I found that I had. As I did with Phil and Thea, in those first few minutes after they arrived and I had given bitter thoughts to their togetherness and their dogs and his plans for Greenhaven. Had I, perhaps, inadvertently blighted their week in those moments? Was it *my* fault that Gaynor had been murdered, as a means of interrupting the lovers and their trysting?

It sounds mad, I know. The normal world insists that we have negligible power over events at best. I believed it to be otherwise. It had been demonstrated to me often enough, after all.

But I absolved myself in the matter of Gaynor. It was too convoluted. It required too devious an intelligence to grant my sneaking wishes in such a way.

I saw Phil drive off at eight-fifteen, Thea kissing him on the doorstep like a nineteen-fifties wife. The dogs milled about, tails wagging slowly, working out what was happening in their usual anxious way. That's another thing I don't like about them. Cats don't know the meaning of worry.

I wasn't surprised when she came knocking at my door at nine o'clock. What else was she going to do? I did my best to be gracious about it.

'How's the bad leg?' I asked.

She didn't have to pause to wonder what I was talking about. 'A bit sore, I think. But she'll be fine. It was her own fault.'

Yes it was, I wanted to say, but restrained myself. 'She probably didn't understand about pigs.'

Thea smiled. 'I think that was the first one she'd met.'

'Perhaps she'll know another time.' Of course, she wouldn't. Dogs are not quick learners – unlike pigs. I ushered her in and shifted the kettle onto the hot part of the Rayburn. 'Tea?' I offered.

'Have you got any coffee?' she asked, as if ready for a negative reply, but determined to give it a try.

'Not really,' I said. 'I keep forgetting to buy some. There's about ten different sorts of tea, though. How about peppermint? Or rosemary and ginger? They're both good in the morning.'

'Peppermint sounds nice,' she said bravely.

'Is Phil going to be out all day? What's going to happen about packing up Helen's things? Will you be doing it without him?'

She sighed. 'I can't, really. I don't know what he wants to keep, or who he might want to give things to. We've already taken everything out of drawers and cupboards, so there are great piles of clothes and linen everywhere. I gather there's a cousin somewhere with some daughters, who might like a few bits and pieces.'

I snorted. 'That'll be Beatrice. If she wanted

anything, she'd have claimed it by this time. She hasn't been back to the UK for twenty years or more. She wouldn't have known Helen if she'd met her in the street. Forget about her and send it all to Oxfam. That's what Helen would have wanted.'

'Some of it's rather good for that. There's a lovely diamond necklace with matching earrings. Haven't you seen it?'

I gave her a straight look. 'No,' I said. 'I never ferreted in her jewellery box, and she never wore any of it. Phil ought to give it to you.'

'Or you,' she said. 'They really are nice. Very simple, but fabulously sparkly. Especially in firelight. We were looking at them last night.'

'So you're at a loose end,' I noted.

She shrugged. 'I'm used to it. I do house-sitting, you know. I can cope with dull days if I have to. It's just – well – not what I expected.'

'And you didn't bring your books or pack of cards or whatever you usually use to fill the time.'

'My computer, actually. I play Scrabble online, or browse websites. That's a brilliant time-waster.'

'Scrabble online?' It sounded faintly perverse, and inescapably sad.

She laughed. 'I'm really rather expert at it. But there are always loads of people even better. I tell myself it keeps my mind sharp.'

'Right,' I said, attending to the tea, once the

kettle had finally boiled. 'And you can always walk the dogs.'

She laughed again. 'Oh, yes. I'll have to walk the dogs. Phil found me a map. I thought I'd give the Macmillan Way a try.'

It was obvious that she wanted me to go with her. But I had other plans. I didn't take her up on the comment, and she quickly got the message.

'So what's with the Mary/Ariadne stuff?' she asked, after she'd sipped the tea and hastily smothered her disappointment.

I explained succinctly. I'd been named Mary after a great-grandmother who had died thirty years before I was born. The soft nothingness of the name had always irritated me, with its air of yearning and sadness. Thea raised her brows at this, and then nodded as if taking the point. 'Then an Irishman I met at a disco told me that every woman called Mary got landed with more than her share of suffering. Every good Catholic knows that, apparently. Well, that was the final straw. I changed it from then on.'

'Why Ariadne?'

I pointed through to my back room, with the piles of fleece and spinning wheel, and folded jumpers. 'She was the spinner,' I said. 'It tells the world who I am.'

'I see,' she said softly, giving it some thought. 'Not many names do that, do they?'

'A lot of pagans take a new name. It's all about transparency.'

'Right,' she said, in an identical tone to the one I'd used about the Scrabble.

We couldn't stay off the subject of the murder for long, of course. She was in a relationship with the Senior Investigating Officer – how could she ignore it?

'Do you think they'll want to ask me more questions?' I said.

She nodded slowly. 'They might. You're the most important witness, I imagine – finding the body and everything.'

'And will Phil tell them about the attic?' I said.

'He already has, although he disagrees with us that there's probably a connection. They'll be checking for fingerprints sometime today. I've got to let the chap in when he arrives.'

'They didn't ask me about it yesterday,' I said.

'No, of course they didn't. Phil hadn't had a chance to report it then.'

'I don't think he believed me when I said I didn't know anything about it. If he didn't, I suppose nobody will.' I looked at her hopefully, but she did not respond to the hint. Instead she drained the tea, and straightened her spine preparing to stand up. As she moved, there was a knock on my front door. For a moment, I thought the sound came from Thea, bumping her chair across the floor.

Then I realised she was looking at me.

'Visitor,' she said.

It was Verona Farebrother, standing with her weight on one leg, a shoulder lightly leaning on the lintel. A study in casual relaxation. 'Hiya,' she said. 'Got a few minutes?'

I let her go in ahead of me, down the little hall, which was at one end of the house, with all the rooms to the left, except for a downstairs lavatory. She wasn't expecting to see Thea and I heard the quick gasp of surprise.

I introduced them elaborately, finding myself acutely interested in what they would make of each other. 'Thea's just here for the week, staying with Phil at Helen's house. Verona's in the pagan group. She's a businesswoman, I suppose you'd say.' I then addressed Verona. 'You're not usually around on a Monday morning.'

'What kind of business?' Thea asked, turning the beam of her lovely face on the new arrival.

'Food,' came the succinct reply. 'Like Ariadne, I've gone for one of life's essentials. People can't manage without food or clothes.' She laughed her brittle unsettling laugh.

'You grow it or something?'

'No, no. Wholesaling. Supplying outlets. I'm just a link in a chain, but I've managed to make myself pretty useful.'

'She's being far too modest,' I interrupted. 'She's

plugged a gap, or whatever it is people say, and is set for great things. She rents a whacking great warehouse near Gloucester and runs a whole fleet of gigantic lorries. Verona's a real tycoon.'

Verona sat down without being invited and put her elbows on the table, clasping her hands together. 'Not quite a tycoon,' she corrected my words. 'It's all still in the early stages. Although,' she went on, encouraged by Thea's interest, 'I can't really lose. I'm not affected by the whims of the supermarket, because I can just switch products overnight. Mind you, I pity those wretched growers and producers. Their lives must be a total nightmare.' There was no discernible sympathy in her tone, just a complacency that she'd had more sense than to try to grow anything.

Thea threw me a quick look, almost an apology. 'Sounds great,' she said. 'Now I should go, if you need to talk to Ariadne about something.'

'Don't let me drive you away,' said Verona. 'I expect you know all about this ghastly business with Gaynor. That's all I came for – to see if Ari was all right.'

I blinked at this. Verona and I had never been on particularly friendly terms. We skirted around each other, playing a convoluted game where she patronised me and I pretended not to notice. Verona was a natural competitor. Once it was made clear that she was not to be challenged, everything was all right. Until then she could be nasty. I could already see that she resented Thea's good looks. Verona's nose was too thin and too hooked, her eyes too close together for beauty. Her skin wasn't wonderful, either.

I brought her a cup of peppermint tea without asking and waited for what came next. It was unlikely that she would stay long, the pressures of business permanently weighing her down.

It quickly became obvious that Verona was more interested in quizzing Thea than in assuring herself of my wellbeing. 'You'll have been left to amuse yourself, I suppose,' she said, 'with your friend being called away.'

I tried to remember what, if anything, I'd told the group about Phil on Saturday evening. I could not recall a single mention of him. Presumably word had spread that he was Helen's nephew as well as a Detective Superintendent. I had a sense of phone calls and pavement encounters and emails all passing on information and gossip. Ursula had recognised him on Saturday evening, and could have told the group who he was as they milled around their cars.

'I've got plenty to do,' Thea smiled. 'Exercising the dogs, trying to sort some of Helen's things.'

'Waiting for the fingerprint man,' I added, amazed at Thea's sudden flash of alarm at my words. Too late – Verona had pounced.

'What? Why?' She looked at the mug I'd given her as if it had bitten her.

Thea's thoughts were lightning fast. 'Oh, nothing to do with the Gaynor case,' she said easily. 'It's all to do with Phil's car. It was broken into last week, and they just want to take my prints for elimination purposes. It's all rather boring.'

'Did they take anything?' Verona seemed less than half inclined to believe her. She turned sideways and stared out of my front window at the house opposite, with a strange expression that looked like curiosity mixed with agitation, as she waited for Thea's reply.

'CD player. He'd forgotten to do the security palaver. He was ever so cross about it.'

I was well out of my depth, stunned by the quality of Thea's lies and at a loss as to why Verona shouldn't know about the discoveries in the attic. But at least I'd learned to keep my lips buttoned.

'More tea?' I asked them both. Two heads were shaken. We seemed to have run out of things to talk about and I felt restless.

'I ought to be getting on,' I said. 'I might have to go and deal with Gaynor's things. Paperwork and so forth.'

'Already?' Verona said. 'You can't register the death, can you? Not until the Coroner's Officer tells you.'

'You sound very clued up,' Thea remarked. 'Not

everybody knows about Coroner's Officers.'

'Least of all me,' I said, with a feeble laugh.

'My brother died last year in an accident at work,' Verona said. 'I had to deal with the funeral and everything.'

'Ah, I see,' said Thea. 'That must have been grim.' I could hear her thinking, *Here's another one for the club.* I had completely forgotten about Verona's brother. It had happened in Birmingham and she hadn't talked about it much, except to Ursula who had only then revealed the death of her own brother, several years before. I remembered shivering superstitiously with fear for my three brothers, who had suddenly seemed to fall into a high-risk category.

'We weren't very close, actually. But it taught me a lot about the procedure.'

Another ragged silence followed and then Verona got up. 'Thanks for the tea, Ari,' she said. 'Call me, won't you, if you need to talk to someone. You must be feeling pretty shaky, still.'

I didn't get up to follow her to the door. 'I'm trying to carry on as normal. I've got the evening class tonight to distract me.'

'It's still on, is it?'

'Of course. Even a murder can't stop an evening class, you should know that.'

Thea waited until the front door closed before demanding, 'Evening class? What evening class?'

I explained about the dyeing and spinning instruction I gave in one of the Gloucester Institute's smaller satellite colleges. 'Pamela from the pagan group comes along.'

'But not Verona?' Thea laughed.

'No. I don't think it's quite her thing.'

'She's a very odd woman,' said Thea.

'Do you think so? I've got used to her, I suppose. She's tremendously ambitious. I think her family must have been very hard up. She's one of those people who thinks money solves everything.'

'Strange for a pagan,' said Thea.

I shook my head. 'Not really. Quite a few of them think they can learn special ways to generate wealth and get what they want. Verona will try anything.'

'She sounds rather scary.'

I thought about this. 'Right,' I agreed. 'I think we are all a bit scared of her.'

Then there was a flurry of activity, with a car pulling up outside Greenhaven and the dogs setting up a racket when a man walked up the front path.

'Oops! There's the fingerprint chap,' said Thea. As she opened my front door, she turned back, 'And for God's sake,' she hissed, 'don't tell *anybody* about the Greenhaven attic.' She gave me a fierce look. 'Have some sense – okay?'

She was gone before I could defend myself, and I was left feeling I'd been a real fool.

CHAPTER TEN

It was still only quarter past ten. I could pick up my normal Monday routines – or so I hoped. There was every chance that the day had been wrecked by what had already taken place.

Usually I felt there was something specific about Monday mornings. A fresh start, a sense of the week lying clear ahead, to shape as I liked. On Mondays I seldom failed to quietly rejoice in my status as a self-employed person. Most people I knew dreaded the start of the working week, another dreary turn of the treadmill, selling their time and their souls to some ungrateful capitalist. Even some of my fellow pagans had got themselves trapped in the system.

There was Ursula, of course, with her geography lessons, and Kenneth, who worked for the Council in some dusty little admin job that made him miserable. Leslie, on the other hand, had found a workable compromise for himself with the National Trust. At least he didn't have to spend all day sitting in an airless office next to somebody he despised. Pamela was almost as admirable an exception as I was myself. She had landed a dream job as chaperone to young film actors during the filming, whether of TV commercials, blockbuster movies or one of a score of drama series. All she had to do was spend whole days drinking coffee and chatting while her small charge got under people's feet on and off the set, waiting for the twenty minutes or so of actual acting that was often the sum total of the day's work. Pamela had to prevent the child from being molested or run over or lost. Mostly they were aged ten or twelve and had a reasonable amount of good sense. To be paid quite respectable money for doing this seemed sheer madness, as Pam herself would say. The job said so much about contemporary western life that we would sometimes spend half a moot talking about it. Riddled with symbolism, looked at from a certain angle, it also led us to frequent acerbic comments about a society that worried so much about the safety of its young, whilst at the same time exploiting them mercilessly.

Daphne worked hardest of all, thanks to Eddie's departure. She was almost at the end of a long tedious course learning to be an actuary, which was so out of character I'm sorry to say I laughed aloud when I first heard about it. 'How does that square with paganism?' I demanded. 'Arguing about piddling details on insurance claims?'

She'd given me a disgusted look and wondered what gave me the right to pass judgement on her profession. At the same time as pursuing the studies, she was working for an insurance company, where she hoped to leap up several rungs of the ladder once qualified. We would seldom permit her to talk about it – not that she seemed to want to. Tedium was not the word for it.

But I did have plenty to think about. First on the list was the visit from Verona and her startled reaction to my mention of the fingerprinting. Thea's hurried diversionary tactics had alerted me to possibilities I had not considered, and the suspicion that I had perhaps told Verona what she had come to find out. From the way she'd looked at her mug, she had apparently become aware of her own prints being left for easy analysis. A wonder, then, that she hadn't insisted on washing up before she left. Except that would have been too obvious a giveaway. She must hope that I hadn't noticed anything, and would routinely wash the mugs myself.

Well, I thought – I won't. I would put the object carefully to one side, just in case.

Just in case *what*, though? Did Verona know Gaynor other than very distantly? Had my careless blabber about Oliver woken some jealousy in her breast? Would Verona risk murdering Gaynor for some secret passion? It seemed highly unlikely. The only passion Verona ever manifested was for her business.

Thea had been right: I was already viewing each of my friends and acquaintances – apart from Stella – as a possible killer. Not only Verona, but all the members of the group suddenly seemed a very credible bunch of suspects. Not one of them had particularly liked Gaynor, for one thing. Obviously it had never occurred to me that anybody might *dis*like her enough to kill her, but given that she presented some sort of threat to one of them, it wasn't beyond imagining that they might. The way her body had been so carefully placed in the Barrow, which we had talked about only hours before, firmly indicated a pagan connection. Anything else was too coincidental to be plausible.

It was hopeless trying to concentrate on ordinary daily matters. Gaynor's cold flesh and empty features followed me around, so I would find myself just standing, halfway from one room to another, and once out in the garden, numbed by the images and sensations that would not go away. By midday I understood that I was the one in need of debriefing. I was desperate to talk to somebody about it, to tell the story of how I found her, over and over again.

It must have been this need that drove me to go to Stow, perhaps hoping I'd meet somebody who would let me talk.

I had almost forgotten the Gypsy Horse Fair, due on the Thursday of that week. I was to have a stall, and should, by rights, have been working on labelling, pressing, displaying the things I intended to sell. Gradually I had become more skilful at presentation, pinning the jumpers onto boards with the sleeves at funny angles, draping scarves artfully around the neck of a wicker woman's head and shoulders. It all took a lot of time, and I often grew impatient with the whole business. My inclination was to throw everything into a glorious muddle like a jumble sale, and let people sort through it for themselves. I'd done that the first time or two to a very mixed reception. The other stallholders disapproved violently and the customers were confused. But the things had sold, just the same.

Now, after what had happened, I couldn't even be sure I'd go through with the stall. It seemed impossible that I could get the work done and stand there smiling for a whole day. Especially as Gaynor would have been my chief assistant. She would have taken a turn at the selling, as well as preparing the stuff beforehand.

Stow was empty, the American tourists somewhere else. October was quieter than the high summer months, but there was never a time of year when they disappeared completely. I've seen six or eight coaches parked in the middle of town in late

November. I left my car in one of several empty spaces and got out and went into one of my fugues, there on the pavement. Gaynor had worked for a while in a shoe shop in Stow, several years ago. We'd met often during her lunch breaks, because I was working – bizarrely it seemed to me afterwards – as a herdswoman on a nearby farm. I had to milk cows morning and evening, and feed calves and see to mountains of paperwork. The middle of every day was my down time. I officially had three hours off, which was not always an easy interlude to fill. Lunch in Stow with Gaynor became a dependable means of passing the time. I had not been prepared for the tidal wave of memories that standing in the town square brought back.

It was too much. I shook myself and climbed back into the car and sat there wondering what I might do next. The police might still be ransacking Gaynor's flat, and I definitely did not want to get involved with that. I could make speculative calls on one or two of my outlets, taking commissions for new items or simply dropping in for a bit of PR. But I knew I would do myself no favours with shadows under my eyes and a lot of difficulty in even smiling convincingly. I scanned the square, thinking how pleasant the town could look if you ignored the traffic and the rather annoying Union Jacks everywhere. And it got even better once you got into the smaller streets. It had alleyways and streets that veered at awkward angles, reminding you of its medieval past. It had no less than four bookshops, though I seldom patronised any of them. I'd never been a great reader, but I sometimes browsed the smaller of the secondhand ones, where the woman always had time for a friendly chat and had her eclectic stock sensibly arranged. I had found a few pleasing surprises in there over the years. None of the others ever struck me as being particularly interested in actually selling anything, even to the tourists.

As I had half expected would happen, if I sat there long enough, a familiar figure came into view. Oliver Grover was walking briskly towards me, carrying a briefcase. He was crossing the wide street beside the library, which at first glance looked like a church or a flamboyant town hall. Before engaging my brain, I was out of the car and waving at him, instantly catching his eye. Only then did I wonder what I would say to him.

'Ariadne,' he said, with a nod. 'Good to see you.'

Oliver was one of three gay men I knew. One of the others was my brother John and the third was a man who ran a boutique in Derby, buying knitwear from me now and then. They had little in common other than a relaxed manner when in the company of women, and an air of not taking life very seriously in any context.

'Hello,' I said. 'Not at work?'

'On my way,' he assured me, waggling the briefcase as evidence. 'The auditors will have started without me, which is no bad thing.'

I had to say it. 'You heard about Gaynor, did you?'

'Gaynor? My little Welsh friend who plays bridge so extraordinarily well. No – what about her?' He was very casual, his glance wandering along the Windrush, where the morning sun was sparkling on the water. He seemed to have something on his mind.

Suddenly it was much more difficult than I'd anticipated. 'She was your friend?'

He shrugged. 'I like her, if that's what you mean. How could anybody *not* like her?' He frowned at me. 'Did you say *was*?'

'Yes, I did.' I partly wanted to shock him into paying due attention, and partly to dodge having to utter the awful words.

'What? Come on, Ari, get on with it. I'm supposed to be somewhere.'

I almost said, *Gaynor asked me to cast a spell to make you fall in love with her*. For a few seconds I badly wanted to say exactly that, instead of the facts that I was already committed to imparting.

'She's dead. Somebody killed her yesterday.'

'No!' His squeal was high and girlish and utterly irritating. 'Who? Where?'

'In Notgrove. At the Barrow. I found her. They

don't know who, if you mean by that who killed her. It's a murder enquiry.' Until that moment, I had completely forgotten that I'd revealed his name during my interview with DI Baldwin. I should tell him, warn him to expect a visit. Although, on reflection, it seemed odd that nothing had yet happened. Perhaps they'd done some sort of background check on him and decided he wasn't worth the trouble.

'Good God! You poor thing! What a ghastly shock that must have been.'

'Yes,' I agreed. 'She was my friend, too.'

'Oh, yes, I remember now. She does – did – your knitting, didn't she?'

I merely nodded, suddenly too choked to say any more. Oliver noticed and patted me clumsily on the arm, looking rather green himself. 'Poor old you,' he said again. 'No wonder you look so zonked.'

I tried to take him at face value, to avoid suspecting him of being a killer. The whole thing between Gaynor and him embarrassed me. Except there *was* no 'thing', I told myself. It had all been in my friend's imagination, a fantasy that would mean nothing to Oliver, the gay accountant and junior Freemason. It was obvious that he was itching to go, and I was just turning away when I remembered our connection. 'Oh, hang on – did you get anything for your gran? She said you'd do her shopping this week.'

He nodded quickly, almost eagerly. 'Everything on the list. I took it round last night. She's on fine form, isn't she? All thanks to your ministrations, I'm sure.'

'Don't be daft,' I said feelingly. 'I don't do much.'

'You undersell yourself,' he said, with his gaze once more wandering across the square.

My flurry of emotion had passed without trace. Now all I felt was irritation. 'Anyway, that's the news,' I said briskly. 'There'll be a vacancy at the bridge club now.'

He winced. 'Don't be like that, Ariadne.'

'I'm not being like anything. I've got no beef about bridge. I might even join up myself.'

'Can you play?' His eagerness was unnerving.

'Not really, no. I have played whist a couple of times.'

'Pooh – whist!' he snorted. 'Fit for old ladies and nobody else.'

'I think that's what most people say about bridge,' I commented. The craze for the game had been a sudden inexplicable tide through the area, attracting people well under forty, and raising suspicions that it could only be a cover for some more sensual activities. Gaynor had assured me that this was groundless on a rare occasion when we talked about it. All they did was play cards, drink coffee and eat iced biscuits. 'There's no need for anything else,' she said. 'The cards are so exciting.'

I had given it no further thought, which I realised now was due to a difficulty I had in reconciling my perception of Gaynor's character with the intense cut and thrust of an evening playing bridge. The Gaynor I knew did not have the wits or the stamina for such an activity. Rather than adjust my assessment of her personality, I had chosen to pretend it wasn't happening. I had never asked myself about the skills involved, simply assuming that people's attitudes to card games were formed in childhood. If their father sits them around a table after supper and teaches them three-card brag or whist or Texas Hold'Em, then they'll have the habit for life. It's a social skill, after all. One that I didn't possess.

But it seemed unlikely to me that Gaynor's restrictive Welsh parents would have introduced her to cards. It had never occurred to me to ask her where she'd picked it up, and what it was she liked about it.

'Better get on,' Oliver said, still rather pale. 'Could you drop in on Gran sometime tomorrow? I'm not going to get there before the weekend, and she's going to want the sheets changing. She said something about winter curtains yesterday, as well, if you can face it.'

I nodded. 'No problem,' I said. 'I like changing curtains.' The sad thing was that this was nothing less than the honest truth.

'It's dreadful about Gaynor,' he said, as if suddenly remembering what I'd told him, and still not quite understanding it. Then he said a very surprising thing. 'But somehow, she's absolutely the sort of person that *would* happen to, don't you think?'

My head jerked back before I could stop it. It was a terrible thing to say. 'No!' I shouted. 'How could you think that?'

He put up the hand that wasn't holding the briefcase. 'Sorry. My mistake.' His face screwed up. 'But – it's true, Ari. She was always so *compliant*, don't you think?'

'That's no reason for somebody to kill her,' I defended.

'No,' he said sadly. 'You're right. Of course it isn't.'

I couldn't properly grasp how I stood with the police, or with Phil Hollis, my longtime friend as well as Detective Superintendent – or with his girlfriend, Thea. It felt as if the facts refused to fit into any existing pattern. Rules were being flouted, because ordinary human relationships overturned them. Phil was on leave and had settled his primary attentions onto Thea. The couple had come to this forgotten corner of the Cotswolds to get to know each other, to test their feelings and take timid glances at the future. They had apparently met during a murder enquiry, some months earlier, and then found themselves embroiled in another during the height of the summer. It was obvious that Phil's work was inevitably going to colour any long-term connection they might establish. From that point of view, the disastrous death of Gaynor had simply confirmed what they already knew. There would be no rest from crime and violence for Thea if she decided to take up with him permanently.

But more apparent, and more immediately interesting from my viewpoint, was the extent of her involvement this time. The suspicion was slow to dawn on me, but I did eventually grasp that she was being used as some kind of minder. She was to keep an eye on me, draw me out, assess my capacity for homicide. Whether overtly requested by Phil, or simply filling in the empty time, she had taken this role upon herself. If I was a candidate for the role of killer, then it made sense for me to be watched. Not exactly tailed by a keen young Detective Constable, but kindly supervised by a friendly woman who refused to be drawn as to just what might be going on. The real surprise was that I didn't have much objection to this. I was badly frightened, both by the sudden intrusion of death in all its uncompromising actuality, and by the perceptions of the police as to what part I might have played in it.

It was reassuring to have Thea and Phil just

across the street, for several obvious reasons. After all, tucked away behind the persistent image of Gaynor's cold body was the knowledge that she had been deliberately slaughtered, like an animal, by a fellow human being. By a human being who was extremely likely to be somebody I knew.

And there was one other thing: I was lonely. This last came as an unwelcome revelation when I went back to my little home. Those whom I called my friends were not really that. There was little true intimacy, and I could trust nobody to deal with this sudden crisis. On a psychiatrist's couch, faced with the need for a quick answer, I would probably have named Gaynor as my second closest friend after Stella. And, if pushed further, I might have given Phil Hollis as the only man I could ever have completely trusted.

CHAPTER ELEVEN

My phone went twice in the hour after I got home, and I answered apprehensively, wondering what further trauma there might be in store for me. The first was my mother, trying to keep reproach and concern out of her voice as she asked about what had happened.

'How did you hear about it?' I asked her.

'It was on Three Counties radio just now.'

'What? Did it give Gaynor's name?'

'No, but it talked about the Barrow, and I knew it was close to you – and you'd be having Samhain ceremonies there next week.' She mispronounced it, as always, saying it as it's spelt, instead of "Sow-en" as it ought to be. I swear she did it on purpose, at the same time being keen to show me that she kept up with my activities like a good mother should. But she was wittering on. 'At first I thought it might have been *you* that was killed.' Her tone was entirely level, stating facts, wanting facts in return.

'I found her,' I said. 'It was a big shock.'

'And you didn't think to call and tell us?'

'I probably would have done at some point.' She didn't need to be told that she was not first on my list of possible comforters. My mother and I had never been very good at adhering to the stereotype. She had reared me efficiently and without undue difficulty. We had even enjoyed each other much of the time. But the apron strings had been long and loose, and although I continued to live with them until I was nearly thirty, we were by then pretty thoroughly detached. I wondered, sometimes, what would happen if either of us became helplessly disabled, needing full-time care. The idea of being each other's default caregiver was grotesque to us both – or so I believed. Maybe I was underestimating her.

'I haven't seen Gaynor for a long time,' she said, with uncertain relevance. 'Was she all right?' It seemed an odd question, as if being murdered was a reasonable outcome after an illness or a period of mental instability.

'She was fine. She'd done some brilliant knitting for me lately. Nothing special happening.' I scrambled for something more meaningful to report and found nothing.

'I heard she'd had some trouble,' she said slowly. 'Only a week or two ago. Something about a stone through her window.'

'Surely not.' I dismissed it without even thinking. 'She'd have told me. It can't have been deliberate. Kids, probably.'

'Mmm,' she said dubiously.

I gave her a bland description of my interview with DI Baldwin, trying to make it sound like a mildly educational experience, touching none of my emotions.

'Well, it's a dreadful thing to happen,' she concluded. 'You'll miss her. Come over any time – you know we're here, don't you?'

It was unprecedented gesture, acknowledging the severity of the event and the effect it might have had on me.

'Thanks,' I said. 'I'll keep you posted.'

The next call was Kenneth, his second since Sunday morning. 'We've arranged a special meeting for tomorrow,' he told me. 'Will you come? It's at our place.'

'I suppose so.'

'Ari, listen to me. You must be badly shaken. We understand that. We want to offer you a healing, a cleansing. Don't turn your back on everything we stand for, now of all times.'

'I wasn't going to. What makes you think that?'

'Well – when I phoned yesterday. You sounded—'

'Ken, I was shocked. I didn't know what I was

saying. I agree with you. I'll be there tomorrow. What time?'

'Seven. Verona can't come, but the others will all be here.'

Afterwards I wondered why he couldn't understand that the best therapy would have been for him and one or two of the others to rush to my side, and encircle me with light and warmth and hope. That an appointed ceremony, with formal preparations and self-conscious attenders, was a much colder exercise than I needed. It smacked of church and detachment and unreality. The words and clothes would be chosen with far too much care. Some meaning would survive, but the visceral human urge to offer comfort and protection would be badly diluted by the delay.

And then I had a visit that came closer to filling my needs. I'd drifted through the afternoon somehow, wondering if Thea would appear and force me to walk the dogs again. But she didn't. I supposed she was trying to get Helen's things into some sort of order.

It was almost five o'clock and I had been thinking about getting up, feeding the cat and myself, and forcing myself to start getting knitwear ready for the Fair on Thursday. I almost didn't answer the door, from some twisted notion of self-sufficiency, grudging the effort it would take to speak politely to whoever it was. For a stupid moment I thought it might be Gaynor and we were back into the realm of normality. But even before I was out of the chair, I knew it couldn't be her.

The familiarity of the face, despite a whole new hairstyle, prompted a rush of complicated feelings that left me paralysed. I simply stood there, staring blankly at her.

'Can I come in?' she said. 'I've just heard the news.'

The voice sparked my brain cells into action. 'Gosh, Caroline. What a surprise.' I let her in with a glance across the street. What in the world would Phil think if he saw his ex-wife paying me a visit?

I took her into my front room and she sat down on the sofa. I could feel my insides churning, with a sick sense of apprehension. 'Why?' I blurted. 'I don't understand.'

She launched into a rigmarole that sounded as if she'd rehearsed it. 'I knew you were in Cold Aston with Auntie Helen, of course. And I knew...the girl who died...was your friend. I called Paddy at the police station, and he told me you'd found the body. It must have been so horrible for you, and they don't ever give enough attention to the person who finds the body, do they? It sounds barmy, probably, but I've been thinking about Emily ever since I heard. You know how that friend of hers, the American girl, found her, and then got sidelined in the mayhem that followed. I always felt bad about that. The poor girl, none of it was her fault, and yet it must have scarred her for life.'

She was saying such nice things to me, but her eyes told a different story. They were full of pain and suspicion. It was as if she needed to test me, to offer sympathy just to see what I'd do with it.

There was a lot of history between me and Caroline. Twelve years my senior, she had watched me grow from a coltish teenager into something more assured and decisive. I remembered, with a rush, how sweet the friendship had once been between us, playing with the children, Caroline talking to me as if I was the same age as her. Then I had hurt her at a time when she was already dreadfully wounded. I had done it almost casually, which made it very much worse. It wasn't possible that she had been thinking fondly of me now.

But I chose to play her game, whatever it was. 'It's nice of you to come,' I said, making the effort to focus on what she had just told me. Her continuing links with the Gloucestershire police surprised me. Her new husband, Xavier Johnson, had nothing at all to do with the Force, as far as I was aware. 'How is Paddy, by the way?' I remembered him affectionately – Phil's partner on the cars for ages. A big fair-haired man, with an understanding smile.

'He's all right, I think. Of course, he's always been fond of you.' Her eyes roamed my room restlessly as she chose her careful words. The strangeness of seeing her again was compounded by the situation. My friend dead, and the people I had once counted my most beloved both here in Cold Aston all of a sudden.

'You knew Phil was here, at Greenhaven, did you?' I asked her. 'With his new girlfriend? They're having a little holiday while they sort out Helen's things at last.'

'I did hear something, yes.' She betrayed no curiosity about Thea, and yet her tension almost made the air crackle. 'So why's he at work? Paddy said he was doing a lot of the interviewing.'

'I suppose because it's all happened right under his nose, and Thea – that's the girlfriend – says it's also because he knows me, and I found Gaynor.'

She flinched at the mention of Gaynor's name and her hands automatically gripped each other. I had been in the kitchen when she knocked, the light in the main room off. Now I switched it on, showing Caroline clearly for the first time. She looked older than I remembered, but more poised and confident. She had lost some weight and seemed fit. Her hair was a rich nutty colour, cut in a clever layered shape that ought to have taken years off. But somehow it just made her look like a fairly affluent middle-aged woman. She wore three or four rings, one of them a clunky thing on her right hand. I remembered the new husband and supposed it was only natural that a woman would adopt a new image to mark the change of partner.

She looked around the room. 'Still knitting?' she observed. Although I tried to keep all the wool and equipment in the back room, things would persist in creeping through to the front.

'Yup,' I said. 'Me and Gaynor.' I had a perverse urge to repeat my dead friend's name over and over, to summon her into the room and not let her be forgotten.

It was still unclear to me why Caroline had come. 'Do you want some tea?' I offered.

She got up, apparently to follow me into the kitchen. 'That'd be lovely,' she said. Then she went to the front window, exactly as Gaynor had done on Saturday. And somebody else in the past day or two had done the same thing, too. For the moment I couldn't remember who it had been. 'It looks very cold and dark over there,' she said.

'There's no power. They're managing with an open fire and camping gaz and candles. They thought it was romantic at first but now they're talking about trying to get the electricity connected.'

'They're here all week, did you say?'

'That's the plan. I expect they'll leave at the weekend. Sunday, probably. They've got three dogs with them.'

'Three!'

'Two of his and one of hers.'

'Baxter,' she said softly. 'Has he still got Baxter? I was fond of that dog.'

'What sort is he?'

'A Gordon setter. Big and beautiful and brainless.' She sighed.

'Sounds like one of them,' I confirmed. 'And a corgi with a long tail. Ridiculous creature.'

She nodded. 'Steve said something about that one. Funny the dogs people choose, isn't it? Do you remember Mavis?'

I shuddered and groaned. 'How could anybody forget Mavis?' I said, trying to laugh.

'Dear old girl,' said Caroline, with another sigh. 'That all seems a lifetime ago now.'

The reference to Steve had opened another window in my memory, too. Phil's son, who I hadn't seen since his sister had died, was another person lost to me. How rich my life had been, all those years ago, compared to what it was now. Steve and I had played ball games in the garden together many a time when he was nine or ten and I was in the habit of dropping round there any time I felt like it.

I made the tea and showed Caroline some of the jumpers and hangings in the back room. She'd bought things from me once or twice when I first started serious knitting. 'You're so amazing with colours,' she said, as if stating a plain fact. 'Really clever.'

'I'll miss Gaynor. She did a lot of these things. She was a much better knitter than me.'

'Gaynor had a lot of talent,' Caroline said, with a rare straight look into my face, as if waiting for me to betray something important. And yet, she was the one who had just done that very thing.

It took me a moment to catch up. 'You knew her?' Why had I assumed that the two had never met? Why was I so surprised? Why did I mind so much that Gaynor had never once mentioned Caroline to me, even when we'd been talking about Phil?

'Oh yes,' she said easily. 'Quite well, as it happens.'

'How? Why didn't you say so sooner?' My head was spinning. Did Caroline know that I had no idea of such a connection? Was she really playing with me, or did it just feel that way?

She tapped a front tooth thoughtfully, giving a stellar performance but not quite hiding her agitation. 'I'm not sure how we first met. Probably just bumped into her somewhere and got chatting. You know how it is around here. People just know each other.'

This was true to some extent, but affluent middle-aged women from Painswick don't generally form friendships with self-employed knitters from Stow-on-the-Wold on the basis of a casual meeting in the street. Then I remembered. 'She knew your husband's name,' I said, the brief exchange coming back to me from Saturday. 'But she never said she knew you.'

'I know!' She was triumphant. 'It was through Xavier. His brother plays bridge. There's a chap called Oliver Grover in the bridge club who does people's accounts. Xavier took him on last year, on Gervase's recommendation, when old Rupert Lack died. He came to the house a few times. The first time, he brought Gaynor with him, and she sat in the kitchen with me and we got chatting.' The story contained too much detail to be spontaneous. She had rehearsed it, I was sure. The tone was just slightly off key, so it sounded exactly like a speech given by a clever actress in a well-written play. Fine in context, but just somehow wrong for the real world. But the information it contained demanded my attention.

I stared at her, my insides forming into lumps. 'When was that?' I choked.

She shrugged. 'A year ago, or a bit more.'

It was impossible. Gaynor riding around with Oliver, going with him on professional visits and never saying a word about it to me. In fact, leading me to believe such a thing was out of the question. What had all that divination stuff been about, then? I reran my encounter with Oliver that morning, searching for hidden clues and ill-kept secrets.

'Did they seem to be good friends? Gaynor and Oliver, I mean?'

Caroline waved a vague hand. 'Oh, I don't know. She never talked about him after that, so I suppose not. Isn't he meant to be gay or something?'

'So I believe.'

'Did you hear about the brick somebody lobbed through her window?' The change of subject was obviously deliberate, but cleverly chosen for all that.

'Just now,' I nodded. 'My mother said something about it.'

'Gaynor didn't tell you?'

I shook my head. 'Must have been kids playing in the street.'

'She was upset. Xavier went and fixed it for her. He's useful like that – turns his hand to anything.' Again the direct look, the sense that she was waiting for me to stumble, or reveal myself, when all the time I wanted her to do the same.

I refrained from remarking that any fool could replace a broken window. Much more important was the revelation that Gaynor had kept something from me. I tried to make sense of these disclosures, all of them leading to the increasingly familiar conclusion that I knew much less about my friend than I'd thought I did. Why had she never told me she was so much closer to Oliver than I thought?

'She kept it a secret from me,' I blurted. 'Have you any idea why?'

She gave me a gentle look, full of sympathy and

sensitivity that was also quite calculated. She was going to tell me something nasty about myself. 'I think she must have been nervous of how you'd react. You can be a bit…brusque, you know.'

It could have been worse. With our history, there were a hundred vicious things she might have accused me of. 'Although she did ask me to do a divination about her and him,' I said defensively.

The reaction was gratifying. 'What? She did what?'

I explained, suddenly unsure of just what Gaynor had been asking me to do. The idea dawned that she had in fact not cared tuppence for the ritual itself. It had been her way of confiding to me that there was something between her and Oliver. I tried to say some of this to Caroline.

'Well, yes,' she nodded. 'That makes more sense. I'm quite sure she would never have actually believed you could make any difference, with that pagan nonsense.'

I tolerated the slur. I knew Caroline had always scorned paganism and made no secret of the fact. We had aired the subject between us many times – not least on the last occasion we'd met.

She glanced again at my front window. All was darkness outside. I hadn't heard Phil's car come back, so I assumed Thea and the dogs were huddled in a back room waiting for him.

'What's she like?' The question fell very casually,

but at least it betrayed a modicum of natural curiosity. I felt a flicker of power at being the pivot between Phil's two women. Hadn't Thea asked me just the same question about Caroline?

'Quite nice, actually. A widow.'

'Good God! How old is she?'

'About forty, I should think.'

'So they've got death in common,' she noted, astutely. 'Let's hope she's better at it than I was.' She paused, and I couldn't think of anything to say. 'I wish he hadn't left the Masons,' she added, softly. 'They'd have given him something I couldn't.'

I gritted my teeth. At last we had reached the subject that Caroline and I had so passionately disagreed on, and which had driven such a massive wedge through our friendship. It felt wrong of her to bring it up now and I would not be drawn. 'I think Thea's quite good for him – from the little bit I've seen so far,' I said. 'She's been very nice to me, as well. Sympathetic.'

'And she's got a dog,' Caroline forced a laugh. 'Dogs *and* death. Heady stuff!' Her laugh grated on my ears. Something was definitely wrong. She definitely wasn't as happy or relaxed as she so valiantly pretended. It occurred to me, finally, that she was grieving for Gaynor, but couldn't bring herself to admit it. Rather than let it leak out, she was doing her best to focus on the couple over the road. 'Will she break his heart, do you think?'

'It's possible.'

Caroline sighed. 'Well, he doesn't deserve that. I can't really wish him ill, can I? He never did anything to me.'

Except give up on you, I thought, but said nothing. Phil and I had both rejected her in our different ways, after all.

'I was a real bitch to him. I can hardly bear to think of the things I said, in those first weeks and months after Emily.' Then she gave herself a little shake. 'But we're not here to talk about me. You and I ought to keep in touch. We could talk about Gaynor.' Again the words were loaded with meaning, and again she watched me closely. I said nothing in reply, just murmured a little hum of non-commitment.

She got up to leave. 'Funny to think Phil's new woman is just over there...' she said. 'He's brave, I'll say that. She might be a right cow, deep down inside. And she'll have worked out that you and Phil go back forever. I bet she's jealous of you.'

Dangerous ground, I wanted to warn her. Ariadne's feelings for Phil were not, and never had been, for open discussion. Particularly as that had been Mary, my past self, buried now under a completely remade person.

'I doubt it,' I mumbled. I wanted her to leave, so I could straighten out all the new information she'd dropped on my head. I concluded that the curiosity about Thea was obviously the reason she had come in the first place – to check up on her ex and his new woman. I'd seen enough of broken marriages to understand that even when they married again the old wounds never fully healed. And jealousy was entirely devoid of reason.

'Well,' she said, 'I really must go. Thanks for the update on Phil and his new female.'

I had not forgotten my evening class, the bag already packed and waiting, with some unusual dyeing materials and a lot of raw fleece. Not that we actually did any dyeing during the class – the small college where the classes took place couldn't quite run to the right facilities for that. But I doled out wool for people to take home and play with, and used it for spinning practice during the class.

Ten minutes before I was due to leave, there was a knock at the door. I was not surprised to see Thea standing there, looking like a lost child.

'Tell me if this is out of order,' she said. 'But do you think I could come with you to your class? Phil's going to be out all evening, and I don't know what I'm going to do with myself otherwise.'

'You just caught me,' I said. 'Come on, then.'

CHAPTER TWELVE

In the car I couldn't refrain from telling Thea about Caroline's visit. 'She knew Gaynor,' I said, two or three times. 'I had no idea.'

'I wish I'd seen her,' said Thea. 'It sounds as if I might like her.'

'She's different. There was something odd about her.'

'Shock, probably. It makes people odd sometimes.'

'Maybe.' I thought about it, the way Caroline had paled at Gaynor's name. 'Yes, that might be right.' I thought about it a bit more. 'And Gaynor went out with Oliver. In his car.' This was like a bruise, a painful spot I had to keep touching. 'And she never *told* me.'

'Some people keep all their friendships separate.'

I was growing impatient with Thea's efforts at soothing me. She was missing the point – deliberately, it seemed. 'I'm beginning to think I hardly knew her at all,' I complained. 'It makes me feel a fool, thinking I was her only friend, when all the time she was swanning around with practically everybody.'

Thea began to speak, and I cut her off. 'And don't tell me that's normal and natural and I needn't get upset about it. I *am* upset, and that's all there is to it.'

'Okay,' she said lightly. 'I won't say anything of the kind. Is this where your class is?'

We'd driven into the parking area, behind the ramshackle building that was a neglected annex to the main college.

'This is it,' I said.

I had seven students that evening, which was five short of the maximum class size permitted, but enough to ensure viability. I did not count Thea, of course. She was there against all the rules, but there was very little risk of trouble as a result. I had been teaching for three years by then and knew the routines. Despite the decline of evening classes from the glorious days reported by my grandmother thirty years earlier, they did still exist, and the payment I received was a useful slice of my income.

The routine had become hedged around with paperwork and injunctions about safety and awareness – whatever that meant – but I'd managed to dodge a lot of that nonsense. Leaving Thea outside the main entrance, I ran into the office and grabbed my register, without speaking to anybody. Then I led the way through the maze of corridors to the Art Room, which I shared with the class on pencil drawing. The other teacher and I were not on good terms, each of us shepherding our pupils to opposite ends of the large room. The college had refused us permission to store spinning wheels and raw fleece anywhere on the premises, so the class valiantly carted their equipment back and forth every week. Those with Ashford wheels had quite a struggle, getting the awkward things in and out of their cars.

But I'd got everybody well rehearsed by this time, and most of them were waiting for me already.

I introduced Thea as an 'interested observer' who would also act as an assistant if necessary. One or two of the women asked her if she was a spinner, and she said shyly that she was thinking of taking it up.

Leading a class like that was mostly a doddle. They brought the results of their efforts during the intervening week, and I explained where they'd gone wrong, or suggested how they might progress. With spinning, almost everybody naturally inclines either to very fine yarn or very thick. I generally took it upon myself to transpose the two, in the interests of versatility, making the thick ones do thin and vice versa. On this, the fifth in the course of ten classes, I introduced the technique of slub, which was wildly ambitious, testing my own skills to the utmost.

Essentially, slubbing involves spinning very badly – making the mistakes you've spent months trying to eradicate. It works best with short staple wool that feeds onto the spool in fits and starts, making lumps and uneven thickness. I had no very high expectations of anybody producing a respectable result, but it's usually quite good fun trying.

Thea settled down with Agnes, an eighty-year-old who remembered her mother spinning, and had always wanted to give it a try. Slubbing was beyond Agnes, to be honest, but she gave it a try anyway. Thea encouraged her, once she'd grasped the idea and with some merriment they tackled the task together.

Inevitably, I spent more time with Pamela, given the events of the day before. She had watched me carefully at first, to see whether I was in any mood to talk. We both realised we couldn't openly discuss the murder of a mutual acquaintance in front of everybody, but there were muttered exchanges.

'Are you all right?' she said first. 'You look pretty shell-shocked.'

'Wouldn't you be?'

'Yeah,' she agreed. 'Course I would. Why've you brought her with you?' She tilted her chin at Thea.

'She wanted to come,' I said shortly.

'Scared to be left on her own?' I wondered

whether Pamela knew exactly who Thea was.

'Why d'you say that?'

Pamela rummaged in her basket of assorted bits of fleece, saying nothing. I looked more closely at her, noticing for the first time that her eyes were puffy and the edges of her nostrils very red. Either she'd developed a cold or she'd been crying.

'What's the matter?' I asked, softly.

She shook her head. 'Not here,' she said.

I moved to Glenda, the youngest in the group, who had already done a previous course of my classes, and was heading for techniques way in advance of what I could teach her. Already she had half a spool of gorgeous slub, in two shades of blue. 'That's perfect,' I said. 'You don't need these classes now, you know.'

'I do,' she assured me. 'I'd get bored just doing it on my own. Besides, it's lovely to get out of the house for a change.'

The coffee break arrived in no time, and we trooped off to the gloomy canteen, where disaffected women slung tepid drinks in plastic cups at us. The coffee was profoundly revolting, as somebody pointed out every single week.

It took some jockeying to get a seat next to Pamela, but I badly wanted to know what she was upset about. If it was the death of Gaynor, I wondered why. As far as I knew, they had scarcely even spoken to each other.

'So?' I prompted, turning my back on the rest of the class, as far as possible. The tables had seats bolted to the floor and everybody had to sit squashed together, pretending to be students.

'I can't tell you now,' Pamela said, peering out from under her fringe like a wild deer in a forest. She glanced sideways at Glenda, who obviously wanted to speak to me.

'Give me a hint,' I insisted. Thea, apparently picking up on what was going on, started talking to Glenda, making some joke that had the whole group focused on her. Within seconds she'd diverted all attention away from me and Pamela. It was a very neat trick and it earned her my respectful gratitude.

'It's between me and Kenneth,' she said in a whisper. 'I've just found something out about him.'

My first thought was *My stars – Kenneth's the murderer!* But that seemed too wild to be possible. More likely, of course, that he was seeing another woman.

'Oh?' I encouraged.

'Ari, I can't say any more. It would be disloyal. But it's not what you're thinking.'

I forced a grin. 'Not sex or murder then?' I said.

She didn't grin back. The single 'No' was uttered in a flat tone.

I remembered what she'd said at the meeting on Saturday. 'Money, then?' I guessed.

Her face flooded with colour, and her eyes went shiny. She nodded quickly, and took a gulp of the dreadful coffee.

On the way back to Cold Aston, I filled Thea in on what Pamela had said. 'What's he like, this Kenneth chap?' she asked.

'Ordinary, even a bit dull. He's got some sort of bone disorder, which makes him move carefully. I'd have thought he was too cautious to get into debt.'

'Did she say he was in debt?'

'Not quite, but I think that's what she meant. She seemed almost scared.'

'Poor thing. It *is* scary when the lenders start getting nasty. Do they own their house?'

'Yes they do, with a big mortgage. We did a special ritual when they moved in.'

'A house-warming ritual?'

'Right. It's a lovely pagan ceremony, as it happens. Going from room to room with scented herbs, introducing the new people to the spirit of the building. It was all wonderfully *happy*.'

Thea sighed in complete sympathy with what I was saying. 'What a wonderful idea!' she said. 'Why doesn't everybody do it?'

'Well, to be fair, most of them do. That's what the ordinary house-warming party is all about. It's just that we make it all more overt. I sometimes think that's the whole basis for paganism. We're mostly stating the obvious, but it's things that people have somehow forgotten, or overlaid with a load of commercial garbage.'

'But things have gone sour for Pamela and her Ken.'

'Apparently. They were a bit tense on Saturday, I realise now, although she was making an effort to be cheerful.'

'Did she say anything about Gaynor this evening?' I was beginning to get used to Thea's abrupt switches of subject.

'No, not really. She just asked me if I was okay.'

'How well did she and Ken know her?'

'Kenneth. He doesn't like to be called Ken. They didn't know her very well at all, to my knowledge. They live in Moreton-in-Marsh, which is a bit out of our orbit.'

'Why did she enrol for the evening class? I didn't get the impression she was very committed to spinning.'

That brought me up short. I had never paused to assess the degree of commitment any of the class had to what I was trying to teach them. It was enough that most of them showed up week after week and kept the whole thing just about viable. Pamela made the trek from Moreton, with her Ashford crammed onto the back seat of her old Volvo, and did her best, as far as I could tell, to produce some usable yarn each week.

'What makes you say that?' I could hear the tetchiness in my own voice.

'I don't know exactly. The way she handles the wool, perhaps. As if she found it repellent. The others all rolled it around, and some even sniffed it once or twice. They *played* with it. Pamela tried to restrict contact with it, using her fingertips, and rubbing her hands on her trousers every few minutes.'

'Yes,' I said, seeing the truth that had been under my nose for five weeks. 'So she does.'

'Which means she wants to keep in with you, or somebody else in the class. Or she wants to get out of the house on Mondays. Or she's made some sort of promise about learning to spin, however distasteful it might be.'

'Yes,' I said again.

'So?'

'So I have no idea,' I admitted. I felt tired and sad and uncertain. The ground had become unstable beneath my feet, and Thea was only making it worse. Thirty-six hours earlier everything had been perfectly all right. My jumpers and jackets were selling well, I had my health and plenty to keep me occupied. Finding the dead body of my friend had brought everything crashing down. 'I think she just likes the idea of making her own clothes,' I said, rather inattentively.

'I'd better tell Phil,' said Thea, in what sounded like another change of subject.

'Tell him what?'

'About your friend Kenneth and his money troubles. It's the sort of thing he should know about. Or do you want to tell him?'

My head was in a muddle with everything that had happened during the day. 'I think it's more important to tell him that Caroline knew Gaynor,' I said.

Thea hesitated, ready to get out of the car. 'Um – I'm not sure I'm the person for that. You'd better come in with me now and bring him up to date.'

I tried to see her face in the dark. 'He might have gone to bed,' I objected. 'Besides, it would be treacherous to pass on what Pamela just told me in confidence. Plus, it's surely irrelevant.'

She opened the car door enough to make the light go on inside. Her face was serious. 'Ariadne, you have a lot to learn about murder investigations. I'm way ahead of you on this. Not just because of Phil, but because I have a brother-in-law who's also a Detective Superintendent, as it happens. I've always taken an interest. My daughter's just joined the force, as well. I'm surrounded by them, whether I like it or not. And one thing I've discovered is that there is no such thing as irrelevance when it comes to a murder. At least, not this sort of murder, where all the pointers are to a pagan significance. You and the others in the group are going to be under scrutiny, whether you like it or not. If one of you has money worries, debts, whatever, then that's important. Take my word for it.'

It was nothing short of a lecture, and I felt suitably admonished. 'Okay,' I said. 'But you do realise that Pamela might never speak to me again if she works out who informed on her.'

'Oh, I think she will,' Thea said. 'If you ask me, young Pamela is really rather fond of you.'

I merely grunted at that, and got out of the car, leaving the wool and spinning gear for the morning.

Thea dragged me across the street and into Greenhaven, where Phil was all entangled with dogs on Helen's big leather sofa.

'Don't get up,' I told him. 'I won't be here for long. Thea thinks I should tell you some stuff.'

He looked at me, open-faced. Not wary or irritated, just encouraging and receptive. I remembered how easy he'd always been to talk to.

I summarised to the point where it sounded more like a text message. 'Kenneth Webster has got money troubles, and your ex-wife knew Gaynor,' I said. Then I looked at Thea and asked, 'Satisfied?'

Phil still didn't get up. He hugged the smaller dog to his chest, and absently rubbed his chin across the hair on its back. It was probably not deliberate, but it made him irresistibly human and safe. The dog sighed blissfully. Thea's spaniel had welcomed her with excessive ecstasy, jumping up at her and wagging its silly tail. These people used dogs as intimately as they did each other, it seemed.

'You've seen Caroline?' Phil said.

I told him about her visit, and my doubts as to its purpose. I added the extra information about Oliver and Gaynor being a lot friendlier than I'd realised. I started to explain about Pamela and Kenneth being in my pagan group, but he waved a hand at me, saying he knew just who they were.

'Have you seen anyone else from the group since yesterday morning?' he wanted to know.

'Verona Farebrother came round this morning,' I remembered.

Phil nodded. 'Thea mentioned her,' he said.

With a sense of superfluity, I proceeded with my report. 'There's a meeting tomorrow evening, but she can't be there for some reason. I expect Daphne and Ursula will both turn up, as well as Kenneth and Pamela.'

'What's it for?'

Good question, I thought. 'I think mainly it's to decide whether we carry on with the Samhain ceremony at the Long Barrow. We're not sure you'll allow us to, of course.'

Phil gave a half shrug, careful not to dislodge the corgi. 'We've done all we need to there – but I imagine it might seem a trifle insensitive to some people if you carry on as planned.'

For the first time it struck me that the Barrow would never be the same again to anybody living in the area. The scene of a violent death generally acquired an aura that could last for centuries – especially if it was already a place of some mystery, with ghostly associations. Perhaps the killer even *intended* that to be so.

'Well, thanks for the information,' Phil said, having waited in silence for me to speak. 'We'd better not keep you any longer. You've had a busy day from the sound if it.' Then he added, 'Oh, yes. Thea thought you might still have a mug with Verona Farebrother's fingerprints on it. Is that right?'

I was too tired to bridle at the suggestion that I hardly ever washed anything up. I nodded. 'And one with your ex-wife's on as well, come to that,' I said. 'I'd better try not to muddle them up.' I didn't want to go out there into the dark, leaving the two of them so cosy and contented. By rights it ought to have been the other way around, with the unheated house and lack of ordinary facilities.

'I'll come and collect them tomorrow,' he said. 'Maybe you could label them and put them in a plastic bag for me?'

I was dismissed and took my leave with a smile from Thea. 'Thanks for keeping me amused,' she said, at the door.

As I crossed the street I looked around, at Greenhaven and the rest of the village, with the fields behind it. Everything seemed to have been sprayed with mildew. I could smell it, musty and moribund. I couldn't remember why I was bothering to stay alive, what I could ever possibly want to do with myself from that point on. People talk about broken spirits, and that was exactly how it felt. Some normally upright thread inside me, which pulsed and gleamed and kept me essentially sound, had drooped like an unwatered plant. I remembered the questions that Baldwin and Latimer had asked me, and their subtle lack of comprehension. They hadn't mocked my lifestyle or rubbished my friends. They'd simply trampled heedlessly over everything I valued, blindly failing to grasp what mattered to me. They'd held a mirror up to my life, which showed it as pointless, a foolish failure in a world where everybody ought to have a proper job and a bland simplistic belief system.

I trudged into the living room without looking back, and noted that the Rayburn had gone out. The cat was nowhere to be seen. The piles of knitwear in the back room looked abandoned, little more than a lot of unwanted jumble.

I remembered the bottle of gooseberry and elderflower in the fridge, that I had not got around to drinking on Saturday. It was a rich sweet wine, good with fruit and cake and ice cream. It was at its best on a hot June evening, not a gloomy October one – but I drank it anyway, pouring out a large glassful as soon as I'd dealt with the fingerprinted mugs. Without them I wouldn't be able to do much entertaining. Almost all the others had chips or cracks in them.

Halfway down the bottle, the magic began to work. The world gained colour again, my head filled with dreams and insights that convinced me I was clever and creative and valuable. Nothing actually *mattered*, not even the death of Gaynor. People died. It happened all the time. We attached far too much importance to the individual, making such a fuss when a single person expired. I put a CD on at random, letting Macy Gray belt out her stuff, not caring if the whole village heard. It was like having someone in the house with me for a few minutes. Then I turned her off again. None of the songs had enough tune and most of the words were indistinguishable. I'm funny about music, anyway. Helen bought me the CD player, not long before she died, and I hardly ever used it. Then I found a stack of disks for sale cheap in Cirencester market, and decided to give it a better try.

The taste of the wine got more and more cloying as I finished the bottle. I could feel it turning thick and sludgy in my stomach. When I held up the glass to the light and tilted it, the liquid was oily, slow-moving. Behind it, the light bulb was diffuse, spooky. It seemed to have a face. I shut my eyes, and the whole world heaved.

But still I felt carefree and pleased with myself. I went to bed, moving carefully, making sure the doors were locked and everything switched off. I fetched myself another blanket – one I'd made from thick and creamy wool, very loosely spun. Nothing in the world could be more comforting.

I woke next morning around nine, with an excruciatingly dry mouth. My head didn't exactly hurt, but it was muffled and dysfunctional. I knew already that the day would have to be abandoned. I was never going to accomplish anything. I might not even get out of bed, except to fetch a large glass of water and drain it in seconds.

Then I went back to sleep.

It was midday when I woke again. I lay there thinking *Cat, pig, Sally*, listing the animals and people who might need me enough to make me get out of bed. No, I decided, they could all manage for a while longer without me. Sally's curtains could certainly wait. The pig would have to find more acorns and worms for herself. And there was no sign of the cat. I sank into self-pity. Nobody cared whether I lived or died. Stella had her job and her family. My parents hardly ever saw me anyway. And Gaynor was dead. The sense that nothing mattered, which had been liberating the previous evening now thrust me into depression. It was all futile, pointless. Nobody would miss me if I died, the same as Gaynor had done. Nobody but me was missing Gaynor. We were superfluous to the world.

Not needed, barely even noticed. Best to just expire, and do some good by fertilising a nice natural burial ground somewhere.

I finally got myself together at about half past two. I went downstairs and unlocked the doors, back and front. There was no post for me. The Rayburn was not just out but stone cold. In the street outside everything was silent and still, although it wouldn't be long before school finished and children would start passing on their way home. In Cold Aston, some courageous mothers still allowed their nine-year-olds to walk half a mile from school to home without supervision. One or two of the kids even waved to me if they saw me through the window.

With a shock, I realised I couldn't possibly be ready for the stall at the Gypsy Horse Fair. I'd rather lost track of days, but when I worked it out, it seemed that this was Tuesday, with the Fair the day after next. A surge of rage against Gaynor's killer, the police in general, and Phil Hollis in particular gripped me. By throwing me into such a useless state, the whole messy business had lost me a major part of my income for the month. From what I'd expected to earn at the Fair, I was planning to cover all the Christmas expenditure as well as running costs on the cottage into the New Year.

I had no desire to eat anything, or to get on with spinning or knitting. The loss of Gaynor was a gaping hole in the whole enterprise. Without her brilliant work, there seemed little point in carrying on. I couldn't do it all on my own, and expert knitters were hard to find. The older women who had done it all their lives were now falling prey to arthritis and rheumatism. If their hands still worked, they had fixed ideas about shapes and patterns that dated back to the Seventies or earlier, and had little appeal for modern customers.

The pagan group had not quite abandoned me, but I did not much relish the planned meeting for the evening. The death of Gaynor was too big an event for our rituals and ceremonies to deal with. All we were, at the final analysis, was a small bunch of people who wanted to retain some faint understanding of how human beings connected to the soil. How the seasons affected us, the sun and moon providing succour for body and spirit. It all crumbled to ash when faced with the violence that people can wreak, the deviousness and greed that we all possess, simply by virtue of being human.

When Thea came to the door at half past four, I almost didn't let her in. What role did she think she was carrying out, running back and forth between me and Phil, barely understanding either of us?

'Are you all right?' she asked, peering intently at me. I had only lit one small lamp in a corner of the room, and the shadows were deep. 'I haven't seen anything of you all day. I've been keeping busy, but

Phil's just phoned to say he can't hope to be back before eight.'

'I'm alive,' I said, in answer to her original question, not caring that this statement carried more meaning than it would normally.

'What's the matter?'

'Hangover,' I admitted. 'I didn't get up until after midday.'

'What a waste of time. Has it thrown all your plans?' She was in the house by this time, roaming around the room as if searching for something.

'Completely,' I said.

'You must be furious with yourself.'

Nobody likes to be told how they're feeling, and my argumentative soul resisted her assumptions, despite their accuracy. Besides, there was an implied criticism in there somewhere. 'Not really,' I said.

She cocked her head at me, her clear eyes catching the light, her wide cheeks making her look like a pretty child. She made me feel like a carthorse, towering over her.

'Well, none of this is very nice,' she summarised, with irresistibly British understatement.

Then she surprised me. 'Let's go to the pub,' she said. 'You could probably do with a drink.'

I physically cringed, hanging back, holding onto a chair. Until that moment I hadn't realised how *ashamed* I was feeling, how urgently I did not want to be observed by my neighbours. 'God, no,' I gasped. 'You must be joking.' Then I saw my clock. 'It won't be open anyway.'

But she was ahead of me. 'You can't hide away from everybody,' she said. 'I know that's what you want to do, but you'll have to live with these people after the business with Gaynor has all been sorted out. Believe me, in the long run it'll be much easier if you get right back into it now. I'll come back at six, and expect you to be ready. I can leave a note to tell Phil where I am. He doesn't think he'll be back until around eight, anyway.'

'But I hardly ever go to the pub,' I said weakly. She hadn't understood on that particular point. It wasn't the public exposure I dreaded so much as another bout of heavy drinking. 'Plus I'm meant to be going to that meeting at Kenneth's.'

'What time?'

'Eight, I suppose.'

'So you can do both,' she said. 'And I'll be home in time for Phil. Perfect for everybody.'

In the event, I didn't go to the pub or the pagan meeting.

CHAPTER THIRTEEN

Sally Grover phoned me at half past five; something she almost never did.

'Ariadne?' she shouted, a relic of the days when telephones were newfangled and not to be trusted. Normally I might have found it endearing. As it was I was poleaxed by guilt at my neglect of her.

'Sally,' I said. 'How are you?'

'What?' She wasn't at all deaf, but somehow her approach to the technology of communications blocked her hearing.

'Are you all right?' I refused to shout. 'Do you want me to come?'

'Yes, I bloody do,' she said, more quietly. 'These sheets are a disgrace and you know I can't tuck them in properly by myself. And Ollie said you were going to change my curtains. The draught's whistling through the summer ones today, and it's given me lumbago again.'

'I'll be there in twenty minutes,' I promised.

'Leave the door unlocked, and I'll come right in.'

Sally squawked. 'I'll do no such thing, what with all these murderers about. You knock like you always do.'

Sally lived in Naunton, which for my money is by far the loveliest of all the Cotswold villages. Phil might prefer Guiting Power, only a mile or two away, but Naunton is the one that does it for me. Bigger than most, it spreads over undulating ground, with the main road comfortably bypassing it. The old village street snakes along parallel to the Windrush, with the jumble of houses mostly on the northern slope. Tourists seldom venture there in any numbers, but it's less deserted than many of the smaller settlements.

Sally lived in a small ancient cottage adjoining the main street and was always in and out of other people's houses, gossiping merrily. There seemed to be fewer second homes in Naunton, too. On sunny days there were generally people in gardens, and once I saw a woman doing her ironing on her small patio outside her side door, in full view of passers-by. There was something about that which endeared me to the place.

I had even said to Helen, more than once, that she had made a big mistake in choosing Cold Aston. 'Naunton would have been much better,' I said.

But Helen liked the wind and the wide open

vistas and the chatter from the school playground. And she did not much like old Sally Grover – or anybody who thought it was all right to drop in on people without due notice.

I ran across to Greenhaven and explained quickly to Thea that the pub evening would have to be postponed. I didn't give her time to ask any questions, but persuaded myself that she wouldn't have long on her own. Whatever Phil might have said, he was unlikely to stay away from her if he could avoid it. It seemed a bit off of him to spend so long on his police work, as it was. Hadn't the man ever heard of delegation?

As I got out of my car in Naunton, another vehicle came towards me, rather too fast for the winding street. In the unnatural glow of the street lighting I was unsure at first of the colour. But I recognised the man at the wheel, as well as the shape of the car. Eddie Yeo was heading straight at me, and for a moment I thought he might hit me. I stood my ground, chest out, and he slowed down, giving me a careless wave as he passed. It was too dark to see his expression, but I thought I could detect the white glint of a toothy smile.

I had never much liked Eddie, but with Daphne as a friend I'd managed to be civil to him while they were married. He was a difficult man to offend, in any case, accustomed as he was to the savagery of the Council Planning Office. Whatever anyone might say to him, he'd heard it before. Little wonder, then, that it had taken Daphne so long to convince him that she really couldn't stomach the marriage any longer. According to her he had gone quite willingly at the end, although nobody had suggested he had another woman to go to.

Sally took a full minute to answer my knock – punishing me, I supposed, for my neglectful behaviour. When she did open the door, she scowled at me unforgivingly.

'I really am sorry, Sal,' I said. 'But things haven't been exactly normal lately.'

'Saw it on the telly,' she nodded. 'And then that Ursula Ferguson told me it was you that'd found the body.'

'You're very thick with Ursula these days,' I noted. 'Gossiping at Bernadette's, last I heard. Seen her again since then, have you?'

'That girl of hers keeps the horse in the field at the back. I give him a carrot now and then. They were seeing to him just this afternoon, as it happens.'

'Well, let's get on with those sheets,' I said. 'I'm meant to be going to a meeting this evening.'

'Bit late then, you'll be,' she said. 'Where is it?'

'Bourton. I might not go, actually.' I'd lost track of the time. Sally's wall clock said half past twelve, which certainly couldn't be right. 'What time is it?'

'Search me,' she grinned. 'Time for my supper, if my tum's anything to go by.'

'Have you got something cooking?'

She shook her head. 'Cold meat, that's all. The bread's stale and Ollie brought that poisonous stuff made out of chemicals instead of proper butter.'

I ended up staying a couple of hours, turning out the fridge, putting some washing away, and giving her stair carpet a good brush. It was good therapy for me, having somebody else's tasks to attend to. Sally was a friendly old thing, chattering on about nothing in particular, making the world seem more stable and ordinary than it really was. I used her phone to call Kenneth and tell him I would have to miss the meeting. He wasn't very happy about it. 'The whole point is so we can offer you our support,' he whined. 'It doesn't matter if you're late.'

But I had decided, and was feeling quite liberated. The prospect of being *supported* by six over-emotional pagans was not very appealing. I thought of them crowding round me, asking questions, pretending to feel the loss of Gaynor as deeply as I did and quailed at my narrow escape.

'Going to the Horse Fair then?' Sally asked me.

'I'm supposed to be running a stall,' I said. 'But I've got loads to do if I'm to be ready in time.' I felt weak at the prospect. 'I might give that a miss as well. It won't be the same without Gaynor.'

Suddenly I seemed to be addicted to cancelling things. I could just lie in bed instead and indulge in total idleness for a change.

It was the first time my friend's name had been mentioned. Sally had made oblique references to the murder, but asked me nothing directly. Now it was as if I'd granted permission.

'You're pally with that important policeman, aren't you?' she said. 'Has he told you who they think it was?'

'They don't seem to have any idea. It's crazy to think anybody would want her dead. She was such a harmless creature.'

Sally grunted at that. 'Not according to my Ollie, she wasn't. Seemingly, she dropped him in some real trouble, a month or two back.'

I stopped brushing and looked at her. 'Are you sure?'

'Course I'm sure. Something to do with some business takeover. She must have seen the papers in his car when he gave her a lift home – he always did, you know, after their bridge evenings – and went and said something to the wrong person. Don't ask me for names, because Ollie wouldn't tell me that.'

'How does he know it was her?'

Sally shook her head helplessly. 'He just does,' she said.

When I thought about it, I could see how Gaynor

might do something of the sort, in her innocence. But *who* could she have spoken to, and what exactly had been the consequences?

More central to my thinking was the unavoidable fact that Oliver had lied to me about how well he'd known Gaynor. He had deliberately played down his links with her, when I'd told him she was dead, if Caroline's story could be believed. It seemed a foolish move on his part – surely he must know that I would find out the truth? If it had been the result of a sudden panic, that might make sense. If he had murdered her, only to suffer all sorts of terrors at being discovered afterwards, that might lead him to tell lies. Except that Oliver was a calculating kind of person, who would think things through much more carefully than that. The murder itself had a calculated aura to it. Whoever committed it would surely have planned what he would say afterwards, making certain it was coherent and credible. Then again, if it was Oliver, he might not have included me in his plans. He might not have considered his line with Gaynor's friend who just happened to have discovered her body.

I gave it up. Here, it seemed, was yet another piece of information I had to pass to Detective Superintendent Hollis. I began to think I was doing a large part of his job for him.

It was after eight when I got back to my own home. The Rayburn was on good form and the front room was warmly welcoming. I poured a modest glass of elderberry and sank into the armchair by the stove. The cat jumped onto my lap and nestled happily against my stomach.

On Wednesday morning, Phil Hollis came to the door at eight, to collect the bagged-up mugs for fingerprinting. I was still in my nightclothes – a pair of men's pyjamas and woolly socks. 'Sorry I'm so early,' he said. 'We're working long days at the moment.'

'No problem,' I yawned. 'I'll fetch them for you.'

The mugs were my two best ones, both made of bone china. 'Don't break them, will you?' I begged. 'The blue one's from Verona. The other one is Caroline's.'

'You think I might need her prints, do you?' he asked levelly.

I matched his tone with care. 'She did know Gaynor,' I reminded him. 'They might come in useful.'

His face was a picture, turning to oak in his efforts not to show his feelings. 'I suppose that is sensible,' he said at last. 'Thanks.' I had noticed that during our recent encounters he had steadfastly refrained from using my name. At least that was better than getting it wrong.

'There are a few more things I should tell you,' I said, almost having to hang on to his arm to stop him rushing off. He paused, with a faint sigh, and I quickly summarised what Sally had told me the night before about Oliver's annoyance with Gaynor over some piece of business.

Phil nodded. 'I'll send somebody to question him,' he said.

I waited for the *again* that never came. 'Haven't you done that already?' I demanded. 'After what I told your Baldwin man on Sunday?'

'Not yet,' was all he would say to that.

As soon as I was dressed I went across the street. On the doorstep I took hold of the doorknob, intending to walk right in, before remembering myself. Helen wasn't there any longer – I couldn't treat the place like a second home. Instead I banged the knocker loudly, setting off all the dogs. Their racket made me wish I'd followed my first impulse.

'What are your plans for today?' I asked Thea when she opened the door.

She kinked her mouth ruefully and asked me the same thing.

'The weather's not bad,' I pointed out. A breeze was blowing, but the sky was blue.

'Okay for a walk then,' she said.

I had never been one for 'walking' as a leisure activity. It was perfectly all right as a means of transport – often more direct than driving and just as quick in the narrow lanes. Cheaper, too. But wandering along footpaths, meeting ramblers and hikers in their comical costumes, was not my idea of fun. I had to walk to visit Arabella because there was no road to the coppice – but Arabella didn't need a visit again so soon. It occurred to me that Thea might expect me to act as a kind of local guide, showing her places of interest, but this role held little appeal for me, either. I might have taken her to the Barrow if it hadn't become imbued with grim associations. It never occurred to me that we might investigate the churches in Turkdean, Notgrove or Naunton, pretty as they doubtless were.

'We could try and find some sloes,' I said, half-heartedly. 'I usually make lots of sloe gin about now.'

'Sounds good,' she agreed.

We were still in the hallway of Greenhaven, with the door open. The cries of children rang from the school playground where they gathered before the day got started. It reminded me of Helen, who had always enjoyed this proof of life and energy close by. And remembering Helen led to remembering Gaynor and how differently the two deaths had affected me.

'How's the sorting going?' I asked.

'Oh, I've given up on it,' Thea said impatiently. 'Phil doesn't agree with any of my categories. He just wants the whole lot disposed of, with no more messing about.'

'In that case why didn't he just use a house clearance outfit, months ago?'

'Good question,' she said, narrowing her eyes crossly.

I felt a pang for Helen's precious possessions. She had loved them all, keeping them dusted and polished, savouring the stories and memories that attached to them. In her middle years she had travelled to romantic places such as India and Guatemala, collecting rugs and cushions in the process. They were faded and patched now, but still very much part of her life story. A story that nobody cared about any more, not even me most of the time. I couldn't share the experiences that were summoned by a hand-embroidered cushion bought in Jaipur or a woven woollen bedspread that had been attacked by moths.

'Have you had breakfast?' I asked, shaking the sadness off with a great effort.

She nodded. 'Yes, thanks. Weetabix and a banana.'

'Right,' I said. The dogs were milling around us, trotting in and out of the open door, plainly hoping for some kind of excursion. They were a pack, noisy and impossible to ignore. The spaniel repeatedly jumped up at Thea, paws scrabbling at her upper thighs, jaws flopping open in an unselfconscious grin.

'I should shut the door,' said Thea at last. 'It's

letting the cold in. Although I'm not sure it's not colder in than out, this morning.'

I followed her through to Helen's morning room, which faced east. It was full of light, as always. I had laughed at Helen's routine of being in here until midday and then moving to the cosier back sitting room for the afternoon and evening – but it had made perfect sense. 'Always make the most of the light,' she said.

For want of anything else to talk about, I told Thea about the mugs. It led to a renewed analysis of precisely who could have murdered Gaynor, with Caroline embarrassingly ;oining the list.

'Phil will be mortified if it turns out to have been her,' said Thea, with a frown.

'But he won't try to hide the evidence, if it points that way,' I said, making it a statement, not a question.

'Of course he won't,' she agreed.

CHAPTER FOURTEEN

The morning continued to resist us. There was no clear plan, no impetus to get outside and do something constructive. Thea and I were still in the house at ten o'clock, trying to decide what, if anything, we could be doing.

'Phil's really sorry about you being embroiled in all this trouble,' she said.

'Only doing his job,' I replied carelessly. 'It's a bummer for you as well.'

'That's true. I've almost written the week off now. It's Thursday tomorrow.'

'Don't remind me,' I groaned. When she made a questioning sound I explained briefly about the Gypsy Horse Fair and how I couldn't face doing it without Gaynor.

'That's a shame,' she sympathised. 'It sounds like fun.'

'Colourful,' I agreed.

'Can't we go anyway?' she asked, suddenly

excited. 'I'd love to see it.'

'But—' I quailed at the thought of being there without the stall. The organisers might see me and wonder what was going on. There'd be a gaping space where my jumpers ought to be, and I'd have to pay for it, in any case.

'Even better,' Thea pressed on. 'Let's do the stall after all. I can help you. I could come over now and we'll get everything ready.'

'But...' I repeated helplessly. 'We'd have to leave at six in the morning. I was going to get everything organised, neat and tidy...' I floundered, thinking of the work involved. No, I decided. I'd been right the first time. It wasn't possible to have everything done in time.

But there was no stopping her. 'Go and get started,' she ordered. 'I'll corral the dogs.'

We spent the rest of the morning folding and labelling twenty-five assorted jumpers and jerkins, eighteen scarves, six woolly hats, one coat, four wallhangings and seven rugs. It took longer than it might have done because Thea kept stopping to admire everything and exclaim about it. 'I want to buy all of them myself,' she laughed. She also made a few suggestions about displaying the wallhangings that I'd never have thought of myself.

Then we stopped, noticed the time and by mutual agreement set out for the pub, Thea readily forgiving me for my non-appearance the previous evening. 'We can make up for it now,' she said.

The Plough was a pleasant enough hostelry, with a single bar, average sort of menu and friendly staff. But when we'd settled down with a pint for me and a white wine for her, she seemed to change her mind. 'Can we go and eat somewhere else?' she asked. 'Somewhere with a view or a garden or something for the dogs. I feel like getting away from Cold Aston for a bit, and there isn't really anything I fancy on this menu.'

I tried to think of a suitable place. 'Hardly any of them allow dogs in,' I said, secretly hating the idea of trying to eat with three sets of watchful eyes and slavering jaws at my elbow. I found her caprice irritating. I felt settled where we were and in no mood for driving around the area searching for a menu to Thea's liking. Another consideration was the state of my fuel tank. I had enough to get to Stow and back next day and that was about it. I tried to limit my visits to the filling station to ten-day intervals, and the time wasn't up until the weekend.

She understood that she depended on me for transport and said no more until her drink was almost finished. I hadn't seen this lethargic side of her before, where she seemed heavy and indecisive. I was hungry and had no quarrel with what The Plough had to offer.

'I'd rather stay here,' I said eventually. 'And I think I'll have the sausage and chips.'

A flicker of her natural grace came through. 'I'm sorry,' she sighed. 'You're absolutely right. I'm being stupid.'

To my horror, her eyes glazed over with tears as she spoke. 'For pity's sake!' I protested. 'What's the matter?'

She forced a weak smile. 'Ignore me,' she said, with a little flip of her hand. 'I get like this every now and then. Life all seems too much sometimes, don't you find?'

I thought about my regular recourse to the home-made wine, and nodded. She did have quite a lot to be weepy about, I supposed, with her new boyfriend disappearing to solve a murder and Cold Aston offering nothing but a lonely pub and blowy wolds.

'It'll be fun tomorrow,' I consoled her. 'The Horse Fair is a real experience.'

'Good,' she smiled bravely.

And it was. Phil helped us to load everything into my car when he got back much earlier than the previous two evenings. Thea and I explained self-importantly that we would have to get up at five-thirty, in order to set up the stall properly at the show.

'What about the dogs?' he asked. 'They'll be shut in here all day.'

Thea thought for a moment. 'Well,' she said, 'I

could take Hepzie with me. Are you going to be out the whole day?'

'Probably,' he said. 'But I expect I could drop back at some point and let the others out for a few minutes.' He sighed, as if she had somehow let him down.

'That'll be okay then,' she breezed, ignoring his scratchiness as she had before, when we'd found the weirdness in the attic. What must that feel like, I wondered. Having somebody so determined to see only the nice, pretending the nasty bits weren't there. Irritating, eventually, I suspected. But then I remembered her gloom at lunchtime and realised I was over-simplifying. Thea could do the whole range of emotions when it came to it.

The unusual thing about her, I was beginning to see, was that she was completely devoid of anxiety. If Phil was disappointed in her, that wasn't anything to worry about. Most women would have bitten their lip, put on a brittle act of conciliation, even altered their plans, in this situation. She did nothing like that. If she even noticed his mood, she dismissed it as his problem, something that would pass in a few minutes.

The Horse Fair was just as much fun as I'd hoped. Even the spaniel was reasonably good company, sitting quietly under the stall for much of the time. Once she'd had my assurance that I could manage on my own for a while Thea took the dog for a walk along the snaking line of stalls, down one side and back the other, with a detour to watch the horses and ponies in the field beyond the stalls. She was gone well over an hour, and came back infused with good cheer. 'It's *wonderful*,' she gasped. 'And I don't even *like* horses. But those piebald ponies, with the little boys on them – they're like elves, with their brown arms and dark eyes.' She went on raving about how poetic and picturesque the whole thing was, until I had to stop her.

'Yes, it's all very grand,' I said. 'And I've sold three scarves and four jumpers while you were gone.'

'Marvellous!' she applauded. 'Aren't you glad I made you do it?'

I nodded with a genuine smile. 'Definitely,' I said.

Then I saw them. Oliver Grover and Leslie Giddins, walking side by side, just that bit too close together for normal comradeship and I made a startling and rapid deduction. Then I gave myself a shake – surely I was imagining it. Leslie had a wife – the admirable Joanne. I was just so surprised to see Oliver with anybody at all, that I'd surely jumped to a false conclusion. But as I watched them fingering some brightly coloured horse blankets and making each other laugh with some jokey remarks, it seemed inescapable. I leaned towards Thea and tipped my chin at the men, trying to make her look at them without being too obvious about it.

'What?' she said quietly.

'Two men at the blanket stall. What do you notice about them?'

She was brilliant. Squatting down to fondle her dog, she managed to give the two a good long assessment without their noticing anything. Finally she stood up and turned her back to them.

'In a relationship,' she reported. 'Definitely. One even touched the other's bottom just then. Brave amongst all these gypsies,' she added.

'Huh?'

'Aren't they terribly homophobic? Or is that a myth?'

I had to think about it. I knew a fair few gypsies, all in secure marriages with huge numbers of children. 'I'd say they prefer not to think about it,' I concluded.

'Well, that's a gay couple, in my humble opinion,' she insisted.

I'd been busying myself with the jumpers, hoping neither of the men would recognise me. They were twenty yards away at most.

'Why? Do you know them?' Thea went on.

I nodded. 'That's Oliver Grover – the one Gaynor fancied. And the other one's in my pagan group. He's married.'

'Oh dear,' said Thea. 'Nasty.'

'It's totally unexpected,' I said. 'I can't really believe it.'

Thea managed a few more glimpses before Oliver saw me and reacted by blushing. His fair skin turned the colour of a particularly successful madder dye, and he put out one hand blindly for Leslie. Not so much for comfort as in warning, I fancied.

'Ariadne!' Oliver said loudly. 'I never dreamed we'd find you here.'

'Thinking of buying a horse?' I asked.

Leslie spun round, his face closer to the hue of old Cotswold stone; liverish in its yellowness. 'But...' he spluttered. 'I thought you were—'

'What? What did you think?'

Leslie mastered himself. 'Well – too upset about Gaynor to cope with doing your stall. But it's good to see you.'

'You too,' I smiled. 'This is Thea. She's staying in Cold Aston for a bit.' I thought it best not to explain her connection with the SIO in the murder case, congratulating myself on my discretion.

Leslie glanced at Thea. 'Yes, I saw you on Saturday evening,' he nodded. 'You were outside with the dogs – I noticed this one especially.' He smiled at her for a second before transferring his attention to the dog. 'Oh, isn't she *sweet*?' he cooed, bending to fondle the ridiculous spaniel ears. I was thunderstruck. Before my very eyes, the shy young husband had turned into a fully camped-up limp-wristed homosexual. It was bewildering.

Oliver kept a discreet distance. His colour had returned to normal and he had obviously persuaded himself that our encounter could be dealt with in a civilised manner. 'Les,' he said, in a tone of fond authority, 'we'd better get on.'

'Oh.' Leslie straightened up. 'Well, nice to meet you,' he said to Thea. He gave me a little wave of farewell before catching up with Oliver, looking into his face exactly like the spaniel looked at Thea.

'You seem rather shocked,' Thea observed, when the men had gone.

'Gobsmacked,' I agreed. 'I had absolutely no idea.'

'So remind me exactly who they are and why this is so important.'

I did my best to explain. 'I look after Oliver's gran – Sally. I've known them for ages. Gaynor told me on Saturday that she thought Oliver might be interested in her. She had some dozy notion that they might get together. When Caroline came to see me, she let drop that she met Gaynor *through* Oliver, over a year ago. She said they were good friends, which I still find very peculiar. Sally then gave me some story about Gaynor getting him into trouble. I told Phil all this yesterday morning. Hasn't he filled you in on any of it?'

'I haven't had much chance to talk to him since then,' she said stoically. 'Do you think Gaynor knew Oliver was gay?'

'Apparently not. She could be very thick about that sort of thing. She had a sheltered life.'

'Did she know the other one? What's his name?'

'Leslie. Vaguely. At least, that's what I've always assumed. I'm not so sure now. She seems to have known a lot more people than I realised. Including Caroline, which is the weirdest of them all.'

'You keep using that word. Everybody knows everybody *vaguely*.'

It sounded like a reproach. 'That's how it is,' I said. 'Friends of friends. You know the name, and one or two basic facts, but you hardly ever actually meet or talk. Although...' I tried to grasp the flow of half-thoughts snaking through the back of my head.

'Although what?'

'I'm starting to wonder how well I really knew Gaynor. I think I might have got her wrong, somehow. You know,' I laughed at myself, 'I've always had this image of her sitting in her flat, just knitting, hour after hour. Maybe playing some music, or watching daytime television, but not seeing any people. I suppose it can't really have been like that. She must have had more life than that. I'm finding things out that I never imagined.'

'And she didn't tell you about any of it?'

'No,' I said, feeling oddly wounded.

From somewhere close by a crescendo of shouts arose. It had been happening all day. Gypsies could be very loud, and in an animated discussion they would simply speak over each other, turning up the decibels to be heard. It was all quite good-natured, punctuated with great laughs. It added to the fizzy atmosphere of the Fair, but it made ordinary conversation difficult at times.

Underfoot the ground had turned to mud a good two inches thick. Sensible people were wearing boots, but a lot of young girls were picking their slippery way along the double row of stalls in high heels. The whole field sloped, so in places it was difficult to keep your footing.

'Lucky you warned me to wear my boots,' said Thea, as a girl of about twenty suddenly sat down heavily in the mud, her feet having skidded from under her. 'Here,' she said to the girl. 'Let me pull you up.'

The winded young gypsy, in a fur-trimmed jacket and cut-off slacks, permitted herself to be hauled out of the mud and propped against my stall. She looked down at herself, twisting to see the damage to the back of her clothes. 'Look at me!' she squealed. 'I'm filthy.'

'It'll brush off when it's dry,' said Thea.

The girl grumbled a bit more, and then turned her attention to me and my stall. I saw her giving my hair a critical examination. It was not the first time that day, and I'd already realised that it made me a misfit in gypsy circles. There was plenty of henna and artificial curl, but nothing as outrageous as my stripes. Then she fingered my wares. Again, I knew only too well that they stood out incongruously from the cheap synthetic clothes and furnishings on the other stalls. I'd brought all my brightest garments, including several waistcoats and scarves, and hats for children – but there was no disguising the handmade aspect. Handmade did not go down well in these circles. Nearly all my sales had been to affluent locals, who were definitely not Roma.

'Well, thanks for helping me up,' said the girl, and she went stiffly away down the hill.

Thea and I sold all but five jumpers and two wallhangings. The money weighed excitingly heavy in the leather pouch I'd put it in, even though half of it was cheques. The two gypsy purchasers had used cash, one woman paying for a scarf in pound coins and fifty-pence pieces. I expressed profound gratitude to Thea for forcing me to make the effort, and offered to stand her a cup of tea and a cake at the stall near the entrance, before we went home.

'Better pack up first,' she advised. 'If we're not going to be here to guard what's left.'

That took five minutes. We put everything in my car that was sitting behind the stall, along with the dog. 'Back soon,' Thea told it, her voice all sloppy. 'She doesn't like being left on her own,' she added to me as we walked away.

I made a sound that was no less sympathetic than I'd intended.

There was no tea tent or anything like it. The only source of refreshment was a mobile caravan thing, sporting a lot of red flags and selling fizzy pop in garish colours. There was nowhere to sit to drink it, apart from a stretch of grass leading to the middle of the field where a few horses were tethered.

'Hello!' came a familiar voice at my elbow, as I stood wondering whether it was worth even getting a drink.

It was Daphne, and next to her was Pamela, the two of them reclined on the grass quite contentedly.

It was not a situation conducive to meaningful conversation. Thea was impatient to know whether we intended to buy some horrible drink or wait until we got back to Cold Aston. There were gypsy caravans all around, with dogs and irritable-looking people, glad that the long day was almost over.

Daphne seemed anxious to speak to me. She stood up and took hold of my arm. 'Have you finished for the day? Did you sell much?' she asked me.

'Most of it's gone,' I said, absently.

Thea and Pamela nodded at each other, without much interest. Daphne raised her eyebrows, and Pamela explained that Thea had been at the evening class on Monday.

Without getting drinks, Thea and I hovered

indecisively near the others. 'I wasn't going to come, after everything that's happened,' I said, thinking Daphne and Pamela might be curious, 'but Thea made me.' I gave her a friendly look.

'Ari, Eddie's here,' said Daphne. 'I saw him looking at a pony. I didn't know what to do.'

'Why do anything?' I asked blankly.

She folded her arms impatiently. 'Think about it. Why would he want a pony? It must mean he's taken up with some new woman who's got kids.'

I did not really want to talk about the errant Eddie. For some reason, people would insist on telling me all their relationship troubles, despite my total lack of wise advice on the subject. Usually I couldn't think of anything to say at all.

'So?' was all I could manage now.

Daphne flinched, and Pamela threw me a withering look. 'It will upset the children if he marries again,' Daphne whined. All I could do was shrug.

Thea showed more interest than I did. 'Eddie's your husband, is he? Ex-husband, I suppose I mean.'

'That's right,' Daphne confirmed eagerly. 'We separated a year ago, but we're not divorced yet.'

'He didn't leave you for another woman, then?'

Daphne shook her head. 'We had irreconcilable differences,' she said, the words in invisible quotation marks.

'It must have come as a shock, seeing him again.' Thea was well into her stride by this time.

'It was as if a spotlight was shining on him,' Daphne said. 'Picking him out from the crowd. I haven't seen him for six months, and there he was, absolutely familiar. It's terribly strange.'

'Did he see you?' I managed to ask.

'No. I got away before he noticed me. I didn't want to give him the satisfaction,' she added obscurely.

'He was with a woman,' Pamela said, speaking for the first time. 'I've seen her before but I don't know who she is.'

'The right age to have pony-riding kids?' I asked. The whole conversation was getting on my nerves. I very strongly did not care what Eddie Yeo might be getting up to. My question went unanswered.

'She didn't look as if she liked him very much,' Pamela went on, impervious to the various looks we were giving her. 'She was telling him off about something.'

Even Thea was on the verge of giving up. 'Well, I expect you'll hear what it was all about sooner or later,' she said. Then she glanced at me, head sideways, clearly implying that she wanted to get back to her precious dog.

I wasn't quite ready to leave. 'Did you know about Leslie and Oliver Grover?' I asked, rather loudly.

Daphne looked at me blankly, but Pamela gave a revealing giggle. 'You saw them as well, did you? What a place to choose to turn up like that. I mean – these are all *gypsies*! They ought to know better.'

'That's what Thea said,' I told them. 'I thought it was funny, them being together.'

'Funny! It's disgusting,' said Daphne.

'So what about Joanne?' I asked.

'She left him, three or four weeks ago,' Pamela said. 'I don't think Leslie wanted anybody to know at first, but her sister works with Kenneth, so we heard about it more or less right away.'

'But I asked after her, on Saturday,' I protested. 'You never said anything then.'

'How could I, with Leslie there?' Pamela said scornfully. 'It was up to him whether or not to tell us officially.'

Suddenly it felt as if everybody was deliberately hiding things from me. What were they so afraid of? What did they think I'd do? 'But he said she was fine,' I protested stupidly.

'It's delicate for him, I guess,' said Pamela. 'You didn't know about it, did you, Daph?' she asked her friend.

'I'd have said something if I did,' said Daphne. 'He ought to be ashamed.'

Thea, not knowing these women at all, had to assess the nuances as best she could. She looked from one to the other, a little smile on her face, content to be out of the loop. Lucky her, I thought. I wanted to be *in* the loop, and was feeling as though I'd been deliberately excluded.

I had had enough. 'Did either of you know that Gaynor and Oliver were friends?' I demanded, looking from one to the other.

They blinked at me. 'Yes, of course. You told us at the moot. You said she wanted us to see if we could...oh!' Pamela grimaced. 'Leslie was there, wasn't he?'

'Yes, but I'm not interested in that for the moment. Oliver's gran told me that Gaynor had interfered with one of his clients, and lost him some business. Does that mean anything to either of you?'

Daphne made a little sound, as if a penny had clinked inside her head. 'Oh, that'll be to do with the Johnson man – Gervase, or whatever he's called. It was *months* ago. I don't know any detail, but it soon blew over, I think.'

I gave her a fierce look. 'How did *you* hear about it?'

She drew away from me and flapped her hand as if I was a large persistent wasp. 'It involved Eddie,' she said reluctantly. 'My kids were having one of their weekends with him when it happened. They came home with some garbled story about Oliver shouting at Gervase outside Eddie's flat, when they were in bed. They were upset, so I phoned Eddie and made him tell me what it had all been about. He said it had all been Gaynor's fault, and I should take my complaints to her. She'd told Gervase that Oliver couldn't handle his accounts as he'd promised, because he was going to be busy with her. All a complete fuss about nothing.'

I put my hand to my forehead, trying to make some sense out of so many random scraps. Caroline had said something about Gervase Johnson knowing Gaynor, hadn't she? It sounded like something she would do, getting the story wrong, failing to understand when she should keep her mouth shut. But the biggest element in the story was the idea that she should tell someone she came first with Oliver. That had to be pure fantasy on her part.

Then, by a sudden consensus we all got up to go. 'They're both pagans, right?' said Thea, as we got out of earshot. 'In your group.'

'Mmm,' I confirmed.

'I thought so. Pamela was wearing a necklace with a five-pointed star on it. I assume she isn't a Freemason, so it must be a pagan thing.'

'There you go again,' I said crossly. 'Making it sound as if Masons and pagans are the same thing.'

'Sorry,' she said insincerely.

In the car, with the dog wobbling about on her lap, she asked about Daphne and Pamela again. 'This Eddie,' she said, 'did he know Gaynor? It sounded just then as if everyone knows everyone around here.'

I spoke without thinking. 'Vaguely, I suppose, yes.' Thea's laugh surprised me for a moment. 'Oh,' I realised. 'Another *vaguely*. But it's true, all the same. He might have met her at my place when he was still with Daphne. I have a lot of people over two or three times a year, in the garden mostly. We have a barbecue and dance about a bit.'

'Should we say something to Phil? About him being here unexpectedly, I mean? His wife seemed to think it was out of character.'

It took me nearly a minute to follow her line of thought, and even then I didn't think I could have got it right. 'You mean Eddie Yeo might have killed Gaynor?' I looked at her, slowing the car. 'But he's on the square,' I protested idiotically. 'A Freemason,' I explained, seeing her blank look. 'The same as Oliver.'

She laughed, a single huff of shocked amazement. 'You can't be serious,' she said.

I had to think about that. My remark had surprised even me, but when I examined it, I found it did accurately reflect my feelings. Masons might be a bit daft, with a lot of delusions about their own status and influence, but they were essentially benign. Just because I didn't want to associate with them didn't mean I hated them the way Daphne did. They raised money for charity, they helped each other and talked a lot about making the world a better place. But more than that, they never really *did* anything. That had been one of Daphne's strongest criticisms. They talked and pranced about, and wore dopey symbolic clothes and jewels, and learned pages and pages of pseudo-Egyptian gibberish – but they were, in my image of them, incapable of doing anything as energetic as killing somebody. I tried to say some of this to Thea.

'But we're not talking about them as a group,' she objected. 'Just two individuals, who happen to be Masons. That probably isn't at all relevant to what happened to Gaynor. Although...' she hesitated. I wondered how much she'd been told about the way Gaynor's body had been arranged in the Barrow, and how tempting it had been to read symbolic significance into it.

'What?' I prompted.

'Nothing, really. It's just that we do seem to come back to the Freemasons rather often, don't we?'

'Not to mention pagans,' I pointed out, with a small sigh.

'You know,' she said, after a bit of silence, 'I thought when I came here with Phil, at least there wouldn't be any mystery. Not like the other places.'

'Uh?' I queried, wondering what she was talking about.

'The house-sitting. I told you. I've been doing it since the spring. I only do the Cotswolds area, but each time it's a matter of walking into a strange house, where I don't know any people, and have to work it all out from scratch. When something happens, it's like being in a dream. Nothing makes sense at first. I thought, this time, it would be much more like a little holiday, with Phil knowing you and the house and everything.'

'He doesn't really, though, does he?' I said. 'Know the house, I mean. And he doesn't know me very well these days, either.'

'That's what I'm saying – I was wrong. All this talk about Freemasons and pagans – those are both completely mysterious to me. Hidden sinister stuff going on out of sight. It's horrible.'

'You should come along to a moot,' I invited. 'You'll see there's nothing at all horrible or sinister about the pagan group. You haven't been keeping up – more people are joining this sort of spiritual organisation, whatever they might call themselves, than are bothering with the Church these days. It's all to do with individual paths and expressing what's really important. We're positively mainstream now.'

'Hmm.' She didn't sound convinced, but at least I'd made the point.

We were waiting to get out of the gateway and onto the small road leading through the town.

Almost all Stow's shops had closed for the day, leaving the pavements thronged with pedestrians heading to and from the Fair.

Something seemed to be holding things up as we sat behind a Range Rover in the gateway.

As we finally emerged from the field, we had a better view. 'Oh look!' said Thea. 'What an amazing car.'

It was Eddie's bright yellow convertible, with the top down, the horn blaring at a pair of horse-drawn traps, moving slowly along the road. 'That's Eddie Yeo,' I said. 'Impatient as usual.'

'Arrogant, I'd say. Who does he think he is?'

'He knows who he is. So does everybody else. You watch, they'll soon get out of his way. Even gypsies don't like to get on the wrong side of him.' I had hardly bothered to look at the object of our conversation. Eddie Yeo was a fact of life, somebody who buzzed about like a wasp, threatening people with refusal of planning permission, flaunting his influence. If it hadn't been for Daphne I'd have managed to ignore him entirely.

'Can you see the woman with him?' Thea persisted. 'Do you know who she is?'

I had to look, then. The car had, as I'd predicted, pulled ahead, dodging around a large group of people who were probably all one big family. Just as it disappeared I registered the tidily layered nut brown hair, and the emerald green knitted jacket. I blinked and gasped and shook my head. 'Impossible,' I mumbled. 'I'm hallucinating.'

'What? Why? Who is she?'

'That's Caroline,' I said.

CHAPTER FIFTEEN

Phil's car was outside Greenhaven when we got back, which seemed to startle Thea. 'Oh – he's early,' she said. Then, after a pause, 'Come in for a bit.' I knew she was shy of mentioning Caroline to him, and hoped I would carry on my role of informant, to let her off the hook. The feeling I'd had before of being the only one who was actually making progress in the murder investigation returned.

Prompted also by a reluctance to go back into my own home, I agreed. The aftermath of a day's selling was always somewhat bleak. The build-up, the exchanges with the customers, the whole busy day could only finish on a down note. I couldn't think of a thing I should be doing, apart from visiting Arabella – a task that was once again becoming overdue. Despite an abundance of acorns and beechmast she was probably feeling hungry for something extra by this time.

Phil was surrounded by cardboard boxes in Helen's living room. The place was unrecognisable, with all the furniture moved, and nothing at all left on shelves or mantelpiece. The air was full of dust and the smell of abandonment. 'Oh dear,' I sighed.

'Where did you get the boxes?' Thea asked. 'How long have you been back?'

'Two hours. Supermarket.' He didn't smile at us. The male, jealous of the females spending time together.

'We're dying for some tea,' Thea said. 'We couldn't find anything drinkable at the Fair, so we came straight back. Ariadne did ever so well. She sold nearly everything.'

'You'll have to light the gaz, then,' he panted, carrying a pile of books to one of the boxes. 'I can't stop this now. We're running out of time as it is.'

Calmly, Thea produced a pot of tea while I tried to help Phil. I knew better than he did where everything was. I pulled open some drawers, and found tablecoths and napkins. 'These are Victorian,' I said. 'Hand embroidered and hemmed. They're worth a bit.'

'Does anybody use tablecloths these days?' he asked.

'I don't know, but they like genuine old table linen.'

He sighed. 'There's far more here than I expected. More of everything. I don't remember her having all these books, for a start.'

I sat down, holding a beautiful cloth on my lap. It was big enough for a ten-foot dining table, the embroidered centrepiece a glorious business of trailing ivy leaves and bright flowers and berries. 'There's something horrible about the way a person's things outlive them, isn't there?' I said, thinking again of Gaynor. 'They just become so much jumble, a burden to other people.'

'Well, they could hardly have buried all this with her. Why didn't she dispose of it while she was alive?'

I tried to imagine the pain and sadness that would come from doing any such thing. The precious possessions, imbued with memories, valued just because they'd spent so much time in your house – given away to uncaring recipients. Pawed over by cynical dealers, if you tried to sell them. 'Don't be stupid,' I said. 'How could she possibly have done anything like that? If you don't want to do it, then call a house clearance person. But don't criticise Helen. That's well out of order.'

'Sorry,' he said. 'I've just had a bucketful of it today, that's all.'

'Why? What's happened?'

I could see him hesitating, remembering my role in the murder investigation. He was suddenly wary, where before he'd just been his natural self. I pretended not to notice, keeping my eyes on his face, my expression only mildly curious.

'Nothing,' he said. 'That's the trouble. We've interviewed everybody we can think of, done every sort of forensic test.' He stopped and looked away.

'I know what you're thinking,' I said emboldened perhaps by Thea's habit of facing things squarely. 'If it was me who killed her, all along, you've just given me a nice bit of reassurance. Or maybe it's a double bluff. You want me to drop my guard and give myself away.'

Phil revealed an internal struggle between the professional senior policeman and the human being. It looked to me as if there was a serious gulf between the two. Finally, he gave me a thin smile. 'Your friend's death is one of those cases that should never happen. It breaks all the usual rules.'

I laughed at that. 'Isn't that the whole thing about murder? It breaks the biggest rule of the lot.'

'Huh!' was all he said to that, but I was pleased that the human being was still at least partially alive.

Thea carried a tray through from the kitchen and began pouring tea. 'We saw some people at the Fair,' she said. 'Oliver Grover, for a start.'

I was impressed at how well she was keeping up, remembering all the names and who everybody was.

Phil seemed to feel differently. He gave her a tolerant look. 'Oh?' he said.

'Ariadne probably told you he was gay, didn't she?' Without waiting for a reply, she romped on, bursting with importance. 'Well, we saw him with a *boyfriend*. It's the first time they've been out together as far as we know.'

Phil looked at me for elucidation.

'Oliver Grover and Leslie Giddins,' I said. 'Definitely an item.'

Phil could hardly help being interested. 'Oliver Grover?' he repeated. 'The chap Gaynor fancied?'

'Right. As far as I know he's never had a proper boyfriend. Nothing that's lasted more than a few weeks. I know his gran, remember. I do for her, more or less as I did for Helen.'

Thea chuckled at this old-fashioned usage. 'The lady wot does,' she repeated. 'It doesn't seem like you at all.'

'I'm in great demand, I'll have you know. I get it from my mother. She works at the hospice.'

Thea ducked her chin in a gesture of admiration but said nothing.

Phil stuck to the point. 'And Grover's gran knows all about his love life, does she?'

I recalled Oliver's look of alarm when he recognised me at the Fair. 'No, not exactly, but she probably would if he took up with anybody seriously. She does know he's gay. At least, I *think* she does.' I couldn't remember any actual reference to the subject between us in all the years I'd been caring for her. It was all by implication, subtle changes of tone, smiles and nods. 'Yes, I'm sure she does,' I repeated. 'We just don't talk about it.'

'He's a good grandson, they tell me.'

I didn't bother to enquire who *they* were. 'He's okay. Not as good as some. After all, he pays me to do stuff he could actually do himself.'

'Which suggests that he's got his own life. Full-time job, the bridge club, other social activities. Time poor, cash rich, it strikes me.'

'That's about it,' I agreed. 'And Sally would rather have me than him doing some of the things. Changing sheets, washing her clothes, that sort of stuff.'

He looked at me appraisingly, probably thinking that a big strong female like me was hardly a more fitting carer than an effete grandson would be. Except Oliver wasn't really effete. Less so than Leslie, anyway. Oliver had an air of confidence, an easy manner, and a well-proportioned body. No wonder, really, that Gaynor had been attracted to him.

Thea seemed gratified that her input had sparked so much discussion. 'They were quite upset that we saw them,' she added. 'The Leslie chap's married, you see.'

'Except his wife's left him,' I corrected her. 'Presumably because he came out to her and she couldn't take it.'

'We don't know that he wanted her to. He might have asked her to go.'

'Hang on.' Phil held up a hand. 'Stop speculating, both of you.' He looked at me. 'Thanks for the information,' he said. 'It might turn out to be useful.' He didn't sound as if he thought it would help in the slightest, which left me feeling both relieved and frustrated. I didn't want Oliver to be the murderer, mainly because of the effect that would have on Sally. But I couldn't think of anybody else who roused more suspicion. And I couldn't get Oliver out of my mind. Random memories came back at me, including the exchanges we'd had about his homosexuality at the meeting on Saturday. Leslie had sat there, saying nothing, taking it all in. What if – and my heart started thumping at this point – what if my careless talk about Gaynor had aroused Leslie's jealousy? What if he, like Ursula, believed Oliver might change and become what Gaynor wanted? After all, Leslie believed in the power of ritual and pagan prayer, more than any of us.

I considered sharing these thoughts with Phil before I went back to my own home, but he had clearly grown tired of his responsibilities for the evening. Thea had joined him on the sofa, snuggling up close, playing with his fingers. But she was too nice to risk embarrassing me by any further demonstrations. I knew I ought to leave them alone for some time together, but there was still more to say. I drew breath to spoil the romantic atmosphere yet again.

But Thea was ahead of me. 'Don't forget all that about Eddie What's-his-name,' she said. 'We ought to tell him about it while you're here.' *And get it over with*, she might have added.

I took over. 'We saw Pamela and Daphne,' I said. 'They'd just seen Eddie, who was looking at a pony as if he might buy it.'

'Eddie Yeo,' Phil repeated quietly.

'You know him?' Thea asked.

'Right,' he said tightly. 'I do know Eddie Yeo.' He looked at me. 'And you do too, don't you, Mary?'

He obviously hadn't noticed what he'd said, and I was feeling too weary to snarl at him again, so I let it go. Thea pretended not to have noticed anything.

'Yes, I know Eddie Yeo,' I said. 'He was in the same Lodge as you.'

Thea gave an exaggerated sigh, as if to say, *Not the bloody Masons again.* I cut across her, again hoping to save her from having to tell him herself.

'He was with a woman,' I said, trying to alert him by my tone. I think, actually, it was Thea going rigid at his side rather than my voice that put him on his guard.

'Oh?' he said.

'Phil – Eddie Yeo was with Caroline,' I said. 'She was in his car.'

He did not react at all except to turn a shade paler. Anybody could see that his ex-wife's name was occurring far too much for comfort in the last day or so. But his brain was obviously firing perfectly.

'So?' he said. 'What does that have to do with anything?'

I left soon afterwards, almost dragging myself across the street. It couldn't have just been the Fair that had worn me out. It was also the emotional upheavals of the whole week catching up with me. And on top of everything else, Phil Hollis had to call me Mary!

First thing next morning, I went to see Arabella, taking another bagful of apples, carrots and boiled potatoes as a peace offering. Her next litter was due in three weeks, and she needed to be well fed before she farrowed. It was awful timing, in any case, and I was not optimistic that the piglets would survive if the weather turned cold. Sometimes I felt that ownership of a breeding sow was one obligation too many. I neglected her shamefully, poor thing.

The coppice where she lived was only accessed on foot or by tractor for the last quarter of a mile. It was a solitary life for her and I'd considered keeping a daughter from the next litter, so she would at least have company. But it was all very vague. She couldn't stay where she was indefinitely and probably the bother of finding somewhere else to keep her would be the final straw. The big decision then would be whether to eat her or try to find her a new home.

Part of the appeal of paganism for me was the acceptance that it was fine to eat meat – but only if you involved yourself in every stage of the process. This came as such a major stumbling block for many that they became vegetarians rather than assist in the slaughter and butchering of animals they knew personally. The morally unacceptable path of allowing others to sanitise the whole business was not an option, or so we insisted in our group. To purchase a bloodless pack of supermarket meat was regarded as the act of a coward. Some years ago, I had arranged for us all to attend the killing of a bullock, owned by my father. Normally, he sent his beef animals to the abattoir like anybody else, and off they went into the food chain, to finish up in Sainsbury's or Marks & Spencer. But I had prevailed upon him to make an exception for one particularly fine Hereford, who I had helped to rear from a calf. I called him Gregory.

The butcher came in a van with his pistol and sharp knives, and I forced everyone to watch as Gregory was almost instantly transformed into four very large quarters of beef, plus a hide that two men could hardly lift. His head, feet and intestines were left for my father to dispose of. The group stood at a short distance, transfixed by the reflexive kicking as the muscles seemed to deny that the animal was indeed dead. The butcher calmly assured them that this was illusory, but I didn't blame them for their anguished scepticism.

Since the catastrophe of BSE, of course, it had become virtually illegal to kill your own animals and to invite a crowd of onlookers might not be regarded as wise. The butcher himself was unimpressed by having an audience. Somebody would talk, he worried, and there'd be all kinds of trouble. But by that time, years after the peak of the BSE crisis – which had in any case turned out to be an appalling over-reaction – the rules were relaxing and I warned everyone not to say much about the experience to their friends and relations.

They talked about it for ages afterwards. For some it was almost the biggest thing that had ever happened to them. They felt proud of themselves for having confronted death in all its redness. I, of course, felt even more pleased with myself. It had been my animal, my idea. I remembered talking about it in the context of human death, as well, claiming that it was just the same, whatever species you belonged to – a thought some found comforting and some disturbing.

Arabella accepted my offerings with due enthusiasm, enduring a lot of ear-scratching and brow-rubbing with placidity. She was always quite gentle with me and I saw her as trusting that the world was essentially benign and would provide for all her basic needs. A small stream ran through the coppice, which she had diverted slightly to make a mud wallow for herself. Once the weather turned cooler, she stopped using it, preferring to lie in the ark I had provided for her – not without some logistical difficulty. I knew where her limits were, all the same. I would not venture inside the ark, for one thing. Such territorial impropriety might well strain her patience. I wouldn't enter into a direct fight with her, either. When I wanted her to go through a certain gateway or into a trailer, I led her with a bucket of food. She weighed three or four times as much as I did, and her muscles were prodigious. Even if she didn't bite me with her jagged tearing teeth, she could knock me flat without a second thought.

I stayed twenty minutes or so, inspecting the fences, talking to the pig as I made a circuit of her domain. The straightforward simplicity of it came as a great relief after the jangled emotions of human business.

Walking back to the village, I remembered Stella. Hadn't I told her I'd call in and tell her the full story of what had happened on Sunday? Since then, I had heard nothing from her and given her scarcely a thought.

* * *

There were times when I wanted Stella with a passion that transcended everything. I revelled in her calm good humour, her self-effacing listening, where I could talk for hours and she would never interrupt with her own stuff. I had wondered for a long time what drew her to me. I saw myself as a very unlikely friend for somebody so professional and focused. Then she said something that explained it.

'Hardly anybody feels comfortable around an undertaker,' she'd sighed. 'They always look at my hands. But not you. You seem to forget what I do, most of the time.'

It was true. And when I did remember her line of work, it was with a small thrill. What Stella did was *real*. It was like when we slaughtered Gregory. Stella saw through the veils of delusion that wrap around almost everybody, and I liked that a lot.

It was Friday, one of the most popular days for funerals. People want to attach the ceremony to a weekend, so they can stay over with the family and do their emotional debriefing. Mondays are the top favourite, using the weekend for preparation as well as obsessive retellings of how the death had happened, what was left unsaid, whether 'Abide With Me' was really a good choice for the hymn. Distant brothers and sons materialise, white-faced and red-eyed, appalled at their own ungovernable emotions, when they'd barely given their sister or mother a thought for years. Stella would describe them with relish, how they literally choked on their own guilt at times, gagging at the enormity of what they hadn't done.

All of which meant Stella was likely to be under-occupied in the office, this being a Friday. The men would be rushing around in the hearses and limousines, florists would be making frantic calls about forgotten wreaths, but hardly anybody would be needing Stella's attentions, unless there was an unavoidable doubling up of funerals, where she had to be the Conductor. This was not a job for a woman in many people's eyes, and although she had done it numerous times, it was always with some anxiety. Personally, I doubted whether the mourners really registered who was conducting the proceedings anyway. The better it was done, the more invisible the individual became.

Stella was in fact loved by a lot of people, despite her dearth of intimate friends. Many of her admirers were aged widowers, profoundly grateful for her gentle treatment during the horrors of burying their wives. They would come back to discuss the headstone or payment or where to strew the ashes, finding a succession of pretexts until they would understand that she would welcome them anyway, just for a little chat and progress report. Anthony Brown, the joint proprietor of the business, had been relaxed about this, having experienced some of the same dependency himself, but gradually it became clear that Stella was almost too much of a good thing. It made him uneasy, the way she gave them cups of tea and let them sit in her office, where members of the public were not really permitted. They might see confidential death certificates or copies of people's funeral accounts. So, reluctantly, she had become less welcoming, slowly disentangling herself from some of the most needy clients.

I had been delighted at the news of the opening of the Northleach office, where Anthony couldn't supervise her visitors. She would generally try to be there on Fridays, ostensibly to catch up with paperwork and make phonecalls.

Taking the risk that she'd be there and available, I drove to the quietly fortunate little town. Northleach is quiet because it has a bypass and traffic doesn't clog its streets. A rare feature, which has made it famous. The result is a village atmosphere where people notice each other and can call across the street expecting to be heard – unlike Painswick, with its stream of vehicles, constant engine sound and oily fumes. Anthony Brown's impertinence in opening a branch of an undertaking business had not gone uncriticised. Some people had been astute enough to see it as a move to exclude competitors, rather than the genuine provision of a service. All the same, Northleach

Church was popular for funerals and it was convenient sometimes to have the coffin waiting in the main street, processing in traditional fashion up to the church.

Stella was at her handsome oak desk, playing Solitaire on the computer, when I walked in. The bell fixed to the door alerted her enough to turn away from the machine, shielding it with her body, but I knew the routine.

'Bored?' I asked.

'Not really,' she said. 'Just taking a bit of a break.'

'Soon be lunchtime,' I noted. 'Shall I get sandwiches?' She wouldn't allow herself to leave her post for more than five minutes, which I often suggested was against employment law, but she never seemed to get the joke.

'I've got some,' she said. 'You can share mine.'

The premises had originally been two shops, knocked together before planning permission to wreak such changes became impossible. A tiny 'chapel of rest' had been created at the back, with space for one coffin. Next to it was a kitchen area, with sink and kettle and microwave oven. Stella went through to make us some coffee, and I followed as far as the door.

'No customers?' I asked.

'Actually, yes. There's somebody in the chapel. We've got a funeral here at four. Some relatives are meant to be arriving from Canada any minute now for a last viewing. It's all a bit tense, wondering whether they'll be here in time.'

A strange urge gripped me to go and look at the body, completely counter to what I'd have expected. After Gaynor, you'd think I would never want to see death again. 'Who is it?' I asked. 'Man or woman.'

'Woman. Sixty-six. Motor neurone disease. The husband told me all about it. Dreadful business.'

'Can I see her?'

Stella stared at me. 'Really?'

I nodded. 'Don't ask me why. Laying a ghost, or something. I'll hide if the people show up.'

'Go on, then. Through there. Don't mess her up, will you?'

I ventured into the minute room, as if entering a shrine. It was completely plain: white walls, vinyl flooring. A vase of mixed flowers stood on a small square table in a corner. The pale yellowish coffin was on trestles, a piece of white fabric like net curtaining spread over it. The top end was folded back, like a bedsheet, and open to view was a square of white satin, covering the dead face. With shaking fingers, I lifted it off, fixing my eyes on the cold flesh thus revealed.

It was, I supposed, a human face, with hair and the top few inches of a neat cotton blouse visible. The eyes were closed, and the lips tightly together.

But it was not really human at all, but was like something manmade, an artefact. It was deader than wood, or even stone. I thought, crazily, that I would rather it had been crawling with maggots, disintegrating back into its constituent parts, than this nothingness. It *was* something manmade, in a way, cleaned up, the natural processes arrested by embalming.

I stood there for what felt like ages, striving to capture the woman it had been. There were lines etched in the thin face, the cheekbones prominent, the eye sockets sunken. She had obviously been horribly ill before she died. But the overwhelming message for me was that none of that mattered any more. It had all passed away, blown to the heavens and forgotten. One of our pagan tenets is that the inevitable fact of death should make us prize life all the more. Seize the moment, celebrate the warmth and movement that will soon be gone. Standing over this dead woman, I wondered if we had it right. Didn't death render everything futile? If we were all going to finish up like this, then where was the point of anything?

I remembered my ghost, the fleeting image of something from a different reality. Why, I wondered, had I not given it more serious thought before this, as a sort of consolation for the death of Gaynor? Because it offered no consolation, I realised. It was utterly irrelevant, an inexplicable anomaly that had come unbidden, and was not amenable to anything I might want or demand. Ghosts which appeared in your bedroom on the night of their passing could perhaps serve a useful purpose. Dead husbands who came up the stairs as you were craving their return in the wee small hours were too transparently wish-fulfilment to be credible. I didn't want Gaynor back enough to conjure her by my own extreme feeling. This thing in front of me was death and it was terrible.

I covered up the face and left the room. Stella was waiting for me. 'Well?' she said, giving me a very intense look.

'I don't know,' I said. 'She isn't like Gaynor was.'

'Is that what this is about?'

'I guess so. I don't really know. I'm in a bit of a mess, I think.' I took the coffee mug in an unsteady hand and went back into the main office.

Stella's manner was not what anybody would immediately think of as sympathetic. She kept very still, but not in a tense way. She just waited for things to settle down, perfectly non-judgmental, happy to let the emotion do whatever it needed to do. It made me feel safe and unhurried.

I didn't cry, although it came very close to that. I sat with the mug between my hands, not drinking it, letting images of death fill my head. I wanted to arrive at some tidy consoling aphorism that would sum it all up, once and for all, and explain what it was about death that made everything so impossible. One or two candidates shaped themselves on my tongue, only to be dismissed as fatuous. Stella had once ranted to me about the ubiquitous passage that people read at funerals, by a bloke called Henry Scott Holland. Everybody knows it, I suppose. *I am not dead, but just in the next room* or some such rubbish. At first I couldn't see why Stella hated it so much, until I thought about my Gran. She was actually dead. There was no 'next room'. It was all a big stupid lie, on a par with stories about gooseberry bushes to deflect children's questions about babies and birth.

And now Gaynor had vanished in the same permanent, total fashion. As had the woman in the chapel of rest. When a body stops pulsing, the eyes stop focusing, the lungs stop inflating, there isn't anything left.

My thoughts came to a full stop, and I lifted my head. 'Murder,' I muttered. 'Killing somebody deliberately. It's beyond words, isn't it? Robbing them of life. It's a *huge* thing to do.'

Stella lifted her shoulders briefly, as if I was stating the blindingly obvious. Which I suppose I was.

'You'd think they'd stand out,' I went on incoherently. 'You know – have some sort of dark halo around them, or a cloud of smoke or a *smell*. You'd think they wouldn't be able to live with themselves – like Lady Macbeth trying to wash herself away. How can they look anybody in the eye ever again?'

Stella smiled patiently.

Something inside me came into sharp focus. 'I have to *know*,' I realised. 'I absolutely must find out who did it. For Gaynor's sake.'

'It doesn't matter to Gaynor,' she said gently. 'Nothing matters to Gaynor any more.'

It was a horrible thought. 'Well, I think it does,' I insisted. Jumbled thoughts about time began to take over. If we weren't so fixated on linear time, with a clear past, present and future, then it somehow mattered to Gaynor's life, *all of it*, that the identity of her killer should be known. It mattered retrospectively, if that made any sense.

'So talk me through it,' Stella invited, with a swift glance at the clock on the wall.

I recollected myself, and where I was. Another new thought hit me. 'Hey!' I said. 'It'll probably be me who has to organise her funeral. I can't think of anybody else who'd do it. So you can have the business.' I grinned at her, aware of how important this would be. 'How about that?'

'I thought you'd never ask,' she sighed, before grinning back.

Instantly my status changed. From a needy friend, taking up illicit working time I became a valued customer, perfectly justified in staying as long as I liked. The minor detail of Gaynor's body still being in police custody, with no suggestion yet of a date for a funeral, hardly mattered.

So I told Stella everything I could think of about Oliver Grover, the pagan group, Phil Hollis and his new squeeze. 'Squeeze?' Stella echoed. 'Is that what they call it now?'

'I think it might already be out of fashion,' I conceded. 'But I like it.'

'What's she like?'

'Nice. Pretty. Clever and unflappable. She's got a dog.'

'Oh, well,' said Stella tolerantly. 'You've got a pig.' She had always found Arabella a step too far. To her mind, keeping a pig was uncomfortably eccentric.

'And she's involved in the murder investigation, is she?'

'Who, Arabella?' The quip was a signal to both of us that my dark interlude was over, at least for the time being.

Stella waited unsmilingly for a sensible reply.

'She's very interested, yes. To be honest, there's not much else for her to do except sort through Helen's things, and she seems to have rather given up on that. Phil goes off all day, when they were supposed to be having a lovely romantic holiday with log fires and oil lamps. She's only got me to talk to.'

'Did she meet Gaynor?'

I had to think. 'No,' I concluded. 'Neither did Phil.'

'And nobody stands out for you, no dark haloes or nasty smells?'

A recently described image coalesced before my eyes. 'Not really,' I said. 'But it did for Daphne – sort of.'

'The one with the Freemason husband?'

'Eddie. She saw him at the Horse Fair, quite unexpectedly, and she said it was as if a spotlight was on him. He was so vivid to her, it shocked her.'

Stella shook her head. 'That doesn't count,' she opined. 'He was her husband for umpteen years. He's bound to leap out of a crowd for her.'

'I suppose so,' I said. Then I told her about the Masonic stuff in Helen's attic, purely because of the association of ideas.

'What's that got to do with Gaynor?' Stella asked.

'Probably nothing. Almost certainly nothing. But it was very strange.'

She gave it careful consideration. 'A message for Hollis is my bet,' she decided. 'Somebody who knew he was coming, and decided it would have a special significance for him.'

'I can't imagine who,' I said. 'Or why. He didn't look as if he was getting the message, either, if that's what was going on. Plus, he might easily never have gone into the attic all week.'

'So if it was some sort of advance confession to Gaynor's murder, it wasn't clear enough for him to understand it.'

'That's ridiculous,' I told her, annoyed that she should turn the whole thing into a bit of jokey nonsense.

'I know. Sorry,' she said.

I didn't stay long after that. She took a few basic details about Gaynor's funeral – a burial in a recently opened natural cemetery that she knew about. 'It's run by a nice couple, Drew and Karen Slocombe. They've expanded onto a second site not far from Stroud, having got one up and running in Somerset. They're popular with pagans, I gather.'

I nodded. 'Yes, I've heard of them. But Gaynor wasn't a pagan. It's just that she'd have liked the atmosphere.' I rode the wave of pain that came without warning. How did I know where Gaynor would have liked to be buried? The subject had never arisen between us.

'Right,' said Stella carelessly. 'Whatever.'

I drove home full of determination to discover who'd killed my friend. There were unresolved niggles in my mind concerning Ursula and Verona, primarily. Ursula always had an edge to her, clever and frustrated as she was. There often seemed to be something on the tip of her tongue, some sharp remark that she was biting back. She had an air of knowing a great deal more than she revealed. Sometimes at a moot she would sigh theatrically and roll her eyes, implying that she saw us all as her intellectual inferiors, but was too polite to set us straight.

And yet she was only a geography teacher. Even when I was at school, there had been little respect for that particular subject. Everybody knew that maths teachers were cruel monsters; English teachers wise and wonderful; games teachers dim-witted obsessives and geography teachers were just pathetic. It's a game I've played a lot at parties and other gatherings, and it almost always works. The stereotypes persist across all schools and all generations.

But Ursula didn't fit. I'd never seen her in action in the classroom, but I suspected she stood no nonsense, and made the subject at least slightly more interesting than most of her colleagues managed to do. She was, after all, exceptional in that she had actually travelled across the world, using every summer holiday to gather up her wide-bottomed daughter and trek across some of the deserts I presumed she made her pupils describe in their homework.

So why would she have any disagreement with Gaynor?

I tried to recall everything she'd said at my house,

the evening before Gaynor was killed. She had defended Gaynor's request for some piece of magic that might attract Oliver to her. She had disagreed with the current ideas about sexual orientation. Not much to go on there, except that she had at least been listening. She had given some attention to my friend and her emotional state. Which was more than Leslie or Verona had done, I realised. They had seemed to ignore the whole topic, as far as I had noticed.

Verona was essentially mysterious. I never fully understood her motives for doing what she did. She was an unlikely pagan for a start. She loved money and influence and always wanted to be the best. But Verona as the killer seemed unlikely. I could not imagine any scenario whereby Gaynor was in her way, or presented any kind of threat.

I had believed I knew these people, what they wanted from life, where they stood on important issues. I also believed I knew how things stood between them – who was miffed with whom, and why. And I did not believe that any one of them had any issues around my friend Gaynor. Most of them scarcely even knew her.

Although, I reminded myself, I was learning that there were other things going on in Gaynor's life that she hadn't told me about. I realised I'd imagined her steadily knitting, hour after hour, during most of her days. She could read at the same time, and sometimes told me about novels she'd consumed, as well as programmes she'd watched on TV. But I never visualised her outside, meeting people, riding around in Oliver's car or gossiping about his clients. I tried to recreate her mood and manner the last time I'd seen her, wishing I'd paid more attention. Was I inventing the restlessness, and air of uncharacteristic decisiveness? A feeling that she was poised with gritted teeth on the brink of some new venture. I thought not. I thought I had been right in sensing a change in her – and it seemed reasonable to assume that this change had something to do with her death.

Which led me to the conclusion that I ought to go and see her flat. Except that of course I did not have a key. And the police might well have sealed it up, after crawling over it for clues. So I'd have to ask Phil Hollis, wouldn't I?

He was not there; I could see by the absence of his car. Poor old Thea must be stranded yet again with all those dogs, even more trapped than she would have been as a house-sitter. At least then she'd have had wheels. I was surprised she hadn't come knocking at my door when she saw – and she surely must have done – that I had come back from seeing Stella. It would be an act of kindness to go over and chat to her.

She didn't answer the door, but there was a lot of

barking from the back, so I walked round and found her in the garden. It was the last hour of daylight, and not particularly warm, but she was sitting there on Helen's old wrought-iron bench, wearing my jumper and writing on a pad of paper. The dogs were all romping wildly on the lawn, rolling each other over and making snarling sounds that I hoped were merely playful.

Thea didn't notice me for several seconds. When she did, she took a few more seconds to focus on my face and remember who I was. 'Oh! Hello,' she said. 'Sorry. I was writing a letter.'

'With a pen!' I exclaimed jokily.

She grinned. 'I know. But we're already living in the Dark Ages here, with no power, so it seemed appropriate. I didn't like to light the lamps so early, so I came out here, hoping I'd be able to see better.'

I looked at the sky. 'And can you?'

'Oh, yes. My eyes adjusted very easily.'

I couldn't think what to say next, aware that she would report all of it straight to Phil. Despite her friendliness I felt distanced, not only from her but everyone else I knew. The taint of having been the person who had found Gaynor's body seemed to get worse with each day. I could hear in my mind's ear people muttering about it and reviewing the relationship I'd had with Gaynor. Plenty of people must have heard me snap impatiently at her now and then. They must have seen me as a bossy domineering character to Gaynor's soft and meek personality. After all, I was about eight inches taller and four stone heavier than her. We must have looked odd together. In the malleable material that was most people's minds, I could easily be transformed into a vicious murderer, I had no doubt.

'I'm writing to my sister, actually,' said Thea. 'Normally I would email her, but I didn't bring the computer with me.'

'No. You said.' Was life so impossible these days, I wondered, without a computer readily to hand? 'Where does she live?'

'Near Bristol. She's called Jocelyn. Have you got sisters?'

'Three brothers.' It was bland stuff, with no discernible subtext. I had no patience for it. 'Did Phil say any more about Eddie Yeo after I'd gone?'

'A bit. The Caroline thing's rather awkward.'

She seemed reluctant to talk about the murder, and I suspected that Phil had told her not to. The thought made me angry. 'It's nearly a week already,' I burst out. 'And they haven't got anywhere at all, have they? I'm supposed to be sorting out Gaynor's things, arranging her funeral. How much longer are they going to keep everything in limbo?'

She shook her head gently. 'I have no idea,' she said. 'All I know is that it's been a wasted week for me, as well.'

Despite the soft tone, I could hear disappointment and worse. 'Are you going home, then?' I asked. 'Are you supposed to be somewhere on Monday?'

She shrugged. 'Not really. But Phil is officially back at work then, so there's no point in staying here.'

I cocked my head. 'What's the difference? I mean, he's working anyway, isn't he? And Cold Aston is a lot closer to the centre of things than Cirencester. He's still got the flat there, I suppose?'

Thea nodded. 'About two minutes from the police station. I hadn't really thought of it like that. I don't think he has, either. It would be nice to stay here a few more days. Especially with the dogs. They like it here.'

All three dogs looked at her, understanding the word. She devoted several seconds to smiling at them in that dopey fond way some people have. The animals smiled back at her. Sickening.

'Sounds like a good idea, then,' I summed up.

'What about you?' she asked.

I raised my eyebrows. 'What about me?'

'Have you got things you need to be doing next week?'

I thought about it. 'The big thing at the moment is Samhain, really. I need to talk it over with the group, if they're still speaking to me after I missed their special meeting the other night. I got waylaid by Sally Grover and never made it. I haven't heard whether anything was decided. We were going to use the Barrow – you knew that, I suppose. Now the police might not let us in. And I'm not sure...' I realised I might not be able to go back to the Barrow without a major personal struggle. The memory of Gaynor's cold curled body would be all too vivid.

'What happens in the rituals?' she asked. 'I hardly know anything about it.'

'They focus on the turn of the seasons,' I explained. 'The onset of winter, and the death of the sun. Other deaths, as well. People used to slaughter the surplus beasts and salt down the meat for the cold months. And burning – they'd burn all the rubbish that had mounted up over the summer. Then they'd have to make sure there was enough fuel to see them through. Firewood and peat. Old people would sometimes go off and die, knowing they'd be too big a burden on the family. It's the season of death,' I finished, not having answered her question.

She had given me her full attention as I spoke. 'That fits with Bonfire Night,' she realised. 'Nothing to do with Guy Fawkes, after all.'

'I think two things came together. That often happens. Like All Saints and All Souls. It sounds like mainstream Church stuff, but it's really not at all. Samhain is the time when the other world nudges up close to this. You can feel the presence of the dead.'

She pouted sceptically. 'Isn't that just because of the fog and the first frosts?'

'If you like,' I said. 'I'm not trying to convince you of anything – just explaining what we believe.' It felt like old ground. Hadn't I already said much of this to her? Perhaps not, since she was listening so intently.

'And you *really* believe that, do you?'

'I *know*,' I said, trying to keep it light. 'It isn't actually belief in anything. It's my real experience.' In spite of myself, my tone intensified. 'I *live* it, every day.'

She smiled. 'You sound like a born-again Christian.'

'No,' I snapped. 'I sound like somebody who has a true faith. It doesn't matter what it is, only that it goes right down to your marrow. When you find something that works, the language tends to be the same across the board.' I heard myself with some relief. On Sunday, hadn't I snapped at Kenneth that I did in fact doubt the sense or usefulness of our convictions? It seemed I had got back on course, almost without realising it.

'Oh,' she said, rather faintly. 'I see.'

It was obvious that she didn't, and in spite of what I'd said, I was niggled by that. 'The rituals are mainly symbolic,' I went on. 'We use masks, which you can interpret in all sorts of ways. The usual explanation is that there are demons and goblins abroad at Samhain and they try to snatch your soul. If you're wearing a mask, they won't get you.'

'Very sophisticated,' she muttered. 'I don't think.'

'I agree, actually,' I said. 'But masks are powerful, just the same. As I often say, don't knock it till you've tried it. You become somebody totally different to everyone around you, while keeping your own self safe and secret, behind the mask. Anyway, that's one thing we do. And we practise divination, plus some singing and dancing. Apart from anything else, it's very liberating. None of the usual daily things matter. It's just the big stuff.'

Thea said nothing for a little while, then she said, 'Big stuff like death, you mean.'

'Right,' I sighed.

She left another silence before asking, 'And you'll go ahead with it all, as planned, will you?'

'I don't know,' I admitted. 'I'll have to speak to the others.'

It was getting dark, and the dogs obviously wanted to go back into the house. We heard a car come up the quiet village street, and stop outside the front of Greenhaven. 'Phil,' we said, simultaneously. Just like wives and sisters and daughters had done for centuries, we put aside our own lives to go and greet the homecoming male. It never even occurred to me to stand back and let

Thea have first contact. I followed her through the back door, only inches behind.

I'd expected her to give him a hug and a kiss, while I waited for the crumbs of a smile and a nod. Instead he almost ignored his girlfriend and looked straight at me. 'Ariadne, I want you to come with me,' he said, his voice strained and harsh.

'What? Why?' I stuttered.

He looked at Thea then. 'Sorry, love,' he said. 'I didn't know she'd be here. I was going to explain to you first, then fetch her.'

'What's happened?' she asked, her voice steady. She was such an *adult*. I would have whinged and sulked if it had been me.

'There's been another killing. We've got another body at the Barrow.'

CHAPTER SIXTEEN

It was Verona, of the chilling laugh and high ambition. Phil did not take me to the Barrow or ask me to identify the body. That had all been done hours ago. They had found her just after midday, when I had been looking at another body in the Northleach chapel belonging to Brown Brothers, undertakers. Stella could give me an alibi if I needed one, I thought wildly.

Instead, I was escorted back to the police station in Cirencester, and handed over yet again to DI Baldwin. 'Routine questions, that's all,' said Phil, in the car. 'Nobody thinks it was you who did it.'

'So why can't you talk to me at home?' I demanded. 'Why do I have to be dragged here all over again?'

'It's the way we do things,' was all he would say.

Baldwin was with another constable, this time a man. He was tall and thin and fair, and I didn't even try to catch his name.

'Tell us all you can think of about Miss Farebrother,' Baldwin said. A tape recorder sat on the table, and he showed no intention of taking notes. Over-reliance on technology, I thought with disapproval. Never a good idea.

'About thirty-two or -three. Lives alone in Moreton, works in Gloucester, running her own business as a food distributor. A real high flyer. Probably lots of rivals,' I added, rather to Baldwin's irritation, to judge by his face. I ploughed on. 'She has a sister – possibly more than one – who lives not far away. I forget where, but it might come back to me. She's quiet, clever, self-possessed.'

'When did you last see her?'

I sighed. 'It must have been Monday morning. She came to my house, to see how I was when she heard about Gaynor. And before that was Saturday evening. She was at the moot. I told you at my previous interview.'

Baldwin nodded, and flipped back through some notes in front of him. 'And what links her to Gaynor Lewis?' he asked.

'Nothing,' I said. 'Absolutely nothing.'

'Except they were both killed at the Notgrove Barrow, and left in the same position, at the same spot.'

'Weren't you guarding it?' I burst out. 'Wasn't it under police surveillance or something?'

'We'd put a tape across the entrance,' he said stiffly.

I snorted. There was nothing to be said.

They stuck to the point. 'You knew them both,' he said softly. 'That's a link.'

I felt chilled. Was everybody I knew going to be picked off, one by one?

'They were both young, single, childless women. Both of a quiet disposition, with few friends.' Baldwin was tapping the desk lightly as he drew each comparison. 'And both unlikely to be too sorely missed,' he added.

It was true. Verona's minimal family had hardly seen her, to my knowledge, for years. She didn't talk about them. Like Gaynor, she seemed happy with her own company.

'You're saying the murderer thought they were expendable?' I said. 'As if that might be some kind of justification, in his own eyes?'

He met my gaze. 'Am I saying that?' he wondered. 'Or have you just jumped to that conclusion?'

I couldn't think of a reply that would sound even remotely coherent. My mind was full of an image of some sinister hooded figure with a grudge against harmless women. One murder was ghastly, two were terrifying.

Then another idea took root. 'And me,' I blurted. 'I'm another one, aren't I?'

He just sat there, pushing his face forward slightly, inviting me to finish the thought. 'The description fits me, as well.'

'Does it?' If I'd hoped for reassurance, I was doomed to disappointment. 'And that scares you?'

'Of course it does.' I laughed shakily. 'Although it seems daft. I mean – what possible *reason* could there be? Besides,' I added, 'I'm much bigger than either of them.' It was stupid, but did in part identify a major way in which I felt different from either Gaynor or Verona. Maybe it was just me, but I'd always felt I had to make *allowances* for small women, as if they were slightly defective or inadequate. Walking along beside Gaynor, I had felt myself to be the normal one, and she the undersized runt. Although it wasn't like that with Thea, I noted. Thea, who was even smaller than Gaynor, but somehow had a big aura, filling more space than her actual body did.

Baldwin didn't take me up on it, didn't refer to this as a point against me. Bigger, and stronger and in possession of several knitting needles – lots of points against me, in the eyes of the police. Except that anyone who knew anything about knitting might realise I never used anything smaller than a 4mm pair of needles.

Phil drove me home again, saying little in the face of my hyped-up condition. I couldn't conceal my excitement, fuelled no doubt by adrenaline, at the abrupt descent into notoriety. 'The papers will be full of it,' I burbled. *'Serial killer in tranquil*

Cotswolds. Knitting needle killer stalks the wold.
You'll be under terrible pressure to catch him.'

'Who told you Verona was killed by a knitting needle?' he asked tightly.

In a TV murder mystery this would have been the giveaway moment. The last persuasive piece in the jigsaw that had me locked up awaiting trial. And it was a good question, to which I had no credible answer. 'I just assumed,' I said. 'Everything else was the same – you told me that. Besides,' I ventured a little laugh, 'there's a partner to the first one out there somewhere. They come in pairs, you know.'

'You amaze me, you really do,' he said crossly. He had said it to me before, when I'd been flippant at a moment when he'd wanted to be serious. I'd joked a lot about Freemasons, for a start. And when his daughter died, I'd tried to keep him going with a robust approach that must have jarred against all the tiptoeing around and embarrassed words of sympathy.

'But you like me,' I said. 'Admit it.'

'I don't like you calling yourself Ariadne,' he said, turning to look at me for two whole seconds. 'I think it's daft.'

I took a deep breath. 'You think paganism's daft, as well. The two go together. Who asked you, anyway?'

Phil Hollis was a Detective Superintendent. That's quite a senior position. He had a lot of people working under him and a terrifying amount of responsibility. He'd moved out of the realm of ordinariness where people routinely addressed him as an equal. He had few genuine friends – at least when I knew him – his wife had gone and married someone else and the path of his new love wasn't running very smoothly. I felt fairly safe in assuming that my straight talking came as quite a blast of fresh air. I might even go so far as to believe I held a unique place in his life. Someone who had known him from his late teens, seen him through a lot of ups and downs, and had been closely connected to his aunt. I knew the secrets, not just about the Masonic fiasco, but one or two more shameful events. I'd always had a habit of being there when things happened to Phil Hollis.

A car very often generates a kind of telepathy when two people are riding inside it. He read my thoughts pretty accurately, it seemed. 'Why are you always there?' he asked. 'It's like having a stalker.' He said it resignedly, with a tiny hint of satisfaction, even.

'I don't do it on purpose,' I said. 'Not any more. I grew out of you a long time ago.'

'What does that mean?' He looked at me again.

'You know what it means. It's changed, over the years. It started as one thing, when I was about twelve, and evolved into what it is now. But there's something that hasn't changed. I *know* you, Phil – maybe better than anyone.'

'And do you trust me?'

I hadn't expected that. I watched the road, trying to find the answer. 'More or less,' I said, eventually. 'Although I'm not so sure you trust *me*. You might think I'm the killer, even now.'

'I think you're centrally involved in whatever's happening here. And even if you're not, you're my best point of entry into the community. You know everybody, after all.'

'It's not a community, not as it's normally meant. People have more intimate relationships with their computers than they do with each other.'

'I used the word carelessly,' he acknowledged. 'It's not important. Besides – I didn't see a computer in your house.'

'No,' I said. 'There isn't one.'

It was dark when we got back. I was hungry and Thomas was annoyed with me. Feeling vaguely sorry for myself, I let Phil go back to his beloved and settled down to a plate of scrambled egg, in the company of my cat. But before I did that, I locked the back door – something I very seldom did before finishing up for the night. And I tried not to imagine shadowy figures hiding under the bed or in a cupboard upstairs. I hadn't felt this level of nervousness since I was seventeen and my parents had gone for a rare visit to some cousins in Norfolk, staying away for two nights. I had been alone in the farmhouse for the first time in my life.

It was an unfamiliar feeling I experienced in my Cold Aston home, based as it was on the hard facts of two unlawful killings of women I knew. A sense of deliberate focused malevolence filled the house. All the stories and traditions of Samhain swirled around in my head. Lucifer walked the land, with his hosts of demons trying to snatch our unwary souls. It was easier to die at this season of the year, our hold on life becoming more fragile. Those who had already died crowded closer to us, pressing against the veil between the two worlds. They wanted us to join them. I imagined Gaynor's wraith, timid and mournful, drawing me to her, wanting to tell me how it was she'd died.

I went to my spinning wheel, taking up a special hunk of pure Cotswold fleece, which I'd been looking forward to working on for months. It was from a two-year-old ewe, who had lived out all winter, avoiding the hayseeds and other rubbish that they picked up indoors. The fibre flowed through my fingers with no need for carding. It was moist and supple and when washed would be a dazzling white. Women had been spinning since neolithic times. It linked me to them, to the persistence of human survival. It made me feel that everything would be all right again. It sent the ghosts back to where they belonged, silent and untroublesome.

There were things I ought to get on with the next morning, regardless of this shattering second murder. Top of the list was visiting Gaynor's flat and making sure everything was secure. The telephone and electricity would have to be turned off. The stopcock should be closed and all the doors and windows locked. It was a routine I'd gone through before, at Greenhaven and one or two other places. Gaynor had owned the flat outright, having bought it with the money her parents left. For the first time, I wondered who would inherit it now.

Verona Farebrother was not my responsibility, but she too owned a property. The sister would have to come and do the necessary, I supposed. Suddenly the whole area seemed full of people sorting out possessions abandoned by their dead owners. It was another aspect of Samhain that I had not considered before. Until that week, I had only been concerned with Helen's things – and then only at a distance.

Returning to my nervous comparisons between myself and the two murder victims, I found myself listing all the others I could think of in the same general category. If you included women of all ages, I easily came up with a dozen, just in the surrounding villages. Women, it seemed, lived alone these days. They somehow acquired a house or flat and made themselves a home in which they were answerable to nobody but themselves. Men must hate it, I realised. Women were supposed to need protection, to give men a reason for getting out there and earning money. If they made it too obvious that they genuinely enjoyed the single life, some fundamental balance was destroyed. When they prospered in the business world and drove flamboyant cars and held their heads up high there must be men out there who itched to slaughter them.

I was describing Verona Farebrother only too well, I realised.

But there would always be women like Thea to give such enraged men grounds for hope. Women who liked being part of a couple, who needed to have somebody else to think about first thing in the morning before they thought about themselves. And good luck to her, I said to myself. Without her and her kind, the social fabric really would come unravelled.

I fell asleep planning the next day in detail. It helped keep my mind off the sounds the house was making, and the conviction that I could hear somebody breathing right underneath my bed.

Saturday morning was upon me before I was quite ready for another day. The murder of Verona had stunned me more than I realised, knocking me into a profound sleep from which I was reluctant to surface. But nudging persistently at me was a sense of urgency. My usual instinct to detach and back away, leaving others to do the worrying and general emoting was overlaid by the knowledge that what was happening was inescapably personal to me. I couldn't dodge it any longer. And the next thing I had to do was go to Gaynor's flat and shoulder my responsibilities as her closest friend – if indeed that's what I was. It wouldn't entirely surprise me to find that Caroline had usurped that position – or even Oliver bloody Grover.

I had forgotten to ask Phil how I could best get hold of a key to Gaynor's flat. I was parking outside before it even occurred to me. Determined not to give up, I checked all the obvious hiding places. It was a ground floor property, with a small garden at the side for Gaynor's use. She had stacked three plastic chairs against the wall, and a row of terracotta pots held straggly plants. I tilted each one to look underneath, then rummaged in the compost around the plants, to no avail. Then I noticed a big stone doing nothing much at the edge of the lawn. It was the usual yellowy-grey hue, typical of the area, and there were signs that it had been moved recently. The grass to one side of it was brown, as if that was where it had been sitting previously. I turned it over, needing both hands to shift it, and found a door key underneath. Only then did I feel a slight jolt of annoyance that Gaynor had never disclosed the hiding place to me. I wondered whether anybody else in the world knew about it.

Making no efforts to conceal myself, I unlocked the front door and went in. There were no immediate signs that the police had searched the place, although I knew they must have done. Gaynor kept it tidy and dusted. She hadn't hoarded knick-knacks or junk mail or old newspapers. She didn't have a cat or dog or budgie, but the house plants in all the downstairs rooms had wilted, and some looked beyond recovery.

She had an old oak writing desk, relic of a Welsh grandparent, where she kept all the usual documents. Fighting to convince myself that I not only had the right, but the obligation, I flicked through all the cubbyholes, looking for a will, or insurance policy, that ought to be consulted as a matter of urgency. Something akin to the feeling I'd had about Helen's abandoned possessions took hold of me, but this time it was skewed by the fact of a sudden and premature death. Gaynor had had no chance to put anything in order. She hadn't had time to destroy or hide anything private. It was all exposed to view, naked without its owner there to shield it. It was a horrible sensation. I expected her ghost to tap me on the shoulder and accuse me of snooping.

One of the desk drawers was locked, which came as a real surprise. Normal people, living alone, don't lock things. Who did she think would try to open it? What could she possibly want to hide so securely?

I satisfied myself with the idea that her father had probably locked it twenty years ago and then lost the key. Nobody would have bothered to try to open it since, until the police, who I imagined had used some sort of device to get it open when they examined the flat for clues nearly a week ago, although it seemed strange that they should lock it again.

I drifted into fantasy, imagining the desk going to an auction room, being bought, still locked, and the new owner taking a hairpin to it and finding some wondrous object like a diamond necklace. I lifted one end of the desk, and waggled it cautiously, listening for movement inside the drawer. It was a foolish attempt. All I accomplished was to put so much weight on one of the legs that it gave a nasty cracking sound, forcing me to hurriedly drop the whole thing. It would be a shame to break it – it was obviously a genuine antique.

I had already found all the documents I needed, including an old address book. On the front page, in childish writing, was the usual many-lined address, culminating in "The Universe." It dated the book to Gaynor's pre-teen years, I guessed. Flicking through, I found myself, alongside six or seven names and addresses from Brynmawr in

South Wales, where Gaynor had gone to school. It was a forlorn little thing, with no entries for anybody in the Cotswolds apart from myself. No Caroline Johnson or Oliver Grover or Gervase-brother-of-Xavier, I noted with satisfaction. There were ticks and dates against my name, which I finally worked out indicated that she had sent me a Christmas card each year. Only four other people got cards from her, it seemed. The only one that looked as if she mattered was a Normanton, Mandy, under the Ns, with an address in Calgary, Alberta. This must be Gaynor's cousin, and the probable inheritor of the flat and its contents.

It seemed a reasonable assumption that nobody had yet contacted Mandy to tell her of the demise of her cousin. I would have to ask Stella – she knew all about such procedures. There was no phone number in the address book, which meant I would have to consult the overseas Directory Enquiries, or else write a letter.

Gradually I became aware of the myriad tasks mounting up, with nobody to tackle them but me. The death hadn't been registered. The utilities hadn't been disconnected. I wasn't sure which to do first, or even how to go about most of them. And I still hadn't been upstairs.

Gaynor's bedroom was even more distressing. Her duvet was folded back, none too neatly, and there was a mug with dregs of tea on the table beside the bed. I peeped into the wardrobe, wondering what I ought to do with her clothes and was struck by how few garments hung there. A drawer at ground level contained folded shirts and two pairs of trousers. In a small two-drawer chest I found underwear, scarves, hankies and a swimming costume.

On top of the chest was a porcelain dish containing the usual dusty collection of rubber bands, small change, dead batteries and odd buttons. Things you took out of your pockets before slinging the garment in the washing basket. There was also a very pretty vase with a single frond of dried pampas grass in it. At least that could go, I thought, with some vague intention of making a start on clearing the place. I lifted the vase and something chinked inside it. Upending it, I caught a small brass key.

The locked drawer must have been nagging at the back of my mind, because I ran down the stairs and tried the key, full of a sense that this was important.

It fitted, and the drawer slid out with utter smoothness. It was stuffed full of leaflets, magazines, some jewellery and a photo.

Fingering them delicately, even warily, I could not believe what I was seeing. The literature was all about Freemasonry – but with the twist that they described Lodges run by and for women. Instructions on how to establish such a Lodge, the restrictions and tolerances accorded to them by the Grand Lodge, the regalia they could use and the secrets they must keep.

The photo showed Gaynor Lewis standing between two other women. A printed label was attached at the bottom, giving the date and 'First official meeting of the New Lodge.'

The two other women were Verona Farebrother and Caroline Johnson, formerly Hollis.

CHAPTER SEVENTEEN

Phil and Thea were sitting in the lamplight when I went over to Greenhaven. It was chilly and they both wore the jumpers I'd given them. They asked me in, politely but with no obvious enthusiasm.

'Sorry,' I said. 'But I need your advice.'

As I described my discovery in Gaynor's flat, producing the photograph with an accusing flourish, Phil seemed impatient and distracted. Before long he interrupted me. 'Yes, yes. We've examined the house already. We found the address book and made copies of all the addresses. We opened the locked drawer, as well and saw what you saw.'

I was stunned. 'And?' I stammered.

His face went still. 'I can't tell you that,' he said. 'All I can say is that it might prove useful in our investigations.'

Thea had listened to everything with total attention. 'Caroline is a Freemason,' she said slowly. 'Did you know? Before seeing the photo, I mean?'

Phil shook his head. 'No, I did not. I'd heard some reports that there was a female Lodge being set up, but it didn't interest me and I had no idea who was involved.'

'But...' I was shouting, still flapping the picture at him. 'This must tell you who killed them. This must be what it's all about.'

They both stared at me. 'Why?' said Phil at last. 'Why must it?'

'You're not accusing Caroline are you?' said Thea with a light *huff* of laughter.

I sat down with a thud on one of the upright chairs standing against the wall. 'I don't know,' I said. 'I can't think. This is so *bizarre*. Gaynor can't have been a Mason. Why would she?'

Phil's face revealed that he knew far more than he was saying. He was way ahead of me and I was once again the clamouring child following in his wake, desperate for his attention and friendship.

'We don't think it's important,' he said softly.

I stared at the floor where the carpet showed the more vivid marks where rugs had protected it from the ravages of ordinary life. Thea had packed the rugs in one of the black bin liners now sitting in the dining room. I almost gave up my quest for an explanation under the pressure of Phil's confident male superiority.

Almost, but not quite. 'Daphne,' I said, as the name flicked into my mind. 'Daphne might have found out. She hates the Masons. She would be furious with Verona if she found out she was dabbling in it.'

Phil and Thea both seemed uncomfortable. 'What?' I demanded. 'What haven't you told me? Why do I feel like an ignorant child here?'

'We're questioning Mr Grover and his – partner,' said Phil. 'They can't account for their movements either on Sunday or yesterday. We know there were certain conflicts between Grover and Miss Lewis. Since then we've been informed about similar trouble with Miss Farebrother. I can't say any more than that.'

Again I had to force my brain to function. 'Oliver's a mason,' I remembered. 'Is that something to do with it?'

Phil clamped his lips together. Angrily I kept up the questions. 'And why the Barrow?' I demanded. 'And knitting needles? That wouldn't be the way they'd do it. You might as well accuse Pamela and Kenneth. At least she knits.'

And they knew the two dead women. And Kenneth had money trouble, bad enough to upset Pamela. I raised my head. 'It could have been them,' I repeated. 'Just as easily.'

Thea got up and threw another log on the fire. 'That's the last one,' she said.

Her voice sounded different – uncaring, as if it didn't matter whether or not they had any heating. I wondered what had happened since I last spoke to her. I guessed it had something to do with their plans for the coming week.

'It doesn't matter any more,' said Phil. 'We'll be leaving tomorrow.'

'Oh?' It seemed very abrupt, and idiotically upsetting. I didn't want them to leave me to cope with the aftermath of two murders by myself. I looked at Thea, hoping she could read my thoughts.

'We've been arguing about it,' she said, disarmingly frank as ever. 'I was hoping to stay on here.'

I knew better than to reveal to Phil that she and I had already discussed the matter. I merely said, 'I'll miss you if you go. It's been nice having somebody in the house.' I looked at Phil. 'And the police protection's been reassuring, too.'

He puffed out his cheeks. 'Don't give me that,' he said. 'I've hardly been here all week.'

'Well, you were quite a lot better than nothing.' They both looked at me, checking whether or not I was being arsy. I smiled. 'No, but really, I hate to see you go.' I looked round at the disorganised room, full of boxes and sad furniture. 'You'll never finish all this by tomorrow, will you?'

Phil groaned. 'We've given up hope of that. I'm going to call a house clearance outfit. They can just take the lot. We've boxed up the bits to keep. It's not a lot, to be honest.'

A kind of panic gripped me at the thought of Helen's lovely things being bundled off to various jumble sales and salerooms. 'No!' I said. 'You can't do that. Why did you leave it a year, if that's all you're going to do?'

'That's what I said,' Thea remarked.

'What about Caroline?' I said, determined not to let her slip out of the conversation completely. 'She might want a few mementoes. She liked Helen.'

Phil took a deep breath, assembling his energies for the female onslaught. 'I don't really think she warrants much consideration,' he said. 'She's remarried now. Her life as a Hollis is over.'

It was an odd way of putting it, revealing his instinctive male sense of ownership over his wife, marked by the surname that she had rejected in favour of another man's. I couldn't begin to imagine how that felt, but he obviously didn't like it. I glanced at Thea, wondering if she was thinking along similar lines.

It was hard to tell, but it did occur to me that she might be entertaining the idea that her own surname could one day be Hollis, in which case she too might feel justified in keeping some of Helen's things.

I lost patience. 'Phil,' I said, rather loudly. 'There are at least three of us who have been too polite and restrained so far for our own good. Caroline, Thea and me. And you've been too distracted to realise that we might well fancy some of this stuff. Not just clothes and jewellery but furniture, rugs, pots and pans. You don't need the money a house clearance chap would give you. It would be hardly anything, anyway. If it's all too much for you, then get out of the way and let me and Thea sort it out. We can get Caroline to come over as well, if she wants to.'

He was genuinely surprised. 'For heaven's sake!' he exploded, looking at Thea rather than me. 'Why the bloody hell didn't you *say*?'

She made no reply, just stood her ground and let his words echo around the room. I could manage no such composure. 'How could she?' I demanded. 'She doesn't know where she stands, what her position is with your family. Have a bit of sense.'

He stood up very straight. 'Listen,' he snapped. 'I've been landed with a double murder investigation over the past few days. I get bombarded with calls, reports, demands, crackpots every five minutes. Nothing's as I planned. Even the dogs have hardly seen me. Quite frankly, the sooner I get shot of all this garbage, the better I'll be pleased.'

This silenced me. I hardly dared look at Thea, for fear she would reveal a sudden distaste – or worse

– for him, if this is how he behaved. Did he always get so stressy when he had to find a murderer? Or was there something particularly bothersome about this one?

Thea smiled at him, a smile full of understanding and forgiveness and unmistakable affection. 'I know, Phil,' she said. 'You don't have to get so aggressive about it. It's not your fault the week's been ruined.'

It was dreadfully sad for a minute or two. The word *ruined* hung in the air. So whose fault is it? I wanted to shout, knowing we couldn't find an answer to that. I felt a sharp stab of rage against the unknown murderer. Even if they – he or she – thought it mattered less because Gaynor and Verona were virtually alone in the world, the ripples still spread far and wide.

'So make sure you catch the bastard,' I said.

'Right,' Phil nodded. 'I intend to.'

I wasn't prepared to leave it there. It was impertinent and inappropriate of me, but I was sufficiently involved to risk it. Phil was being unnecessarily grumpy with me and I wanted to understand why.

Thea was standing close to him, a hand on his back, an intimate touch that spoke volumes about her abiding fondness. I imagined her fingers, slowly stroking him through the jumper, sensual and proprietorial. He was a lucky bloke. I could see him leaning back into her touch, a distant look in his eyes.

'Are you saying you think you're close to making an arrest?' I asked, using words from countless television dramas.

He wanted me to go. We were standing in the hall, all three of us, and I was inching my way towards the door.

'We're running some forensic tests,' he said. 'When I get the results I might know enough to take action.'

I remembered the mugs carrying two sets of fingerprints. 'You'll already have found Caroline's prints on things in Gaynor's flat,' I guessed.

He nodded. 'Doesn't mean anything. We know they knew each other.'

I remembered something else. 'The stuff in the attic. What about that?'

He put up a hand. 'I can't reveal what we've found. Surely you understand that. A careless word now could mean the whole case collapses.' He was almost pleading with me. 'You have no idea how careful we have to be these days.'

Thea moved, just a slight forward tilt, but it felt as if she was urging me to leave. Phil was between us, looking at me but in physical contact with her. Suddenly I understood something: he had not moved on from twenty years ago. He couldn't grasp that I was no longer the same obsessive teenager I'd been then, despite what I'd tried to tell him in the car the day before. Knowing this made me volatile and foolish, but also somehow *dear* to him. It was pleasing to be loved, after all, and perhaps he had known more than I realised about my feelings then. I had to put him straight, if only for Thea's sake.

'Phil, I'm not sure how to put this, but I should point out that we're not youngsters any more. I'm thirty-six. You don't have to treat me so carefully.' I floundered, aware of putting myself in a very embarrassing situation if I didn't watch out.

Thea, sweet Thea, came to the rescue.

'Ariadne's trying to tell you that she's grown out of the crush she once had on you,' she said, her tone suggesting that he was the one risking embarrassment, not me. 'Although I'm not sure why she feels she has to say it *now*.' She raised an eyebrow at me.

I groaned. 'There's never going to be a perfect moment, is there?'

Thea gave a look of commiseration, and Phil shook his head. 'I'm tired,' he said. 'I'm going to sit down.'

Thea came outside with me, which I hadn't expected. 'We're not leaving until after lunch tomorrow,' she said. 'So I'll come over and say goodbye in the morning.' She leaned closer, glancing along the dark deserted street. 'I think he's right about Oliver Grover, you know,' she whispered. 'It makes good sense.'

'Not to me it doesn't,' I argued. 'And he'll have to come up with some very good proof to convince me.'

CHAPTER EIGHTEEN

Unlike the previous night, I slept badly and was up before seven next morning, fuelling up the Rayburn for the extra heat I awarded myself at weekends. The gloomy prospect of Thea and Phil departing demonstrated how lonely a life I led. The news of Verona's death seemed to have stunned everybody into silence. No one had phoned or visited me to talk about it. Either they were too shocked, or they suspected that I'd done the wicked deed – or they'd simply forgotten all about me. I fiddled with the airlock on one of my wine demijohns and knew I'd have to seek human company or drive myself mad worrying about murder and wrongful arrests.

For no better reason than that she was the closest geographically, I walked to Turkdean at nine, in search of Ursula. I went slowly, but it still took barely half an hour to get there. It was an unsocial time to call on somebody, but the situation seemed to justify unsocial behaviour. However, after several loud knocks on the front door, I started to think my journey had been in vain.

'Urgghh?' came a voice from above my head. Stepping back, I looked up to see Annie leaning out of an upstairs window. 'Is your mum in?' I asked.

'Dunno,' said the girl, plainly only just surfacing for the first time that morning.

'Oh.' I hesitated. 'Well...'

Then the front door opened and a very sick-looking Ursula appeared. I called up, 'It's okay, Annie. She's here.' The girl disappeared without another word. 'What on earth's the matter?' I demanded of Ursula. 'You look terrible.'

'Haven't you heard?' She looked at me as if I was insane and possibly dangerous. 'About Verona?'

'Yes, of course I have. But—' I wondered briefly whether it was monstrous of me not to be as obviously distraught as Ursula was.

'She was *murdered*,' the woman wailed. 'The same as Gaynor. What in the world is going on here?'

I pushed my way in, leaving my boots inside the front door, and most of my spirits with them. This was going to be a grim and gruelling conversation.

Ursula led me into her front room, where the curtains were still closed and no discernible heating in operation. She slumped onto a sofa where she had obviously been for some time, and left me to choose between two matching armchairs. 'I'm so *scared*,' she shivered. 'Absolutely terrified.'

'But why? Has somebody said something? Have you been attacked?'

'Not for myself, but for Annie. Somebody's slaughtering young girls, out there. I can't let her out of my sight until he's caught.'

There were several things wrong with this. 'But Gaynor and Verona weren't young girls. They were both over thirty,' was the obvious first point. 'And they lived on their own. It's silly to be scared for Annie. She's only fifteen and she lives with you. There are no similarities at all as far as I can see.'

People never like to be told their fears are foolish. I've seen it before, the way they bridle, and accuse you of being feckless or wilfully blind. They talk about risk and say *but what if…*a lot. *How would you feel if it was you?* is another favourite. It's all impossible to argue with, and I didn't even try, at least to start with.

'It's a living nightmare,' she moaned, more than once. 'Here in these quiet little villages. It's obscene.'

For the first time I realised that nobody had spoken about the possibility of rape. It had not even occurred to me that the killer might first have assaulted his victims. Gaynor's body had been so nicely arranged, her expression so relaxed, I didn't think it was a factor at all. But Ursula was probably making the predictable assumption that sex must have been at least an element in the crimes.

'Obscene?' I repeated.

She flipped her hand impatiently. 'Depraved. Barbaric. I can't think of words strong enough.'

'You're doing quite well,' I assured her. 'Now calm down a bit, and let's see if we can come up with something useful.'

She stared at me through her odd glasses. They had a very prominent horizontal line across the lenses, which distorted her eyes. I always found them unsettling. 'Useful?'

I did my best to explain. We were local to the site of the murders. We knew the victims. We probably knew their killer – she flinched at that and rammed a hand over her mouth as if to stifle a scream. 'So we might be able to think of some motive, or suspicious connection that the police haven't managed to find,' I concluded.

'What connection?' She sounded so stupid I could have slapped her.

'I don't know. They were both single and living alone, for a start.'

'One rolling in money, and the other living from hand to mouth.'

I wanted to tell her about Caroline and the Masonic connection and Phil's suspicions of Oliver, but he had asked me not to. I didn't think it would reassure her much, in any case.

'Have you discussed it with the others?' I asked.

'Not since I heard about Verona. Before that, it was only Daphne and Pamela, really. Kenneth did phone, but I hadn't got time to talk to him. He sounded rather upset.'

'What day was that?'

'Oh, I don't know. Probably Wednesday.'

'I saw Daphne and Pamela at the Horse Fair on Thursday,' I contributed. 'And Eddie Yeo.'

'Oh, yes,' she agreed carelessly. 'I've seen him. I heard he's been going around with some woman.'

I swallowed. 'I think that was Caroline Johnson, and I don't believe there's anything in it.'

Too late I remembered that Ursula also knew Caroline from when she taught the Hollis kids. She seemed to find my news unremarkable, however, just nodding. 'It'll have been business, then. Eddie probably wanted to speak to Xavier about something. People do gossip, don't they? After all, she's way too good for him.'

'Is she? He's quite a big noise, surely.'

Ursula sniffed scornfully and said no more. She was a lot calmer than when I arrived. We sat quietly for a minute, and then Annie came in, still wearing a short nightshirt. 'You're here then,' she said to her mother. 'I thought you were out.'

'I'm here,' Ursula said.

'But you *were* out,' persisted the girl. 'I called you an hour ago and you didn't answer.'

'I haven't been out,' said Ursula. If she hadn't

thrown a nervous glance at me, I would never have taken the slightest notice. As it was, it became suddenly obvious that she was lying and didn't want me to know. She was such a fool. She could have said she'd gone into the garden, or even to the loo.

Annie, like most children, was quick to detect parental deception. 'Liar,' she said, easily. 'You're always such a liar.'

Ursula blustered. 'What a thing to say,' she protested. 'To your own mother.'

'It's true,' Annie shrugged. 'Off to see your boyfriend, I suppose.'

'Early on a Sunday morning?' Ursula tried to sound mocking. 'I don't think so. Anyway, I wasn't out. Leave it, will you. Go and have some breakfast.'

I had not known that Ursula had a boyfriend. And she hadn't wanted me to know. She turned her back to me, hiding her face. I couldn't imagine that it was important, so I left. She hadn't even given me a cup of tea.

With a feeling that I ought to steer clear of Thea and Phil for a while longer, even if it meant they went off without seeing me again, I drifted back to Cold Aston along the tree-lined road, which always felt like the approach to some gorgeous mansion. In fact, there was a manor house in Turkdean, as well as a Manor Farm, which must have created the wonderful avenue of trees originally. If I'd been a local historian, I'd have known for sure just who and when and how. As it was, I simply enjoyed the sensation of being alone on a country road with the wind rising, giving the trees an energy and character that I found exhilarating. I scuffed my feet through the dead leaves on the verge, and let my thoughts wander. Starting with Ursula's mystery lover, I was soon into my own plans and timetables. Having sold so much at the Horse Fair, I now had a serious shortage of items for the Christmas rush. At least two of the local shops were going to be clamouring for originals in the next few weeks. Without Gaynor, I wasn't at all sure I could satisfy the demand. But at least I had the buttonless coat, rescued from Gaynor's flat. And – the unworthy thought came unbidden – I would not now have to pay the knitter for doing it. If it sold, as I expected it to, it would be pure profit.

Before going back to the cottage, I called in at The Plough, which had just opened. I wasn't a very frequent drinker there, but they knew who I was. I couldn't claim close friendship with anyone in the village. Several of Helen's chums acknowledged me, but it didn't go further than that. I was strange in their eyes, with my paganism and the pig and the stripy hair. They never seemed to know what to say to me. I could easily imagine that some of them might think me capable of murder.

A couple in their early sixties were having a pre-lunch drink in the bar, sipping carefully and not talking. I knew them vaguely. He had just retired, and was making a nuisance of himself everywhere he went. He'd got heavily into Neighbourhood Watch, for one thing, going round to everybody, haranguing them about being careful about locking doors and windows. She was an amateur painter, producing some very unoriginal watercolours and trying to sell them at fetes and table-top sales. Since her husband's retirement she had looked haunted, forever chewing her lower lip and sighing a lot.

They looked up when I went in, seeming relieved to have company. 'Hello,' the wife said. 'We haven't seen you for a while.'

'No,' I agreed.

'Terrible business, that murder,' she went on, dropping her voice. 'You must have been so *shocked*.'

'Murders, you mean,' said her husband. 'There've been two, remember.'

The woman looked astonished. 'What?' she said.

'Two. They found another body at the Barrow on Friday. It was on the evening news.'

'You never told me!' she shrilled. 'I had no *idea*. Who was it?'

The man looked at me as if for rescue. 'Some girl,' he muttered.

'She was called Verona Farebrother, and ran a business in Gloucester,' I said. 'I knew her, the same as I knew Gaynor.' I tried to laugh. 'I'm beginning to take it all rather personally.'

'I didn't know,' the woman continued to complain. 'I feel such a *fool*. Henry, how could you not tell me?' She gave him a look of pure hatred. 'You do it on purpose, keeping things from me.'

'Don't be stupid,' he said, with insolent calm. 'I just assumed you would have heard.'

'Who are the people in Greenhaven?' the woman asked me, abruptly. 'Do you know them? Is it a relative of Helen's?'

'Her nephew,' I told her. 'And his girlfriend. He's actually a police detective. Rather senior, in fact.' I stopped, thinking I might already have revealed more than Phil would have liked. 'I think they're leaving today.'

'How convenient! Is he investigating the murder? Murders, I mean.' She threw another poisonous look at Henry.

'He is, yes.'

They hadn't really known Helen very well. They did not attend the funeral, and had made no particular attempt to offer me condolences. Perhaps that was why I found their interest now so irritating. Why, I asked myself, was I speaking to them at all?

Henry stuffed a pickled onion from a dish on the

bar into his mouth and spoke before it was properly disposed of. 'You've got in with them, by the sound of it,' he commented, with a knowing nod. 'Clever girl.'

It was like a punch in the belly. The insinuation was unbearable. I leaned over him, my broad shoulders casting a shadow across his upper body. 'I've known Phil Hollis since I was twelve,' I shouted. 'I knew his wife and his children – and his Aunt Helen. I'm his *friend*.'

'Hush, dear,' pleaded the woman. 'Henry didn't mean anything. Did you?' she demanded of him.

He was wiping his mouth with a napkin, as if I'd spat at him. 'Hollis?' he said, looking at me. 'His wife wouldn't be Caroline, would she?'

His manner was exactly as if we'd just exchanged pleasantries at a Buckingham Palace garden party. Being shouted at by a large, slightly mud-stained female was clearly well within his comfort zone. And it was entirely effective.

'Yes, as it happens,' I muttered.

'I knew Caroline, when she was Mrs Hollis,' he said. 'Now she's Mrs Johnson. I saw her at the Horse Fair on Thursday.'

'So did I,' I nodded.

'With that Yeo fella from the Council.' He beamed at me in triumph. 'And I've just seen him again, this morning, with that Mrs Ferguson who teaches at the big school, from Turkdean. They were sitting in a car having a real old ding dong.'

It was too much. None of it made sense and I just wished the whole of Gloucestershire would go to hell.

'I expect she was trying to persuade him to let her have planning permission for something,' said Mrs Henry brightly.

'Yes,' I said, rather loudly. 'I expect she was.'

Thea was standing beside Phil's car when I got back. He was in the driving seat and the dogs were not in the vehicle with him. I made a tentative judgement that the argument had been resolved in Thea's favour. I stood at a little distance, waiting to catch her eye. 'Staying, then?' I said, when she did finally look at me.

'That's right,' she nodded.

Phil didn't seem to be harbouring any grudges. 'It makes sense,' he endorsed, from the open car window. 'If only so she can keep an eye on you.'

I hadn't expected to be factored into the decision and felt quite touched, even if he'd only meant it jokingly. 'Ha ha,' I said. 'You mean because I'm still a suspect?'

He took a deep breath, steadying himself. Then he looked at Thea. 'See you soon,' he said. She leaned down for a final kiss and I turned my attention to the dogs for a moment. Those dogs had a great knack of *milling*. They circled each other, sometimes one of them giving a stiff little jump, the spaniel perpetually flirting with the others. Collectively they presented a constant presence of skirmishing energy that I found persistently irritating.

I felt burdened by the events of the morning: Ursula's mysterious behaviour in particular. I ought to have told Phil that Ursula had just been seen in a car with Eddie Yeo, but his manner had not been inviting. Let him get on with his own business, I decided. I wasn't qualified to investigate murders. Anything I said or did was as likely to impede as to assist, and I was thoroughly sick of the whole thing.

Thea and I were left on the main street of Cold Aston with three bouncy dogs for company. 'So what happens now?' She asked the question that had been on my tongue.

I thought there was a serious risk of a rerun of a few days ago when we'd lost all enthusiasm for lunch, walking, driving – anything. I felt that it had already been a long day, and it wasn't even half over. I had no answer to the question.

But Thea seemed energised. 'Well, we're spoilt for choice,' she said. 'Finish the work on Helen's things; go somewhere interesting for lunch; talk through the murders and come up with the obvious solution; walk ten miles along one of these footpaths – or all of the above.'

'Or none,' I said. 'I've already walked three miles this morning and had a beer much earlier in the day than usual.'

'We might go and visit Caroline,' Thea said with a nervous look at my face.

I smiled. 'Don't you think Phil or one of his minions will get there before us? They've probably got her in that interview room with Baldwin and Latimer as we speak.'

'Baldwin and Latimer? Sounds like a make of fruitcake.'

She was already cheering me up. I described the detectives in detail, making her laugh.

'Actually,' I said, after a moment's thought, 'I keep thinking about Daphne Yeo.'

'Eddie's wife,' said Thea to show she was still keeping abreast of it all. 'Why?'

Before I launched into an explanation, I tried to lead her across to my house. But instead she insisted we go into Greenhaven and at least make a pretence of working.

'Daphne is the *angriest* person I know,' I said. 'I can actually imagine her sticking a knitting needle into somebody.'

'But would she sully the Barrow like that?' Thea wondered. 'I mean, as I understand it, it's a sacred place to you pagans. Wouldn't it ruin the vibes or whatever, to kill people there?' She paused. 'Or is that what it was always meant to be – a place of sacrifice? Would it be the normal natural place to perform an execution?'

'Hold on,' I pleaded. 'You're jumping all over the place. Sacrifice. Execution. Where did these ideas come from?'

Thea was moving around the room, collecting the last few things from the mantelpiece and putting them on the central table. 'I've been thinking about it,' she said. 'It all seems so ritualistic, two identical killings in the same place. It doesn't feel like the work of a furiously angry person at all. More like somebody making a very strong point.'

'Well, it hasn't worked very well, has it? None of us seems to have got the point so far.' I shuddered. 'Do you think they'll go on killing people until we understand the message?'

'Not at the Barrow, anyway,' said Thea. 'There's a twenty-four-hour police guard on it now.'

'I still can't understand why there wasn't before.'

'Nobody ever dreamed it would happen again. And they did send regular patrols past, to make sure it wasn't being over-run with gawpers. They thought that would be enough.'

I had more sense than to overdo any criticism of the police, so I just mumbled a faint *s'pose so* to that.

'Where does Daphne live?' she asked a few minutes later, moving to Helen's big dresser and checking that there was nothing left in its cupboards.

'Stow,' I said. 'She's got two teenage kids.'

'Does she know Caroline?' Thea frowned, trying to remember the connections between the various individuals.

I had to think about it. 'Presumably not, since she didn't recognise her at the Horse Fair when she saw her with Eddie. She just said he was with a new woman.'

Then I remembered the latest snippet from that morning. 'Eddie certainly seems to be spreading himself around. He was seen with Ursula Ferguson this morning, arguing with her in a car.'

Thea looked blank. 'Do I know her?'

'The one from Turkdean who used to teach Phil's kids. She was over here like a hare on Sunday evening. Phil gave her a cup of tea before you and I got back from our walk.'

'So she's the most local to the Notgrove Barrow,' Thea realised. 'Out of all your pagans, anyway.'

'Just about,' I acknowledged. 'But Oliver's gran lives in Naunton, which is only a couple of miles away, and the others are all within easy driving distance.'

Thea's look was of blank incomprehension. 'Is she a pagan as well? Oliver's gran?'

'What? Oh, no, of course not. I didn't mean that.'

'So what *did* you mean? Is Oliver a pagan?'

'No, no.' I put a hand to a sudden throbbing pain

in my head. 'I have no idea why I said it – it just popped into my head.'

'How peculiar,' Thea said, with another strange look at me.

Lunch was inexorably looming. I had food enough in my house, but it would all need cooking, and I wasn't in the mood. On the other hand, I wasn't keen to spend money in a pub, especially on a Sunday lunchtime when it might be crowded and noisy.

Thea, however, had apparently worked it all out. 'Listen,' she said. 'I've got a plan.'

It turned out that Thea had seldom been to Stow-on-the-Wold, despite living for much of her life in the next county. 'Why would I?' she demanded, looking around at it. 'Once or twice is probably enough to get the general idea.'

We meandered along the pavements, pausing to look in the shop windows, making rude comments about the prices and the shameless appeal to tourists. We had persuaded Daphne Yeo to come and meet us at the Queen's Head on the main square, and she had reluctantly agreed that she might manage to be there shortly after one. We went into the organic shop next door to the pub, where Thea bought some provisions and I considered how much money I might be making from my own garden produce if these prices were typical. But the fact that we were the only customers made me think again. The fruit and veg looked dusty and past its prime, and there were repressive notices all over the shop forbidding prams and justifying the locked freezers.

'Bit depressing,' I muttered to Thea as we left. 'What did you buy?'

'Some very expensive apple juice and a cake made of carrots,' she said.

'More money than sense,' I accused her. 'If you want food, just ask me. I've got mountains of it.'

She was quite excited by the Queen's Head. 'I'm still researching Cotswold pubs,' she said. 'So far I think I like The Butcher's Arms best, but I'd never be able to find it again. It's somewhere near Bisley.'

'Never heard of it,' I threw over my shoulder as I asked for two pints of the local brew.

'I'll pay,' she said, and I let her without a quibble.

Daphne was five minutes late, looking worried and preoccupied. I introduced her to Thea, reminding her they'd met briefly at the Horse Fair. 'Hi,' said Daphne, with little show of interest. We went to sit in the small area between the main bar and the open air bit at the back. For a moment we considering going outside, but the sun had disappeared and it looked chilly. There were fewer customers than I'd expected, and we had no trouble getting a table in a recess, with just space enough for three.

It was the first time I'd seen Daphne since Verona's death. I was still having trouble absorbing the fact that Verona too had been murdered, and was gone forever. It was as if my emotional limits had already been reached with Gaynor, with no space left for further shock or grief. The only feeling that had grown with the second death was fear.

Daphne wasted no time. 'Have they caught him?' she demanded, in a low voice, as soon as we were settled.

'Who?'

She stared at me as if suspecting I was deliberately teasing her. 'The murderer of course,' she hissed. 'Who do you think?'

'No, they haven't,' said Thea in a normal voice.

'Why did you want to see me anyway? It sounded very sinister.' She gave me a wild look. 'You don't think it was *me*, do you?'

I decided it would be too complicated to play games, and wouldn't get us anywhere anyhow. 'Daphne, you've been so angry lately. I know it's all about Eddie and your separation, but now people are dying all around us, well…' It was impossible to voice my thoughts. They already sounded stupid inside my head.

Daphne turned very pale. 'What?' She was no longer whispering.

'He's obviously putting himself about rather a lot,' said Thea. 'People are talking about him being with at least two different women. This sounds awful, I know – but what if he'd been with Gaynor and Verona as well? How would you have felt about that?'

I blinked at this, realising Thea was way ahead of me. She'd thought through far more motives and scenarios than I had. And she was a lot braver in making her accusations. She didn't even *know* Daphne. How could she be sure she wouldn't find herself on the receiving end of a steak knife or a broken beer glass?

There was a horrible hush, and then Daphne laughed. It sounded quite genuinely amused. 'Eddie doesn't "go with" women,' she said. 'And if he did, why should I care?'

'What do you mean?' I demanded. 'What are you saying?'

Daphne seemed perfectly relaxed. She swigged her beer. 'Not that he's gay, if that's what you're thinking. He's just not interested. Never has been, really. If you knew the trouble I had to go to to get those kids...' She rolled her eyes and Thea giggled.

'So he didn't know Verona or Gaynor?' Already I was crossing Eddie Yeo off the suspect list, and trying to bring myself to replace him with Caroline Johnson. But that had so many painful implications I found myself grasping for other names. Kenneth, perhaps. Or even Leslie.

Daphne gave me a patient look. 'Ariadne, I don't

know who he knows, do I? I haven't seen the bastard for six months. The kids go off with him at weekends, and come back saying practically nothing. I gather he's doing well at work, fingers in all the usual pies, slapping all the right backs. I'm getting along fine without him.' She smiled. 'I'm not even as angry as I was. You pointed that out yourself last weekend.'

'So what do you know about Caroline?' Thea asked, leaning across the table.

Daphne's response was blank. 'Who?' she said.

Before we could go further, the food arrived. We all had baguettes, mine filled with tuna. Eating out was sometimes tricky for me, partly because of the cost, but also because I routinely produced much better food than the average pub or restaurant did. I had even made my own ham the previous winter, steeping it in brine and molasses for a terrifying six weeks, and eating it for the next three months with no ill effects. It was infinitely more delicious than anything you could hope to buy. Tuna was one of the few things I was never going to produce for myself.

I finally got us back to the subject. 'You don't know her then?'

'I might by sight. What's her surname?'

'Johnson. She's the woman he was with at the Horse Fair.' I checked myself. 'And you did seem rather disconcerted then, to think of him with a new woman.'

She shook her head. 'Not that. It was just so strange to see him, out of the blue.' She took a bite of the bread and turned to Thea. 'Are you separated or divorced?' she asked.

Thea shook her head. 'Widow,' she said briefly.

'Ah. Sorry. Well, I hadn't realised what it would be like to see him again unexpectedly. Whatever I might feel about him now, there's a terrible familiarity that you can't escape from. That's why I was in a bit of a state on Thursday. I don't suppose it'll be the same next time I see him.'

I tried to guess what Thea was thinking. Was she jealous that at least Daphne's husband was still alive? Or was it cleaner and simpler to be widowed? Had she saved herself all the mess and muddle of a divorce in years to come? And where did she fit Phil into such questions?

'Have you got anybody else?' she asked Daphne.

Daphne choked slightly and shook her head. 'Do me a favour,' she said. 'I'm not that daft.'

I remembered that I had been inclined to wonder if Daphne herself had been the killer. That, more or less, had been my reason for asking her to have lunch with us. In a few minutes, the whole theory seemed to have crumbled to dust. I had known her for four or five years and had always liked her. She seemed steady, intelligent and determined to make a good life for herself by her own efforts. As a pagan she was more interested in the preservation of ancient wisdom than in gaining anything for herself. She was essentially a rural person, enjoying the vagaries of the weather and the changing seasons.

'Oh, well,' I said carelessly. 'That's you in the clear, then.'

She changed in seconds, her eyes boring into mine, her nostrils flaring. She looked at Thea and then back to me. 'Are you working for the police or something?' she demanded. 'Is this some sort of interview, with me as a murder suspect?'

Thea put a calming hand on Daphne's arm. 'Of course not,' she said urgently. 'It doesn't work like that, you know it doesn't. Ariadne didn't mean it to sound the way it did.' She gave me a withering look, which I didn't think I deserved.

Daphne calmed down only very slightly. 'You always manage to wind me up,' she accused. 'You never give it a rest, do you?'

Give what a rest? I wondered, startled by this attack. What was she talking about? It wasn't long before she enlightened me.

'Forever on about Eddie, for a start. And arguing with me every time I open my mouth. I don't know what I've done, apart from rubbishing your precious Freemasons, but I've had enough of it.'

I couldn't breathe for the injustice of it. All I could think was that Daphne must have gone mad. 'You're crazy,' I spluttered. I was worried that Thea might believe what Daphne was saying, but couldn't find words to defend myself. 'Completely mad,' I added. 'I've got no brief for the Masons, any more than you have. Why would I?'

Thea was having no luck with her efforts at restoring calm. Daphne pushed herself up from her seat, red in the face, her curly hair looking as if it had a life of its own. 'I'd better go,' she said. 'I don't know why it is, Ariadne, but you always seem intent on having a dig at me.'

I couldn't let her have the last word. 'You're wrong,' I insisted. 'Horribly wrong. I don't support Freemasonry – of course I don't. Whatever gave you that idea?'

She snorted at me, like a dragon. 'Liar,' she snarled. 'You and the others, forming your ridiculous women's Lodge. Don't think I haven't heard all about it.'

I felt sick. 'What makes you think I'm involved in that?' I managed.

'Don't try to deny it,' she threw at me, already walking away. I couldn't call after her – other people in the pub were already much too interested in our row as it was. It wouldn't have done any good, anyway. She'd just have ignored me.

Thea hardly moved. When I looked at her, she seemed frozen – I assumed with embarrassment or something like it. It so seldom happens that people get into real fights in public, at least in picturesque

Gloucestershire they don't. Extreme anger, violence, rage are all kept firmly out of sight in our circles.

Finally, Thea spoke. 'I see what you mean,' she said. 'That is a very angry lady.'

'It isn't true,' I assured her. 'Honestly, it's a downright lie. I had no idea there even *was* a women's Lodge until yesterday.'

'So who do you think told her about it?'

My mind was blank. 'I have no idea,' I said.

Apparently we were still on course for the remainder of Thea's plans for the afternoon. We finished our lunch, with me still feeling shaky at the unprovoked assault from Daphne. The weather was better when we emerged onto the town square, with the impressive library dominating the top end and a few more people strolling about.

'Home, James,' she ordered. 'Next we walk those dogs.'

Trekking across the fields again with Thea reminded me how imminent Samhain was, with the mists and imaginings that went with it. I wanted to clutch hold of its significance, and not let it flit by without due observance. At least I was in the right setting – much more so than being shouted at in a pub, anyhow.

The dogs were ecstatic, remembering the path and confidently bounding ahead of us. The absurd long-tailed corgi waddled cheerfully behind the others, occasionally moving up a gear and bounding in a comical motion like a speeded-up toy. The spaniel flittered back and forth, the long hair giving it a fuzzy outline, the crazy ears flapping. I had gathered up some beans and apples for the pig, filling a carrier bag with autumn bounty for her.

'I'll have to get some proper food for her this week,' I noted.

'Proper food?'

I laughed at myself. 'What a thing to say! I meant commercial pig nuts. She needs building up before she farrows. And there won't be much left in the woods by this time.'

We had become good enough companions to be able to walk along without saying much. I watched her now and then, assessing her. She was in her early forties, still lovely, but soon destined to fade. In her case, I could see that it wouldn't matter. She had so many virtues that had nothing to do with looks, that losing them might almost be a relief. I could imagine how burdensome it could be, attracting people simply by letting them see your face. Not that I'd ever had that problem. They looked at me, yes, because I was big and vivid and confrontational. But they weren't magnetised like they were with Thea. Just spending a few minutes on the pavements in Stow had demonstrated how it was with her. They softened at the sight of her. They slowed their steps, and somehow *bathed* her in approval. And not just the men.

But there was a large unspoken matter lying between us. Daphne's accusations still rang in my ears and I assumed Thea must be hearing the same echo. She must at the very least have questions for me, to straighten out the ragged contradictions over the tortured business of Freemasonry. I had tried, I assured myself, to avoid telling any direct lies. I had convinced myself that the details I had failed to mention were in any case irrelevant. I had foolishly overlooked Daphne and her obsession.

Three or four times, the spaniel came back to Thea, and stood on its back legs, reaching up to adore her. She always stopped, bent down and fondled the mottled black and white face. Usually she crooned a few words of nonsense at the same time. It was all perfectly easy and unselfconscious. Fancy letting yourself go like that, I marvelled. Fancy allowing such naked love for an animal its full expression. I felt tears prickling, the third time it happened. Alarmed at myself, and the obvious onset of some sort of insanity, I picked up a stick that was lying by the path and started whacking nettles and dry dock stalks.

'Watch out,' came a voice that was not Thea's. 'I've got a nettle down my neck.'

I turned, and not far behind me was Ursula

Ferguson, approaching from the left, which was roughly the direction of Turkdean.

'Well, you shouldn't creep up on people,' I said.

Thea had been slow to realise we'd got company, having gone trotting ahead with the dogs. When she did finally stop and turn to see what was happening, she jumped. 'Where did you spring from?' she gasped.

Ursula pointed back the way she'd come. There was a dip, which might have once been an old road or waterway, which had hidden her from view. 'I've been trying to catch up with you,' she said. 'But I didn't like to call out.' She glanced around as if wary of invisible marauders.

'Which one are you?' Thea asked, with a visible effort to attach a name to the face.

'I'm Ursula. The one who taught the Hollis children when they were at school.'

'Got it!' Thea clicked her fingers. 'Nice to meet you.'

Ursula smiled briefly. 'Actually, I thought you would have gone by now. Weren't you only staying the week?'

'Phil's gone,' said Thea. 'I'm staying on for a bit. We didn't finish the job properly, you see.'

'Job?'

'Clearing Auntie Helen's house,' Thea elaborated. 'But I'm taking a break. We've just had lunch in Stow.'

Ursula looked as if she had no need of such information. She looked hot and worried. But she was unfailingly polite. 'I like Stow,' she said. 'When you think of the state the rest of this country is in, you can hardly fail to appreciate the wonderful little towns we have all around us.'

'It's certainly very law-abiding,' said Thea, trying to be diplomatic.

'Oh yes,' I said, feeling increasingly angry. 'The only law that gets broken around here is the one about killing people.'

We were within earshot of Arabella's domain. She could hear us, and I could just detect her questioning grunts, as she asked herself who might be coming to visit. 'Better hold onto the dogs,' I said to Thea. 'After last time.'

'Don't worry,' she assured me. 'They'll keep their distance.'

Arabella was unmistakably hungry. She surged towards my bag, frustrated by the intervening fence, which seemed suddenly rather insubstantial. 'Sorry, babes,' I said. 'I've been keeping you on short rations, haven't I? We'll move you back to the village this week, where I can feed you up.'

She gobbled the apples and beans with no ceremony whatsoever. Watching a pig eating is a salutary experience. They appear not to use their tongues at all, but operate the lower jaw like a shovel, sometimes tossing food up and grabbing it just before it lands, getting a better hold. The clichés and references people use about pigs' feeding habits are perfectly apt. You can argue that pigs are not dirty, but you can't claim delicate table manners for them.

'Heavens,' said Ursula, rather faintly. 'She made quick work of that.'

I was still wondering why Ursula had come to join us the way she did. Had she seen us across the fields and decided on a whim? Had we coincided with a more purposeful trek onto the upper levels of the wold? 'Do you often walk up here?' I asked her.

She shook her head. 'I don't usually have time. I wanted some space to think. Annie's got her ghastly music turned up to deafening pitch and I had to get out.' This was quite a change from the paranoia of the morning, but I was tired of seeing conspiracy everywhere. In fact, I was feeling generally weary, after a full week of the worry and confusion that followed Gaynor's death. All I wanted to do was slump in front of my spinning wheel and let the world get on without me.

'You haven't met Arabella before, then?' Thea said.

'Oh, yes. When she was in Ariadne's back garden, I saw her quite often.'

'What did you need to think about?' I interrupted, surprised that Thea hadn't switched into detective mode herself and picked up on

Ursula's remark about needing to think.

'You can have three guesses,' said Ursula.

'I gather you were with Eddie Yeo early this morning,' I said, still in my no-beating-about-the-bush mode. 'Before I dropped in on you at nine o'clock.'

'What if I was?' she flashed. 'What's it to do with you? And it was half past nine, not nine o'clock.'

'I just can't imagine what you and Eddie could have to talk about,' I said.

'Can't you?' she asked me. 'What do I have to talk about with half the people around here?'

'School, I suppose,' said Thea. 'You must know most of their kids.'

'Precisely,' said Ursula. 'Tom Yeo is a boy with problems, causing a lot of disruption in class. His father has been asked to attend several meetings and totally failed in his duty. I took it upon myself to flag him down this morning when he came through Turkdean. I didn't want him in the house, waking Annie, so I sat in the car with him and gave him a serious drubbing about the boy.' She took a long self-satisfied breath. 'And I think I can say I finally got through to him.'

'Well done you,' said Thea.

'He even ended up promising to start fundraising for the Biology lab, at his Lodge. We need a lot of new equipment, and the Head says the budget can't stretch to it.'

Thea threw me a look, as if to register that she knew this was a delicate area between us, which would soon have to be confronted. 'We had lunch with Daphne today,' Thea said to Ursula. She made me think of poker players, throwing down an unwanted card, leaving everyone to guess whether it was significant or not. 'We wanted to talk to her about Eddie.'

'Oh?' said Ursula. 'And what did she say about him?'

Thea laughed gently. 'That he doesn't much like women, apparently. Which is a bit of a surprise, considering he seems to spend a lot of time with them.'

'You mean you wanted to find out what's going on between him and Caroline,' said Ursula, with a dash of impatience. 'Well, they've always been friends, haven't they? Their fathers knew each other, or something. What's all the drama about?'

The word *drama* was still in my ears when there was a sudden shout. Thea's dog set up a frenzy of barking, which badly upset Arabella. And that made her repeat, with considerably more serious consequences, her clumsiness of a few days earlier.

There was some crashing about in the undergrowth, which confused the pig even further. With a long series of loud warning grunts she rushed off to investigate.

When a large sow makes that particular noise,

even her beloved owner knows the only thing to do is to back off. Pigs are very heavy. And they can run faster than most people assume.

Arabella had never really taken to men. Mostly this was due to unfamiliarity, but I think she must have been ill-treated as a youngster. But she had no malice in her. All she meant to do was see what was going on in the woodlands she regarded as her territory. But she never could see very well, and somehow the man and the pig – just as the pig and dog had done – found themselves on a collision course. We heard the impact. The pig emitted loud sounds of concern, and the human being gave one scream of agony and then fell silent.

'My God,' said Thea. 'She's killed somebody.'

Somehow all three of us managed to clamber over the fence and run to see what was happening under the trees. Thea's dogs waited cautiously on the safe side of the barrier, which earned them my respect, even in the midst of the crisis.

We found Kenneth sitting on the ground cradling his right leg.

'It wasn't her fault,' he said through gritted teeth. 'It's my stupid bones. But I'm very much afraid I've broken something.'

For a few seconds the three of us stood gaping, each waiting for the others to take action. For some reason I expected Thea to be hugely efficient in a crisis, well versed in first aid and a thoroughly calming presence. In fact, she showed no initiative at all, and it was Ursula who stood forward and asked Kenneth if he thought he could walk at all.

'Of course not,' he grated.

'Haven't you got a mobile with you, any of you?' Thea demanded.

Ursula and I both shook our heads. Kenneth seemed to find the question too ridiculous to bother with an answer. 'Haven't you?' I said.

'I left it at the house,' she admitted. 'One of us had better run for help, then. I suppose I'll do it.' The logic was opaque, but we all seemed to feel it made a sort of sense.

'If you cut across that field there —' I pointed, 'you'll come to a farm just behind those trees. It's only ten minutes if you run.'

'What if there's nobody in?' she said. 'I won't know where to go next.'

'It's a normal working farm,' I said. 'There's always somebody in.'

'The dogs'll follow me,' she worried.

'Let them,' I said, glad to have them out of the way.

She went off at a trot, cutting the awkward figure that running women generally do. The three dogs scampered merrily round her, until she shouted them out of her way. I watched her for a full minute before attending to the casualty. He was beyond pale and into green. 'What on earth were you doing here anyway?' I asked him, trying to remember what we'd been saying and whether he might have overheard anything important. Had he somehow followed us, and if so, why?

Arabella had found something edible in Kenneth's bag, and I leaned down to examine it. It looked like a jumble of nuts, mushrooms, sloes and haws. The pig was finding much of it less than delicious, or so it seemed from the way she nosed through it without taking much into her mouth.

'There's your answer,' Kenneth choked. From his greenish colour I understood that he must be in considerable pain.

'I see. Gathering nature's bounty,' I said, trying to sound as if this was perfectly normal. 'I think haws is going a bit far. They're utterly tasteless.'

'Jam,' he mumbled.

'Jelly, actually,' Ursula corrected. 'And it's still tasteless, even then.'

'Kenneth,' I said, 'does this have anything to do with the rumours about you being short of cash?'

'Ariadne, *please*,' Ursula insisted. 'It really isn't the time for that.'

But I'd guessed that it would help to distract him if I could keep him talking. He seemed to be of the same mind. 'If you like,' he said. 'Free food, you see. Can't spend anything till the end of the month.'

'Well,' I consoled him, in terribly bad taste, 'at least now you'll get some free meals in hospital.'

He managed to laugh, which endeared him to me and seemed to make him feel a bit better too.

Ages seemed to pass, while Kenneth twitched alarmingly, his legs jittering as if with extreme cold. But the pain was apparently easing. My main – though unspoken – worry was that Arabella would be in serious trouble, and so would I by association. Although Kenneth had admitted that it wasn't her fault, she had caused him injury and the woods were open to the public, with a footpath running through them, not to mention the Gloucestershire Way just to the north. There was no place for homicidal sows in this pastoral scene. My best hope was that I'd be ordered to confine her where she could do no further damage. She looked so innocent and unconcerned in the middle of the disaster she'd wreaked, as if human beings were irrelevant and even perhaps invisible to her. She was such a peaceable animal, self-possessed and contented. It was sheer bad luck that Kenneth had managed to get under her feet as he did. And it had to be Kenneth, of course. Anybody else could just have rolled aside, with no harm done. His brittle bones simply weren't up to such a steamrollering.

At last a battered Land Rover came into view, driving in a straight line across open fields. A grizzled farmer emerged from one side and Thea from the other. 'Ambulance be coming,' he said, in

an accent one seldom heard any more. He must
have been over seventy and I was surprised to note
that I didn't recognise him.

'Will it be able to drive out here?' Ursula asked.

'It's an air ambulance,' said Thea, with a hint of
importance. 'Helicopter.' We heard the whirring in
the sky a few seconds later. Thea and the farmer ran
out into the open field and started waving.

A landing helicopter is a thrilling event. The
noise and wind and aura of crisis made everything
seem overwhelming. Afterwards I couldn't properly
remember the sequence of events, but they bundled
Kenneth onto a stretcher and into the bowels of the
machine. At the last moment, Kenneth stirred
himself and fished in the pocket of his trousers. He
produced a set of car keys and handed them to me.
'It's in that layby on the main road,' he panted.
'Someone'll nick it if it's there for long.' Then off
went the helicopter like a frenzied bee. We were left
just looking at each other. 'We'd better get hold of
Pamela and tell her what's happened,' said Ursula.
'I'll do it.'

Thea and I trudged back to Cold Aston hardly
speaking. The dogs had apparently got the
message that there was no more fun available,
and they followed us meekly, heads down. We felt
drained and shocked, and there didn't seem to be
anything much to say. The afternoon was fading,
and neither of us had much idea of what

happened next. 'It'll have to be reported, I suppose,' said Thea. 'The hospital will have to alert the police.'

'Poor Arabella,' I sighed. 'I'm sure she didn't mean any harm.'

Thea retrieved her mobile phone from Greenhaven, rather rueful at having failed to take it with her on our walk. 'Phil's going to tell me off about that,' she said, showing little sign of apprehension at the expected chastisement.

By an unspoken agreement, she came into my house, having shut the dogs in Greenhaven. It was half past three, and the sky had clouded over. Inevitable thoughts of the dark evening ahead began to loom.

'Isn't Phil coming over this evening?' I asked her. Something about the way they'd parted earlier in the day seemed to imply something ominous.

'That's what I'm going to ask him,' she said. 'It depends how busy he is.'

She spoke to him unselfconsciously, in my main room, starting with a brief factual account of the accident to Kenneth's leg. She laughed at something he said, and then, with a glance at me, reassured him that there was no need to worry. There were several minutes more, which I tried not to listen to, but he had obviously asked her about my pig, among a lot else. Then she asked him if she would see him that evening. The threads of need, or desire, or even anxiety were barely discernible in her voice.

She was quiet for a while, listening to something lengthy from her lover. 'All right,' she said. 'Good luck.'

CHAPTER NINETEEN

It was a short interlude of calm. We were both on edge, waiting for something to happen. 'I wonder if Pamela's going to be furious with me,' I said. 'Letting my pig almost kill her fiancé.'

'Why was Daphne so beastly to you?' Thea asked, at last. It was uttered casually, as if it followed naturally on what we'd been saying, but I knew it was an important question.

'She got it wrong,' I said, needing to convince her. 'I was never remotely tempted to join Caroline's silly Lodge. I truly never knew she'd got it off the ground. She approached me two or three years ago, very obliquely. I hardly even understood what she was talking about. I don't know where Daphne got the idea that I was involved. That's the thing with the Masons, you see. It's so much whispering and false rumours, all kinds of stories get around.'

'But it was a secret – the all-women Lodge. You had no idea that Gaynor and Verona had joined?'

'Right!' I almost shouted. 'I still can't believe it.'

'And Daphne thought you'd joined them as well. She was so furious about it.'

'She's been scratchy with me for most of the time I've known her,' I said. 'But I don't think she really believed I was a secret Mason. She would have said something earlier. I think she's only just been told, by somebody who's trying to stir up trouble, or else she's just got hold of the wrong idea.'

'And it all blew up because you said she was in the clear as the murderer,' Thea remembered. 'That really pressed a button.'

'Do you think she was protesting too much? Could she still be the one?'

'I don't know.' Thea shook her head. 'But I think we can delete Ursula Ferguson. That story about Eddie's troublesome son sounded convincing to me. I think she's much too bound up with her job to have time or energy for murder. She's just a typical teacher.'

I winced. 'That sounds a bit dismissive. Don't you like teachers?'

She grinned. 'I'm in awe of them,' she corrected. 'They're like another species to you and me. I only know two or three, but they always seem completely immersed in school – it's like trying to do three demanding jobs at once. They never even have time for their own kids or friends and anything really. They might murder some ghastly offensive kid in a fit of insane rage, but not a carefully planned ritual like Gaynor and Verona.'

'Hmm,' I said. 'But Ursula does find time for the pagan activities. She's really very committed.'

'Is she?'

I thought about it. Compared to Daphne or Pamela or even Verona, Ursula actually devoted very little time to the group. She came to meetings, giving us her attention for a few hours and then disappearing until the next time. 'Maybe less than the others,' I admitted.

'And Oliver Grover – what do we think about him?'

'I think I might just have believed he'd killed Gaynor – though that was hard enough – but I can't see the slightest reason why he'd go for Verona. If he thought she'd found him out over Gaynor, would he do an identical ritualistic killing? What would that be about?' I shook my head forcefully. 'No, I'm deleting him as well.'

'What about Leslie?'

I sighed. 'Leslie's too *limp*,' I judged. 'It defies belief that he could ever kill anything. He almost fainted at the bullock slaughtering.'

'The what?'

I explained. Thea gulped a few times, and changed the subject.

'And Kenneth?' she said.

'He was gathering free food in the coppice. He

said he couldn't spend any money until next month. Sounds as if he's had his credit cards confiscated.'

'People in debt do desperate things,' she observed.

'But I can't see how it could lead him to perform two murders.'

'Not unless somebody paid him.'

We thought about that for a moment, and then both shook our heads.

Then the phone rang.

It was Pamela, screaming at me. In actual fact, she didn't scream, she kept her voice level. But she was definitely very upset. She said terrible things about poor Arabella and assured me that there would be a charge made against me for irresponsible pig ownership.

I managed to ask after Kenneth's leg. 'It's responding slowly to treatment,' she said tightly.

'I really am dreadfully sorry,' I said, ignoring a little voice in my head insisting that you should never say that if you were in danger of being sued for something. It sounded like an admission of guilt. The truth was, I genuinely did feel considerable sorrow about what had happened to Kenneth.

'I should hope you are,' she said. I could hear the sounds of traffic down the phone and asked her where she was.

'The hospital, of course. You have to go outside

to make phonecalls. I had to come on a bus, would you believe?'

I remembered the car, which Kenneth had entrusted to my care. 'Oh – the car,' I said. 'I'd better go and fetch it.'

'Could you bring it here and take me home?' she asked.

My mind always goes into paralysis when one of those IQ-test situations arises. 'If George and Jim are at Point A with two cars, and Cyril needs to get from Point B without passing his ex-wife's house at C, then how many car journeys are required, given that George is still a learner driver?' sort of thing. They seem to occur in real life quite regularly. I looked at Thea, realising that however it was to be managed, she would be required to help.

'Give me an hour or so,' I said to Pamela.

'Thanks,' she said. 'It's Ward B12. You can ask at reception.'

Thea's mind was obviously in better shape than mine. 'Right,' she said. 'It's simple. We'll both go to the layby. One of us will drive Kenneth's car, and we'll go to the hospital together, in both cars.' She paused. 'No, wait. I'll go to the hospital, and you can go to their house and wait there, to collect me when I turn up with Pamela. She can give me directions, then.'

'It'll take *ages*,' I grumbled.

'What else is there to do?' she asked. 'And I

suppose she thinks you owe her.'

She went across the road for a coat, and to give the dogs an early supper. 'And I'd better see if anybody wants to widdle,' she added.

It all happened in the same sort of dreadful blurry unbelievable fashion as the pig and Kenneth thing had. I was rushing, and rather cross, I suppose. And I didn't think I needed to look behind as I turned the car round. I did it every day; it was routine. If I sometimes mounted the verge outside Greenhaven, then so what?

There was a thud and a shattering succession of agonised howls somewhere at the back of the car. With an unbearable sense of guilt and dread, I switched off the engine and got out, but not before I had remained sitting there for a good thirty seconds. Thea was there before me. The big black and tan dog was writhing in her arms, still howling.

'It's Baxter,' she said tightly. 'I think you've broken his hip.'

I had to defend myself. 'I couldn't see the bloody thing – he must have been right behind me. He wasn't there when I got in the car.'

'He was probably coming to say hello,' Thea said, in a voice overflowing with grief. 'He wouldn't have expected you to be reversing.'

'We'd better take him to the vet,' I said. 'The one I use is in Cirencester – we'd better go there. Get him onto the back seat.'

I had to help her. The dog was heavy and wouldn't keep still. The noise it made filled my head with steam, until I could barely see, and certainly couldn't think. Thea got into the back with the animal. Then she had a thought. 'My phone,' she said. 'I'll have to get my phone.'

The car was still sitting straddled across the street, blocking any traffic that might want to pass. The other dogs were somewhere about, but I couldn't see them. I didn't dare move, in case I did more damage.

Thea was quickly back. 'Don't worry,' she said. 'He'll be okay. If he can make that much noise...'

I couldn't believe she was being kind to me after what I'd done. I almost wished Phil was there, to give me a bollocking. I could do with being yelled at just then.

At least I knew where the vet was. But I didn't have their phone number. Thea was ahead of me. 'We ought to call the vet and warn them we're coming. There might not be anybody there on a Sunday afternoon.'

'Try Directory Enquiries,' I said.

Thea fumbled with the phone, the dog still moaning maddeningly. 'They've changed it all, haven't they?' she remembered. 'I don't know what you have to do now.'

'Nor me,' I said. There had been a lot of adverts and leaflets when the change happened, all of which

I'd ignored. 'We'll just have to turn up and hope for the best.'

Suddenly I could smell something very nasty.

'Has he crapped himself?' I asked.

'A bit. He's distraught about it, poor boy. And it's mostly on my jumper.'

Needless to say, it was the jumper I'd given her. 'Bloody hell,' I said.

It was a nightmare journey. The dog whimpered and made a stink; Thea soothed him and I kept my foot down, window open and mind empty.

There was a special bell at the vet's for out of hours emergencies. When we rang it, a woman appeared and ushered us in with admirable composure. 'I live in the upstairs flat,' she said. 'I get all the out of hours work.'

'Bad luck,' I sympathised. 'I hope they pay you properly for it.'

She glanced at Thea, and didn't say anything. Obviously my comment was too insensitive to dignify with a reply. I was panting from carrying the heavy dog from the car. 'Can we get on with it?' Thea pleaded.

They disappeared into a consulting room, leaving me to flip through a stack of old magazines and read notices about worms and fleas.

They were ages. I heard the dog howl once or twice and the low murmur of voices, but nothing more than that. Fed up with the magazines, I decided to go and stand outside for a bit, just for a change of scene. Thea would come and find me when she wanted to be driven home. Only then did I remember Pamela, waiting at the hospital for us.

Cirencester was quiet, the chilly wind keeping most people indoors. The streets are all well-proportioned and tasteful, not so much self-conscious as self-possessed. Everything is solid and assured and well maintained. The power of money is mainly used to good effect, keeping the shops fully stocked and the park looking tidy. I almost never bought anything there, even on market day, but I was not averse to a bit of browsing from time to time. Now, waiting for Thea and Phil's suicidal dog, I wandered into the main street for a few minutes.

The first person I saw was Leslie Giddins. He was alone, walking towards me with a mobile phone clamped to his ear. I observed the process whereby he saw me with his eyes, but did not register who I was, his mind on the phone conversation. He came close enough for me to hear what he was saying, before he was aware of me.

'I know,' he was saying. 'Your grandmother comes first, I understand that.' Then it happened. 'Good God, Ariadne's here. Right in front of me.' He moved the phone away from his head and smiled at me. 'We were just talking about you,' he grinned.

'Oh?'

'This is Oliver. He's had to go and see to his gran. She fell over, or something. I'm afraid he—'

I snatched the phone from him. 'Oliver? What's the matter? Is she all right?'

'Ariadne? Where are you? I mean – where've you been? I've been trying to phone you all day. Gran's had a fall.'

'Has she broken anything? Where is she now?' I was startled by how distraught I felt at the idea of Sally being hurt.

His voice was low, as if Sally might be listening. 'I don't think it's terribly serious, to be honest. She missed her chair and sat down heavily on the floor. She says her hip is badly bruised, but she won't let me look. That's why I wanted you to come.'

'Did she call the emergency people?' Sally had a special gadget, which she was supposed to hang round her neck and use to summon help if she fell or felt poorly.

'No. She called me. She won't have the doctor – says he'll send her to hospital and she'll give up and die if that happens. You know how she is.'

I looked at Leslie, who was standing patiently waiting for his phone back. No prizes for guessing where Oliver had been when his grandmother tried to contact him.

'Listen, Oliver, I'm up to my eyes in stuff just now. Everything's happening at once. I can't really be of much use to Sally, anyway. She'll have to swallow her pride and let the doctor see her.' I endured the stab I felt at my own treachery. The awful thing was that Sally had every reason to resist medical attentions. She and I had both seen what happened to Helen at the very end.

'She won't do that,' he said. 'I can stay here tonight, and make sure she doesn't get any worse. And all day tomorrow, if I have to. But after that—'

'We'll worry about that when the time comes,' I said. 'Maybe it is only a bruise. Can she stand on it? Does her leg look straight?'

'Straight? When were Gran's legs ever straight?'

I laughed. Sally had been bandy-legged ever since I'd known her.

'Her foot isn't crooked, is it? If the hip's broken, the ligament that keeps your ankle straight doesn't work any more, and your foot looks weird.'

He paused. 'Hang on a minute,' he said. Then, 'No, her foot looks perfectly normal.'

'Good. Look, I'll have to go. I'm sorry, but she's got you. She'll be okay.'

'I hope you're right,' he said.

Before he could disconnect the phone, I had a thought. 'Wait – Oliver!' I shouted.

'What?' His voice was low and impatient.

'This probably isn't the right moment to ask, but it's been nagging at me most of the week. You know Gaynor.'

'Of course,' he snapped, and I winced at my own crassness.

'Sorry. Well what exactly did she do that lost you some business? Sally told me about it. Said you were furious with her. Then Daphne told me she'd heard about it, and it involved Gervase Johnson somehow.' I was speaking quickly, trying to keep it light so it didn't sound like an accusation.

'Ariadne, this really is not the time to talk about it. But as it happens, I can explain in about twenty seconds. You seem to have blown it up out of all proportion. It was nothing much. It wasn't really anything to do with Gervase, either. Gaynor just spoke out of turn. She didn't mean to. Wrong person at the wrong moment, that's all.'

'Was it to do with the Masons?'

He made a clicking noise. 'Well, yes, in a way. She let drop that I was on the square. He was so outraged he took his custom elsewhere. I was angry with her for about two days at most. Gran just happened to get an earful because she was the next person I saw after it happened.'

'Did you know Gaynor had joined the Masons?'

'Of course I did.' Of course he did. It explained nearly everthing.

'Okay. Thanks for telling me,' I said. 'Now go and see to Sally. Tell her I'll be round tomorrow.'

I handed the phone back to a forlorn-looking Leslie. 'Poor old Sal,' I said.

He sighed. 'We were going to the theatre this evening.'

'Why are you here then?' I wondered.

'Shopping,' he said as if that was obvious. He did have a bulky Waitrose carrier bag in one hand. 'It's my turn to cook.'

I had no patience with his dull domestic little plans. 'I must go,' I said. 'I'm due at the vet's.'

He didn't ask for more detail and I was in no mood to give an account of recent events. Somehow Leslie and Oliver had become insignificant bystanders in the rollercoaster that the day had become. Even if they had murdered Gaynor and Verona, it seemed to matter a lot less than Thea's distress and Sally's hip and Kenneth's pig-inflicted injuries.

Thea was talking to the vet woman in the reception area when I got back. There was no sign of the dog. Help! I thought. They've had to put it down. Phil was never going to forgive me.

I couldn't think of a safe way to phrase the question, so I just looked. 'I thought you'd gone off without me,' she said, only half joking.

'The dog?' I ventured.

'He's got to stay in overnight. The vet thinks the hip's just dislocated.' The parallel with old Sally Grover was inescapable. How strange life could be, I thought, ramming events at us in teasing conjunctions, forcing us to make comparisons.

'That's good, isn't it?' I ventured.

Thea sighed. 'Could be worse,' she conceded.

The vet picked up the vibes between us and smiled cautiously. 'He should be fine in a few days,' she said. 'He's a gorgeous dog.'

'He ran out right behind me,' I burst out. 'One minute everything was clear, the next—'

'It happens,' said the vet. 'Setters tend to act on impulse.'

It was a very diplomatic thing to say, I had to give her that. It wasn't going to help the atmosphere on the drive home, though.

Thea sat beside me in her smelly jumper, trying in vain to reach Phil on the phone. 'I tried twice at the vet's and he wasn't answering,' she said. 'When I phoned the police station, they said he was unavailable to take calls. What does that mean?'

'He must be out on some sort of mission,' I said. 'Staking out somebody's house, having to keep quiet.'

'I don't think so,' she said, her voice cold.

'I saw Leslie Giddins just now,' I said, in an effort to start a new subject. 'He was talking to Oliver on the phone. His gran's hurt herself.'

'Oh dear.' There was little interest in her tone.

'And Pamela's going to wonder where on earth we've got to.'

'I forgot all about that,' she said, reviving slightly. 'What're we going to do?'

'I don't know,' I admitted. 'It's nearly six already.'

'So?'

'Nothing, I suppose. Somebody else might have given her a lift by now.'

'She'll still want the car.'

'Mmm,' I said. 'Well, I'm thirsty and hungry. I'm not doing anything until I've had some tea.'

We went directly back to my house and I put the kettle on. Thea had decided not to disturb the two remaining dogs, if we were going out again in a little while. 'They'll be confused,' she said. We could hear the spaniel barking.

'She must have smelt you,' I said.

Thea looked down at her jumper in horror. 'Oh, God. I'll have to go and change, won't I.'

'I can lend you another one,' I offered. 'If you promise to keep it clean.'

'I'll do my best,' she grinned.

'Did you get any coffee?' Thea asked me, when I'd turned my attention back to the kettle.

'Bugger,' I groaned. 'Sorry. There's only tea, I'm afraid.'

I expected her to shrug and accept a mug of nice strong Indian brew, but she surprised me. 'No,' she said. 'There are limits. I can put up with rampaging pigs, damaged dogs, stinking jumpers, but only if I get a decent cup of coffee at the end of it. I've got a jar of Gold Blend over the road. I'll have to go and get it, whether it winds the dogs up or not. I won't be long. It's getting dark – I hope I'll be able to see in that house.'

'Take a torch,' I told her, getting on out of a drawer.

When I realised ten minutes had passed, I merely thought she'd gone to the loo, or been distracted somehow. Maybe Phil had finally called her on her mobile.

But the dogs were barking again, which seemed peculiar. Thea knew we were meant to take Kenneth's car back. Twelve minutes was too long to readily explain. I went to my door and looked across the street.

You can't tell what's going on inside a house just by looking at it from outside, especially when there's no electricity and no lamps had been lit inside. So I went over and tried to open the front door. It wouldn't budge. Why on earth would she lock it? What were the dogs barking at?

I went around the back, my mind paralysed by the strangeness. There were no answers to my questions and I wasn't in any state to make inspired guesses. The dogs had gone quiet, at least, which seemed like a good sign.

The back door was locked as well. 'Thea!' I called out. 'Where are you?' That started the dogs off again. I banged hard on the door. 'What's going on?' My head filled with a picture of Phil bending over the lifeless body of his beloved, blaming me even more than he was going to blame me about his dog.

I couldn't let it happen. I remembered the ladder and the wonky bathroom window, and got myself up there in seconds. The window came open quite easily, but I was almost too big to squeeze through it. I had to dive in head first, which was awkward and undignified, and left me in a tangle on the floor, my legs practically in the loo. I hoped I'd been quiet enough to avoid notice, even by the dogs. I stayed in a heap, not daring to move until I was sure of what was going on.

Somewhere I heard voices. 'Lucky we locked the doors. Has she gone?' a man hissed.

'Probably,' said Thea. 'But she'll know something's wrong. She'll call the police.'

Too late, I realised I should have done just that. Much more useful than sprawling on the bathroom floor.

'Why did you come here?' she asked, her voice sounding impressively steady.

'We needed to fetch something. I thought you were out.'

'Oh. What about the dogs? They wouldn't have let you in.'

'Shut up. I'm not explaining it all now. It doesn't matter. You're just stalling for time.'

I assumed he'd got that right. Thinking about it, the most likely explanation was that he'd crept in the back and quickly shut the dogs in one of the rooms downstairs. Then the dogs must have started barking when they realised they'd been tricked.

A woman's voice joined in. 'We thought you'd gone,' she said.

My heart was thundering so drastically by then that I could hardly hear what they were saying. The voices were familiar, but the identity of the speakers seemed to matter to me less than the fact of their intrusion and the idea that Thea was in danger. The rooms were unlit, but it was less dark than I'd expected. Half of me wanted to get to my feet and simply march right into the room and demand an explanation. I think the locked front door was the strongest reason preventing me from acting on the instinct to rescue my new friend. Instead I crawled very quietly and carefully out of the bathroom and onto the landing, where I could hear everything more clearly. Having made myself consider the situation logically, I was forced to admit to myself that Thea and I were trapped with these people and although I certainly hadn't thought through precisely what could happen if I charged in and made a lot of fuss, I had enough remaining wits to understand that it would almost certainly make things worse.

'We came here to get something,' said the man

again, with laborious significance. 'Something we left in the attic.'

So I had been right all along! The Masonic trinkets belonged to Eddie Yeo – whose voice I was now sure I recognised, despite not having heard him speak for nearly a year. He had a high voice, with careful vowels where he'd eradicated his Gloucestershire accent.

'They're not there any more,' said Thea sturdily. 'Phil took them away for examination. He found your fingerprints on them.'

The woman made a little moan and I realised Thea was addressing her, not Eddie.

'There! See what you've done, you silly bitch,' snarled Eddie.

The woman gave a choked sound, and I tried desperately to fill in the gaps caused by not being able to see their faces.

'You killed Gaynor and Verona, didn't you?' said Thea, with what seemed to me appalling recklessness. 'For some stupid reason to do with Freemasonry.'

I was so eager to know whether she was talking to one or both of them that I almost gave myself away.

The woman spluttered again. 'What?' she gasped. 'What are you talking about? Eddie didn't kill anybody. It was Ariadne who killed them.'

'You genuinely think that, do you?' Thea

sounded almost sorry. I was totally sandbagged by Caroline's firm assertion, as if it was plain fact. 'What a fool you must be,' Thea added calmly.

Eddie laughed nastily. 'You've got that right,' he said.

'Eddie!' Caroline's voice was shocked, confused, but still a long way from revising her opinion about me, I feared.

Thea seemed to have thrown every scrap of caution out of the window. 'It wasn't Ariadne, you idiot, it was Eddie. I think he brought you here to kill you as well. He wants to wipe out that whole group of women Masons. Isn't that right, Eddie?'

This time it was Caroline who laughed, though with no hint of mirth. 'He wouldn't do that,' she said. 'That's stupid.'

'So why has he brought you here? What did he tell you was going to happen?'

'Actually, I brought him,' said Caroline. 'I'd already decided I couldn't keep the new Lodge going without Gaynor or Verona. I was going to let him have the regalia and so forth.'

'You really did meet here, then, you three women? In Helen's attic? But why?'

'It had good vibes,' she said simply. 'And it fitted all the criteria. It was Gaynor's idea, funnily enough.'

'But weren't you worried that Ariadne would see

you? She lives right across the street.'

Caroline gave a loud sigh. 'We met on the nights she did her evening class. But the truth is, I was still hoping she'd join us,' she said. 'That was another reason why it seemed such a good place.' She made a soft little whimpering noise, for some unknown reason.

Eddie made a noise rather like a snarl. My stunned brain slowly came to the conclusion that if I *had* joined Caroline's Lodge, I might be lying in the Barrow's long grass as well as the other two.

Thea's voice suddenly sounded closer and I realised she was edging towards the door. 'He made it look as if Ariadne had killed them,' she said. 'With the knitting needles. And you fell for it. But surely Phil must have told you it couldn't have been her?'

'I haven't spoken to Phil,' she muttered.

'So you let this wretched little man talk you into suspecting your friend?'

'Mary stopped being my friend nearly three years ago,' she said harshly.

'Well, you've got it wrong,' Thea repeated. 'The murderer is right here in front of you.'

It still felt like wild fantasy to me. How could the irritating, pompous, self-satisfied Eddie Yeo *possibly* have committed two murders?

'But why would he? What would he have against those two girls?'

'Ask him,' Thea invited.

A short silence followed. It was getting much darker with every minute that passed. Then Caroline said quietly, 'You're my friend, Eddie – aren't you?'

He replied with a loud tirade that suggested his control was cracking. 'You think I could be a *friend* to someone as sick as you? *Friends* with a woman intent on perverting the Craft – polluting it in that disgusting way. Wearing our symbols, defiling our rituals. All I did was clean them out of the way, your revolting little Sisters. They had to go, it was obvious.'

Another stunned silence, and then, 'You *executed* them,' whispered Caroline. Thea spoke next. 'That's right! He stabbed them through the heart with the closest thing he could find to the ritual knife the Freemasons use. Because he saw them as traitors.'

'Really an execution, then,' said Caroline, sounding terrible.

'They were in her bag,' said Eddie. 'It made it seem right, somehow. I saw the points, sticking out.'

This was too much for Caroline. 'You're a monster!' she suddenly shouted. 'A stupid, bigoted, crazy monster.'

The slap was so explosive I almost felt it on my own skin. Both women shrieked, so I wasn't sure which had received the blow, although Caroline was the obvious choice.

Then Caroline spoke rather thickly. 'You can't hope to get away with it,' she said. 'Although maybe you think you will. You seem to have some kind of power complex.'

It did me good to hear her. It made up my mind for me. I'd never manage to get out of the house without them hearing me, not by window or door, and by the time the police could respond to any call I made, things might have moved on to a point where someone got killed.

'She's right, Eddie,' I said, showing myself in the doorway. 'Now have some sense and stop behaving like a lunatic.'

Eddie Yeo was a bureaucrat, for all his silly yellow car and ideas about the sanctity of male bonding. He was not particularly fit and neither was he very quick-witted. It seemed almost banal that he could have slaughtered two healthy young women out of some obsessive notion that not even his most rabid fellow Mason could have approved.

He had a knife in his hand, however, which I had not anticipated at all. In the gloom it had taken me a few seconds to register just what it was. Slowly I focused on a long pointed thing, with a blade that looked extremely sharp. I cocked my head at it, aiming for the less-than-impressed gaze that women throughout the ages have used to wither the male ego. 'Makes a change from knitting needles,' I said calmly.

'You...you...!' he said thickly, and the hatred on his face came as a serious shock. I forced myself to think.

'You hoped the police would suspect me of killing two women who were my friends,' I accused him.

'You flatter me,' he said, avoiding my eye. He opened his mouth to say more, but then closed it again. I took him to mean there had been no real plan behind the murders. He had simply wanted to annihilate Caroline's Lodge. And there was quite enough Masonic mumbo-jumbo to make him think he was justified. Reams of quotations from so-called ancient texts babbling about Betrayal and people being stabbed through the heart if they revealed secrets of the Craft. It was all part of the initiation rituals, with the knife pressed against the bare breast of the new recruit to warn him of what would happen if he transgressed.

The mystery of his involvement with Caroline still nagged at me. If I had understood things right up to then, she was his next potential victim. And he *had* just slapped her face. I examined her cheek in the poor light. It looked red from the blow.

'You truly didn't realise it was him?' I asked her.

'I had no idea,' she said with evident sincerity. 'I was totally convinced it must have been you – or just possibly somebody else from your pagan group. I *hated* that group, you see. They seduced you away from where you truly belonged – with me and my new Lodge.'

'Huh?' I choked, remembering what she'd said a few minutes earlier about hoping I'd still agree to join her. 'But I've never given you reason to think I might.'

'Verona thought you would. She could see how it was the obvious next step from paganism.'

'So why tell Eddie about what you were doing?'

'I didn't. Nobody did. We struggled to keep it a secret from anybody in the area. Gaynor especially was adamant that nobody should know about it – least of all you. But despite what people think, Freemasonry isn't really a secret society at all. I had to register my Lodge, list the members —'

'How many members are there?' I demanded. 'Only the three of you?'

'Three new initiates applied to join us this month, as it happens,' she said with dignity. 'By this time next year we'd have reached double figures.'

'And were you going to execute all of them, one by one?' I asked Eddie, aggressively. I found that despite his knife, I was not afraid of him.

Slowly, as he listened to us, his wrist had relaxed, until the point was directed more and more towards the floor. There was little risk, I judged, that he would try to use it, now there were three of us. But its very presence suggested that he had indeed been intending to kill Caroline, there in Greenhaven's attic. The idea was horrible.

And then, with a sense of everything coming into sharp focus, I allowed myself to remember how much I had hurt her when she had begged me to join with her in forming a new female Masonic Lodge. She had appealed to our friendship, reminding me how close we'd been, what fun we'd had when her children were small and life was fresh and good. And I had refused, not so much from a distaste for Freemasonry, as a refusal to become so permanently bonded to her. I couldn't face a friendship as all-consuming as that threatened to become. And between us, working as some dreadful emotional glue, was the lost Emily, the dead daughter who was an integral part of those happy memories. She had only been dead a few months when Caroline approached me with her proposal. I rejected the suggestion with unnecessary violence. And in so doing, I might have saved my own life. This last thought made the whole thing infinitely worse.

It could only have been ten or fifteen minutes since I had climbed through the bathroom window. The dogs were still quiet, and nothing seemed to stir in the street outside. Cold Aston was coldly ignoring us as we enacted a surreal climax to a horrible story. I don't think any one of us had the slightest idea of what might happen next.

Eddie was becoming more and more agitated, and he started to wave his knife with fresh vigour. 'I could slaughter the lot of you,' he said, in an obvious attempt to convince himself.

I almost laughed in his face. 'The Cold Aston massacre,' I said. 'You'd be famous for centuries.'

'That's enough,' said Thea. 'There's no need to say any more.' She seemed to be more upset than any of us. The room was very dark, lit only by the street lamp outside. Our eyes had adjusted, but suddenly I realised I could not see any expressions clearly.

Eddie made an angry snort, as if thwarted. 'Stay here,' he ordered us, brandishing the knife again. 'I'm going. You'll never see me again, any of you.' He pushed his face close to Thea's. 'You lied about Ariadne calling the police,' he accused.

'No,' she said. 'I truly thought that's what she would do.'

It didn't seem to matter. I felt limp and dirty and very *very* unhappy. 'Let him go,' I said.

He went, and for a few moments all we heard was footsteps, a yap from one of the dogs and the front door opening. Then there were bright lights and shouts and more barking, as if Eddie had triggered some bizarre new reality.

They arrested him without much of a struggle, and Phil came up the stairs with a bright torch. He shone it on our faces, one by one, and then took Thea into his arms.

CHAPTER TWENTY

We couldn't have a proper conversation by torchlight. There were too many pools of darkness, too many shadowed faces and unbearable emotions. Inevitably we all trooped over to my house, including Caroline, with the dogs somehow bringing up the rear.

We made Phil explain himself first. 'It was Ursula Ferguson,' he said. 'She had a call from Pamela at the hospital, when she couldn't get hold of Ariadne, and she came over here to see if she could find you. There was nobody here, and only the dogs in Greenhaven, the whole place dark. So she drove Pamela home, and then came back here. She found Ariadne's car, but still no sign of you two.'

'She ought to have guessed we were in Greenhaven,' I said.

'Well, she did, at it happens.'

'Why didn't she just knock on the door?'

'Because the house was in total darkness. And

she didn't want to set the dogs barking like she had the first time.'

'What on earth did she think was going on?' Thea demanded.

'The mind boggles,' I said, with a bitter laugh.

'But she didn't give up,' Phil continued. 'She went round the back, and saw the ladder. She actually climbed up as far as the window, and heard voices. Enough to know there was something highly unpleasant happening. So she contacted the police.'

'And you just sat outside waiting for something to happen,' I accused. 'He might have killed us all.'

'It was a calculated risk,' he said. 'We had no reason to think he had a weapon, for a start. We couldn't storm the house without alarming him, which was likely to be much more dangerous than just letting him walk away.'

'And,' said Thea thoughtfully, 'unless Ursula heard everything, you couldn't be entirely sure who exactly was the criminal. It might yet have been Caroline.'

'Precisely,' he said, with a fond smile at her, and a rueful grimace at his ex-wife.

It was late in the evening when we dispersed. Caroline had stayed on much longer than I had expected. She had phoned Xavier, her new husband, who promised to come and collect her.

The aftermath of Eddie Yeo's arrest was threaded

with all kinds of extraneous considerations. The two damaged hips could not be ignored – Phil's distress at his injured dog never quite left him, and I was weighed down even further by Sally's accident.

But the main obstacle to a full and frank debriefing was embarrassment. Thea seemed to be aware that she had missed something between Caroline and me, but didn't like to ask directly what it was. Instead we stuck firmly to Eddie Yeo's extraordinary attitude to female Freemasons. Caroline managed not to look at Phil throughout the whole conversation, but she did give an account that would probably satisfy a criminal court, when it came to it.

She had always admired the Freemason brotherhood, as Phil well knew. Her father had been a Grand Master, and she had grown up quite familiar with much of the symbolism. It had seemed almost inevitable when the idea eventually dawned on her that she might establish a Lodge of her own. The procedures already existed and she had little difficulty in gaining the acquiescence of the authorities in the Grand Lodge. Then she had set about discreetly recruiting her members.

'I knew Eddie didn't approve, but I had no idea he took it so personally. I still can't believe he decided he had to take it upon himself to destroy it completely. He was always rather pleasant to my face, when I saw him around.'

'What were you doing in his car at the Horse Fair?' Thea asked her.

Caroline giggled with threatened hysteria. 'That, oddly enough, was nothing at all to do with the Masons. He wanted Xavier to do him a patio in his new house. He was giving me a drawing of it. I do some of the admin for the business, you see,' she added vaguely.

Something reminded me of another niggling loose end. 'And what about Gaynor and Oliver?' I demanded. 'Why was that such a secret?'

'Secret? I don't think it was a secret. They were just pals, as far as I know.'

'But what was in it for *him*? Why did he drive her around when he was working?'

Caroline gave me a severe look. 'You have never appreciated Gaynor, have you? You always thought she was a pathetic little mouse with nothing to offer anybody. But Oliver thought she was good company. He encouraged her to join my Lodge, as well, of course. He liked her stories of her childhood in Wales, and she made no demands on him.'

'But she wanted to. She wanted to be in a proper relationship with him. She asked me to do a divination...' I trailed off helplessly. 'And when I told him she was dead, he didn't seem to care at all.'

'He cared,' said Caroline. 'We all cared.'

I looked at Phil. 'Didn't you suspect it was him,

right from the start?' I wanted to know. 'Right from when we found the stuff in the attic?'

'He was on the list,' Phil nodded. 'But the timing was all wrong. And there were none of his prints on anything.'

Then there was a knock on the door, and I opened it to Xavier Johnson. Small, smiling, he had a boyish, rather pixie-like manner. 'Come for Caroline,' he said. 'I hear there's been a bit of bother.'

She was at my side before I could turn round. 'Thanks for being so quick,' she said. 'I'm ready to go.'

'Won't you come in for a minute?' I remembered to say.

Caroline gave me a look. Then she tucked her hand through Xavier's arm in an old-fashioned gesture and steered him out into the street.

Thea left Greenhaven the next day, giving up on the impossible task of finding homes for all Helen's things. Phil had delivered his injured dog to his sister at Painswick, where he would get some dedicated nursing.

'Where next?' I asked her, remembering the house-sitting work.

'I'm not sure,' she said. 'But I have just seen that somebody's advertising for a sitter in Blockley, next March. Sounds like my sort of thing.'

'Blockley's nice,' I said non-committally. 'Maybe I'll come and see you while you're there. Meanwhile, be nice to Phil, won't you?'

'Yes, Mary,' she said with a disarming grin. 'I'll be very nice to Phil.'